The Puppet Contingency

Steve R. Romano

Editor/Cover Art:

Heidi Bosch Romano

Lunamont Visions Books
Porterfield, WI 54159
LunamontVisionsBooks.com
books@lunamont.com

Printed in the United States

Publisher's Cataloging-in-Publication Data

Romano, Steve R.
The Puppet Contingency / Steve R. Romano

p. cm.

ISBN-13: 978-0-578-89036-4
ISBN-10: 0-578-89036-4

1. Fiction / Science Fiction / Genetic Engineering
2. Fiction / Science Fiction / Crime & Mystery
3. Fiction / Science Fiction / Hard Science Fiction

Chapter 1

The Puppet Contingency, Phase 1

Rick tore his gaze away from the glass enclosure where their subject lay wired to the network. A shiver ran down his spine as he realized there were fates worse than death.

He stepped up behind Susan and placed his hands on the back of her seat as he peered over her shoulder. He studied the readouts on the multiple screens displayed in front of her.

Information flowed from the network in seemingly random bits of data. But to the trained eye, that data stream contained the sum of humanity's achievements over the past eighty years in quantum holographic science.

Rick trusted Susan implicitly and hoped she didn't feel his hovering over her shoulder was anything but his own curiosity needing to be satisfied. After months of failed trials, he had to believe that this time it would be different.

Susan felt Rick's nervousness as she began reading aloud the vitals for the record: "Brainwave activity is holding steady between 0.5 Hz and 3 Hz, delta range; temperature is 98.1° F; heart-rate is 58; oxygen is 97%; blood pressure is 118 over 66.

Rick scanned the bio-readings carefully before making his next decision. "Bring the subject's brainwaves to theta and prepare for simulation," he ordered.

Susan's fingers danced over her virtual keyboard as she introduced a cocktail of drugs into the subject's bloodstream via computer-controlled injectors. She watched her monitors closely as the brainwave frequency changed from 0.5-4 Hz to 4-7 Hz. "Subject's brain activity is holding at theta frequency. I am activating aural implants and olfactory stimuli. Visual cortex input and oral stimulators are operational."

Rick gave her shoulder a gentle pat, reassuring her she was doing an excellent job.

Susan Chen was the life sciences specialist in charge of monitoring the test subject's biorhythms. A short, bobbed haircut nicely framed her even-featured face. The warmth she radiated added to her attractiveness.

With no shortage of potential suitors, she had little interest in dating. However, she found herself attracted to one team member in particular. A relationship with that person would definitely be discouraged if discovered. Dating within the group was strictly forbidden because of the potential for upsetting the dynamics of the group. Thankfully, Susan's passion for her work took priority over her personal life.

Being chosen for the project had been an unexpected change in Susan's life, but one that she had welcomed once the full scope of what they were trying to achieve had become clear. In short, she loved her job.

"The subject is ready and waiting," she reported.

Rick turned to the next member of the team, Dr. Phillip Thompkins, their resident neuropsychologist in charge of the test subject's mental health. "Phillip. Status please," Rick requested.

Phillip placed his hands on his screen's personally modified keyboard. To the average scientist, his custom symbols and pictograms made his keyboard resemble some sort of other-worldly language. No hindrance to him, he swiftly entered commands to initiate the necessary sequences.

"The patient is entering an induced theta frequency and is now in a semi-hypnotic state. I am monitoring his brainwave activity. All indicators show that he is responsive to external stimuli," Phillip reported. "Test memory upload initiated," Phillip continued. "Memory wipe is in effect. The patient will have no recall of his past life at this time. Artificial memories have all been successfully uploaded. He's reached baseline point, and is in essence, a new man," he said, pausing briefly. "Ready to proceed," he announced. He turned to Rick and smiled. "He's as normal as you are. Subjectively speaking, that is," Phillip added teasingly.

"Of course," Rick responded, followed by an almost imperceptible groan at Phillip's jab.

The lab was laid out in a semi-circle with Rick's seat strategically placed in the center. He stepped back from the group and sat down at his command chair, making him feel as though he was the captain sitting at the bridge in the archival footage of an ancient sci-fi show that he'd come across and enjoyed. From his elevated perch, he could easily see each of his crew's consoles.

Rick (known as Dr. Richard Denzer, formally) graduated from Massachusetts Institute of Technology with top honors for his thesis in the field of quantum gravitational dynamics.

After college, he traveled around mainland Greece and its surrounding islands visiting the various ancient ruins. He was often mistaken for a native, him being of small stature and having similar features to the dark-haired, dark skinned Greeks.

Rick had a winning smile and could be exceptionally witty at times. He loved playing sports, but wasn't particularly popular, preferring to study rather than engage in social activities.

A classified government branch recruited Rick shortly after graduation. He spent the last twenty years of his career working on top-secret projects involving particle manipulation using the holographic principle of string theories. Specifically, the use of optical transition dipoles on organic molecules defining how they will react to a confinement field.

It was his theory that they could manipulate elementary particles via light waves and sound waves in such a way as to cause restructure and cohesiveness at the sub-atomic level. He proposed that the description of a volume of space can be thought of as encoded on a lower dimensional boundary to the region with a quantum gravitational horizon allowing the creation of three-dimensional quantum images at a selected location without the aid of a site-specific projector. In layperson's terms, solid things can be created on the quantum level using only water molecules, micro-particles, sound waves and light waves, then appear instantly at another location without the use of an on-sight projector.

In his initial lab tests, everything had worked beautifully, but something unexpected and frightening had happened. The government had become intrigued by the implications of these results, then stepped in and took over the project.

As with all government projects, nobody is without constant scrutiny. Any research team member could significantly skewer the results of any given experiment acting on their own agenda. That's why the government gave Dr.

Phillip Thompkins (Phillip) the added responsibility of monitoring the team's mental health.

Phillip was a very popular guy in school—the class clown to be exact—personality plus. His hair was already thinning in his late twenties and his facial features were just right for someone who wanted to make a living in comedy, but his heart lead him into the field of psychology, his wanting to help others deal with life's stresses. His minor in science made him the perfect candidate for the project, having strengths matching the criteria for the job.

Rick hadn't wanted to keep secrets from the team, but Phillip had convinced him that everyone would behave less self-consciously if they weren't aware that they were being observed for any possible emotional issues, especially considering the unusual nature of the test subject. Phillip made Rick realize this when he expressed his genuine feelings: "After all, we are dealing with a living soul in what I could perceive as unethical in many ways. Basically, Rick, we are playing God."

Phillip's statement had burned in Rick's mind, stuck there like a thorn. It was only because Rick believed in what they were doing that he could force himself to focus on the larger picture.

On Rick's left was Charles "Chuck" Adams at console number 1. Chuck was the newest member of the team, who Rick had recruited from Vid-Tec eight months ago.

A prodigy from the University of California, Los Angeles, Chuck had studied computer science and had graduated at the top of his class. His outside-the-box approach had earned him numerous awards and the jealous respect of his peers.

Chuck was married to a sweet-natured, plump woman and they had two rambunctious young boys who always vied to be the center of attention.

Chuck was an average-looking guy who was a bit out of shape. His only unusual feature was his hair, which grew much too fast. His wife regularly trimmed his overgrown eyebrows and thinned out his wild, wiry hair before he, as she put it, "starts looking like a crazed, redheaded Santa Claus."

As a hobby, Chuck loved to play with indoor train sets. Oftentimes, his teammates teased him mercilessly because of his childlike personality which made him such an easy mark. His wife took her shots as well claiming that "I'm raising three kids, counting Chuck," whenever she was asked about her family life.

Liked by his co-workers, Chuck's only downside is being so self-absorbed at times that he forgets his manners. In particular, he has an annoying habit of forgetting everyone else's birthdays, while expecting them to fuss over him when his special day rolls around.

"What's our status, Chuck?"

"The program is online and all systems are looking good," Chuck answered with obvious pride.

As if Rick were their conductor and they his orchestra, the technicians "played" their individual screens in perfect harmony. Information flowed to Rick from every display.

At console number two was Mick Forester. Born in Australia, he had a slight build, but was very fit from swimming and hobby diving. He possessed a dry wit which often surprised people because he rarely, if ever, smiled. He moved to the United States as a teenager where he'd enrolled at Yale University and graduated with honors.

After a tour in the Air Force, Mick was recruited by the project as a security specialist.

"Initiate security protocols, Mick," Rick ordered.

Mick's hands manipulated his virtual controls as he locked out the elevator and shut down all incoming communications. Only the highly encrypted satellite uplink remained open. "All security procedures are activated," Mick reported. "The cube is locked down."

The cube, as Mick nicknamed it, was the sealed room that was located two-hundred feet beneath the old Denver, Colorado, airport. Above ground, the vacated terminals (with their controversial wall murals) still existed, along with the facility's old airfields and hangers.

They had converted one of the original concourses into a mall with restaurants and entertainment for anyone who wanted a night out on the town.

A small portion of the airport was still operational, but with nearly everyone capable of flying their own air-cars, domestic travel by jet aircraft had nearly vanished.

Only several large airports existed in the country, and those few serviced international travelers, only. Denver was one of them, and it made a perfect cover for this secret lab.

"Anyone topside?" Rick asked Mick.

Mick studied numerous security feeds which showed all points of entry into the dilapidated hanger that concealed the elevator entrance.

"All monitors show 'clear' status. We've got the whole place to ourselves," Mick replied.

Susan occupied console number 3, and to her right at console number 4 was the resident holographic expert, LeRonda Cameron.

LeRonda studied computer programming at the University of Southern California where she showed a high aptitude for dimensional mathematics as outlined in her senior thesis.

Almost a year earlier, Rick recruited LeRonda at a casual meeting set up secretly by a friend at the university.

Of African descent, she was tall, shapely and exceptionally good-looking. Her journey had been difficult because of the stereotype that her professors couldn't get past: beautiful woman aren't supposed to be smart. Fortunately, Rick had seen past her defensive exterior and had convinced her that there were better places for her to demonstrate her intelligence.

"LeRonda, how are we looking?" Rick queried.

"Quantum projectors are online in the test cylinder," LeRonda replied confidently.

Rick surveyed the room. He felt a touch of pride at the professionalism and expertise of the team he had assembled. But it would all be for naught without the one man who was making all of this possible. Rick's eyes settled on their subject in the glass-enclosed, sterile room attached to the lab by an airlock. Inside of that chamber, he could see their test subject enshrouded in his cocoon of wires and probes.

The attending physician, a sweet young doctor named Mary Dawson, fussed over her patient, monitoring his vital signs and ensuring his life support system was functioning properly.

Rick admired Mary's dedication and found her delicate frame very attractive. Although he had to admit that the bulky sterile suit that she wore did an excellent job in hiding it.

Mary and her patient were the last members of the project team. The team knew next to nothing about Mary's patient—the man inside the chamber. All they had been told was that he had been a soldier, wounded in battle. Privately, Rick was fully briefed on their patient. Rick knew that the medics who'd brought the grievously wounded soldier into the field hospital had expressed little hope for his survival. In fact, they didn't really understand how the last bits and pieces of this human-being could still be alive. His butchered remains had scarcely resembled a human body. The only explanation the battlefield surgeons could come up with was that the soldier's self-contained battle armor had done its job and had kept him alive for several days until they had found him. Although his body was essentially dead, by some miracle, his mind remained active and that was how he had ended up here as part of the experiment.

Rick and his team were working on a hypothesis that, if successful, could give this wounded soldier and others like him a semblance of a normal life, albeit an artificial one.

The government had an original idea of what to do with the technology that wasn't as altruistic. But Rick was the only one privy to that information.

Rick pulled his gaze away from the patient and addressed the team. "All right, everyone. Prepare for Phase 1," Rick announced.

Rick rose from his chair and went to a recessed alcove at the back of the room. A retina scan of his eye opened a sliding panel revealing a biometric reader. Rick placed his palm on the glass scanner. Red laser light illuminated his fingers as the beam swept across from below.

Almost immediately, an indicator light changed from red to green and a small steel door popped open. Inside the safe was the key to the project.

Once the safe was opened, Rick removed a delicate crystal the size of a human fist. The artificial rhombus had taken years to perfect and cost millions in research and development. As he turned to the projector, Rick couldn't help marveling over the inner complexity of the crystal. If eternity could be captured, then certainly the inner facets of this crystal were where it would be found.

To his left was a similar recess. Carefully, Rick inserted the crystal into a padded holding clamp. The clamp closed gently around the precious gemstone. Its robotic arm rotated 180 degrees. Beneath an array of lasers, it locked into position with a pneumatic hiss.

Rick let out a long breath that he hadn't realized he'd been holding. The special crystal, although innocent in its beauty, held more information than ten supercomputers from the past.

Rick returned to his command seat. "Start program on my mark: five, four, three, two, one!"

A blue glow appeared as the lasers powered up. "Let there be light!" Rick whispered under his breath.

Beams of pure light pierced down into the crystal. The crystal blue light refracted inside the artificially made facets of the prism in ever expanding numbers until a quantum image was constructed. The image was perfect in every detail from any angle. Ten thousand miniscule versions of a man were visible inside the crystal matrix.

"Give my creation life!" Rick thought to himself. He'd picked up that line from watching an ancient horror movie he'd found in the archives. A part of him hoped he wasn't walking in the same shoes as the mad scientist in that movie.

"Imagers are responsive. Starting beam sequence for satellite transference of data stream," LeRonda reported. LeRonda's hands hovered over her virtual keyboard. "Mark." She pressed the button.

The information in the crystal was beamed to a satellite in high orbit above the planet and then, in secret, instantly redirected to a second remote site. Although Rick had been informed of the back-up protocol, he had no actual knowledge of site two's role in the experiment.

Information flowed to the test chamber on the other side of the main lab's wall.

Everyone's eyes were glued to their monitors. At first, it appeared as though nothing were happening. The seven-foot-tall cylinder of transparent resin remained empty. Then, almost as if by the intervention of supernatural specters, a swirling of matter began to take on form. It grew larger by the second.

Shapeless at first, it inexorably morphed one digital molecule at a time. Bones appeared followed by ligament, veins, muscle, flesh and sandy blonde hair until it formed a complete human being. The resemblance to the subject in the medical suite was uncanny. They could have been twins. Nobody said anything. The sheer awe of the moment seemed to take their breath away.

The naked man stood there with his eyes closed, unaware of his surroundings. His only sign of life was the rhythmic rise and fall of his muscular chest as he breathed.

Rick's whispered voice broke the tension. "What's our status, Susan?"

"All life signs are normal," she said in an awed hush. Her eyes naturally traveled down his body. "He's perfect." She said under her breath as she admired every aspect of his physical form.

"Phillip, you're next," Rick directed.

Phillip swallowed his nervousness as he pressed the key that would activate a two-way speaker. "Can you hear me, Jon?" he asked the man, softly.

The man in the cylinder showed no outward reaction.

"Susan. Are the aural stimulators on-line?" Rick inquired.

"AI systems show normal," Susan replied.

This was as far as the team had ever come after months of failed trials. Successful completion of today's test was crucial before the next phase could begin.

"Try again, Phillip," Rick ordered.

"Jon. If you can hear me, nod your head," Phillip persuaded.

The lab was silent, except for the hum of the ventilation fans and the muffled beeping of medical monitors in the med chamber. The passing minutes felt like years.

Rick pressed the intercom switch that tied him into the medical suite. "Mary, any reaction from our subject?" He looked towards the room.

Inside the chamber, Mary moved from her patient's side to a panel on the clear wall. She depressed a virtual switch with her gloved hand. "He's not showing any signs of awareness at all."

"Damn," Rick whispered, shaking his head, ready to admit defeat.

After every setback, he'd really thought they had beaten the odds this time. All the computer models had shown a remarkably high success-to-failure ratio, but it seemed that they just weren't going to get past this point. If the consciousness of the subject could not be inserted into the quantum hologram, then the project was for naught.

Phillip's voice abruptly interjected itself into Rick's ruminations. "Look!"

All eyes focused on the view screen as they watched in awe. Inside the chamber, Jon's chin dipped ever so slightly and then rose again, indicating a simple but significant nod in answer to Phillip's question.

Mary noticed an almost imperceptible movement of her patient's head at that exact same moment. A chill ran down her spine.

Chapter 2

Rick smiled. The test simulation had gone perfectly. "That was excellent work, everyone. Please follow your shutdown protocols and let's call it a day. I don't know about any of you, but I'm exhausted, and I'm sure our patient could use a break as well."

In the sealed test cylinder, Jon's quantum body disappeared one bit at a time.

Rick stood. "I'll expect reports from all of you on my desk by 0900 hours tomorrow morning. Oh. And Susan, I would like you and Phillip in my office as soon as you complete your system shutdowns."

Rick stood up and gazed around the room. "Good job, today. Try not to celebrate too much, tonight. We have another hard day ahead of us, tomorrow."

LeRonda smiled as she leaned over to Susan and whispered under her breath. "If he only knew."

Susan grinned at their shared secret. "Work hard, party harder." The two women bumped fists.

Mick's hands flew over his controls. "Next round's on me!"

"Easy for you to say. To you, it's always the next round," Chuck teased. "Who's up for pizza and beer?" Chuck glanced at Mick and did his best Aussie impression. "That's Fosters to you, mate!"

"Hilarious," Mick answered deadpan with a straight face.

Chuck continued the shutdown sequence on his console, but before he hit the last key, he glanced around nervously at the others in the room. They were all preoccupied with their own terminals, especially Mick.

Chuck casually inserted a crystal drive into a port on the left side of his console, out of view of the others. He moved his finger over the "copy" icon and touched the screen.

He could feel his heart hammering in his chest as the files downloaded to the crystal. It seemed to take forever. If he should get caught, the consequences would be severe. Life in prison would be a holiday compared to what would happen to him.

The computer flashed that it was finished. Chuck pulled the crystal out of the port and quickly slipped it into his pocket just as Mick turned his way. "Hey, Chuck. That was the worst Australian accent I've ever heard."

"That wasn't Aussie, Mick," Susan chimed in. "It was Chinese! I should know," she joked.

The others all joined in the laughter, even Chuck. And Mick almost smiled.

One by one, everyone got up from their darkened workstations. Coats were grabbed from the backs of chairs and car fobs jingled as they filed towards the elevator.

"Come on, Chuck. You're holding up the show!" LeRonda beckoned.

"On my way," Chuck responded as he grabbed his denim jacket from his chair back and rushed towards the elevator, close behind the others.

"Hey, Susan. Will you and Phillip be dropping by later?" LeRonda called out.

Susan yelled back over her shoulder. "I hope so. It depends on what Rick wants and how long it takes."

"Count me out, this time," Phillip answered. "See you tomorrow."

The elevator doors closed and the laughter coming from inside the paneled box quickly faded up the shaft.

Susan and Phillip entered Rick's office to find him already seated at his desk, going through reports for the day. "Please, sit down." Rick set his work aside and leaned back in his chair. "I wanted to get your unofficial feelings about today's run. Susan, how did our patient respond to his physical environment?"

"By all indications, he was alive," she said. "His physical response to Phillip's question certainly showed cognitive function. His reaction was as normal as yours or mine would be. I detected neither undue stressors in his bio-readouts nor any other indication that he found his 'reality' lacking in any way," she stated succinctly.

"That's good news. Tomorrow's test will be a little more detailed, so it's extremely important that you keep a sharp eye on our patient. We don't want a repeat of our last failure," he warned, but no one needed to be reminded of that horrific event.

"I'll stay focused, boss," Susan reassured.

"I know you will. Thanks for staying a few minutes late. I'll look forward to a complete report in the morning; but for now, go out and de-stress. You've earned it."

"Thanks, boss. See you guys tomorrow."

Susan collected her things and stepped out of the room. As she moved towards the elevator, she couldn't help glancing over at Jon, encased in his bio-chamber. Mary was busy with her daily routine of caring for him. Mary's back was to the window, and she didn't notice Susan's probing eyes. Susan felt a slight shiver as she caught the briefest glimpse of Jon's half body before Mary finished covering it.

Susan hurried to the elevator, turning her thoughts towards more pleasant topics, envisioning the Mai-Tai's that were awaiting her arrival.

Rick sat contemplatively for a few moments until he was certain that they would leave him and Phillip undisturbed. He pressed a button under his desk. A soft click issued from the door lock as a small indicator light simultaneously changed from green to red, and the computer-controlled transparency screens turned opaque. The room was now secured for privacy.

"You know why I wanted to speak with you?" Rick asked pointedly.

Phillip answered equally pragmatically, "Of course."

Rick stared at Phillip, who to his annoyance, had the ability to appear both superior and eloquent at the same time. "... and?" Rick prodded.

Phillip cleared his throat. "The patient responded as if he believed 100 percent that his implanted memories were real. It is, of course, too early to tell just how much of his consciousness was transferred to the hologram, but the very act of a physical response shows tremendous promise." He paused before continuing. "Rick," Phillip said with enthusiasm. "He finally responded both virtually and physically to a direct question! We've never been able to get any response from the previous subjects, except the one..." Phillip caught himself, leaving the rest of that sentence unspoken.

Rick cleared his throat. "Yes, I understand. In your professional opinion, is it relatively safe to continue to the next phase of the experiment?"

Phillip leaned forward with his elbows on the table and rested his chin in his hands. "You are, I presume, referring to our patient's safety?"

Rick waited for him to continue.

"Currently, I have witnessed no significant abnormalities with his thought processes nor his emotional state. But we've got a long way to go," Phillip stated blandly, as if he were reciting the obvious.

Rick could always extract the pertinent information from any conversation and cut to the chase. "Exactly, what do you mean by 'no significant' abnormalities?"

Phillip leaned back, crossed his legs and straightened the impeccable crease in his trouser leg. "Well, I noticed that he's been having some trouble sleeping."

"I thought we had already resolved that problem. Isn't he supposed to be in a near comatose state when at rest?" Rick was feeling a bit irked by Phillip's comment.

"Yes. But the human brain can never be completely shut down. There is always some activity, even at the lowest levels of consciousness. Let me reiterate my position on this when I say that this sleeplessness will not affect the program; however, I would be remiss if I didn't caution you about restricting his dream state too much. Human beings need to dream in order to keep their sanity," Phillip lectured. "It is my recommendation that we continue with the induced delta sleep when our subject is offline so that his natural healing processes can continue. However, at some point we should seriously consider giving the patient a gamma wave induced period of REM sleep."

"I'll keep your recommendation in mind," Rick said. "What about the team? Have you noticed anyone exhibiting feelings of guilt or signs of remorse about what we're doing with our patient?"

"So far, no. At least none that I've observed or documented," Phillip answered quietly. "I believe it's safe to conclude that they all believe in what they're doing and hope that it could bring Jon some semblance of a normal life again."

Rick pressed his palms together and interlaced his fingers. "Have you given any thought to what would happen if we succeed?" He leaned forward. "I mean, what if we completely transfer the consciousness from the patient to the hologram? What happens to his body over there?" He nodded his head towards the darkened window and what lay beyond.

"That's the million-dollar question, isn't it," Phillip stated flatly. "Is consciousness the soul, or is it just the mind?"

"We've come a long way in answering that question, but do we really know anything beyond the biblical references?" Rick mused.

"The ancient Essenes believed that when the soul left the body, the body would die. Many other ancient religions described the same concept." Phillip gathered his thoughts. "However, with the discovery of quantum theory, many in the scientific community who didn't previously believe in the soul, changed their viewpoint on the topic when science began to prove religious concepts as being true. Supporting evidence came from several near-death case studies, which showed that the consciousness could exist outside the body. Patients were reporting with startling accuracy that their out-of-body consciousness witnessed all the procedures the doctors had followed in order to resuscitate their unconscious bodies, which were lying on the operating table below.

Rick listened with keen interest. "Although the same ideas have existed for thousands of years and are well documented, as you said, it's only in the last century that science has actually confirmed what religion has been teaching all along."

"I agree. Take, for example, the study of telepathy and telekinesis. We've known since the twentieth century that these are actual phenomena, proof that the conscious mind is acting on a plane outside the body. What science has been having difficulty with is locating the energy source. Yes, we can certainly measure the results and see the evidence, but we can't define the mechanism." Phillip paused.

Rick interjected. "Science has demonstrated that the discovery of quantum vibrations in microtubules inside brain neurons, which governs neuronal synaptic function and connects the brain processes to a proto-conscious quantum structure of reality, suggests that space-time allows consciousness to exist apart from the brain or body."

"That's true Rick, but religion suggests that there is a time limit on just how long the body can exist without the mind, soul, and consciousness connection. And I think that is where our real problem lies. Just how long can we maintain Jon's physical body while at the same time he is living in a virtual world? And if the Essenes are correct, then what happens to Jon's body when we've robbed him of his soul?"

Rick stared at the wall, deep in thought. In a near whisper, he spoke. "We're playing God here, aren't we?"

"We crossed that line today," Phillip agreed.

"Yes, I suppose we did," Rick said.

"What lines will we cross tomorrow?" Phillip posed.

"Whatever ones we have to, Phillip. This experiment must and will succeed," Rick stated firmly.

Phillip looked quizzically at Rick. "Sounds kind of cold to me."

"That's our job, like it or not," Rick replied.

"Of course," Phillip answered. "Besides, whatever happens from this day forward will be on *your* shoulders. As you said, *I* just work here," Phillip said sarcastically.

The remark irked Rick and he responded more sternly than usual. "I expect daily written reports on everyone. And, I expect to be notified *immediately* if anyone shows signs of having second thoughts about our work here. Baulking over performing necessary procedures could be disastrous to the project. Are we clear on this?" he snapped.

"Crystal," Phillip replied.

"That will be all." Rick pressed the button which unlocked the door and Phillip left. He could hear Rick's phone ringing just as the door closed behind him.

Rick waited for the door to lock before he answered his phone. "Yes?"

"You have a problem," the voice warned.

"Talk to me," Rick ordered.

"We detected a download from your site."

Rick sat up straighter. "Which console?"

"Number one."

"Dammit! Are you sure?" Rick asked, even though he knew that there could be no error.

"There's no doubt. We'll send in a team."

"I'd prefer to deal with this myself," Rick said.

There was a long silence on the line and just when Rick was thinking they had severed the call, the voice came back. "You are going to deal with this," the voice ordered.

"Understood," Rick answered. The phone line went dead.

Chapter 3

By the time Susan got to Mama Romano's Pizza bar, the party was in full swing.

"Hey, Susan! You made it!" LeRonda shouted above the din as she waved Susan her way.

Susan smiled as she wound her way through the tables to join her teammates.

The bar was packed with people and everyone seemed in high spirits, or high *on* spirits, whichever the case may be.

Susan gave LeRonda a big hug. "Wow, this place is really hopping tonight!" she shouted in order to be heard above the din of cheerful people and the karaoke singer.

"That's because it's Friday!" LeRonda laughed.

"Geez! For a moment I forgot what day it is," Susan said, befuddled. "It's so easy to lose track of time working in the cube."

LeRonda pulled out a chair and the two ladies sat across from Chuck and Mick. Mick leaned closer to Susan. "How did your meeting go with the big boss?"

"Fine. He just wanted a prelim report on today's run," Susan answered.

The server interrupted before Susan could say more. "What'll you have?"

"A Mai-Tai, please."

"And a round of shots of Tequila!" Mick added.

"No, Mick. Really. I…" Susan tried to decline, not wanting to drink too much.

"Just the one," Mick reassured. "This is a celebration, after all. Today, we broke the mold and walked into a new future! Who knows what tomorrow will bring; so tonight, let's do this!"

"Yeah! What he said," Chuck added.

LeRonda smiled at Susan. "Looks like you're out voted."

They talked idly about nothing in particular until the server returned with their drinks. As she set the drinks around the table, she asked, "Anything else?"

"Two large pizzas: one with the works, and one with… what would you like, ladies?" Chuck looked across the table.

"Make the other one Hawaiian style with a thick crust," LeRonda answered.

"I'll put your order in right away. The pizzas should be ready in about twenty-five minutes. Can I offer you an appetizer while you wait?" the server asked.

"How about the bread sticks with marinara sauce?" Mick suggested.

"Sounds great." The others chimed in.

The server hurried off with their order.

"I'd like to propose a toast," Chuck said, picking up his shot glass.

The others all held up their glasses and looked expectantly at Chuck.

Chuck cleared his throat. "To the best group of people I've ever worked with. Today, we performed a minor miracle, and I for one can't wait to see what's going to happen tomorrow." Chuck gazed at each person before continuing. "I want to remember this moment, forever, because we're making history!"

"Hey, Chuck. Maybe someday there will be a picture of us above the bar with a note that says *'This is where we made it happen!'*" LeRonda joked.

"Hold on, everyone!" Chuck said, gesturing wildly to get their attention. He turned to the table next to theirs and handed his phone to the nearest person. "Hey, buddy. Would you mind taking a picture of us?"

"No problem," the guy said with a broad grin.

Chuck moved over and stood behind Susan and LeRonda, putting his arms around them. Mick turned in his seat to face the camera. They held up their glasses for the toast as the picture was taken.

"Here's to us!" Chuck shouted before he took a swig of the strong liquor.

"To us!" The others all said in unison.

Chuck retrieved his phone and thanked the stranger. "I'll be right back." He went towards the bar and was lost in the crowd. Several minutes later, he returned with a smile that reminded LeRonda of the proverbial cat that ate the canary. "What are you so happy about?" she teased.

"You'll see," Chuck said with a grin.

Their breadsticks arrived and they ordered more shots. Then came the pizza and more drinks.

"Hey, look, everyone!" Chuck shouted excitedly as he pointed to a large poster that was being pinned up behind the bar.

Everyone turned to see. "It's us!" LeRonda said with excitement.

"This calls for another round!" Chuck said, delighted with himself.

Susan punched him playfully. "You big buffoon!"

Everyone laughed, including Chuck.

Susan had been laughing so much that her face began to get sore. "You guys, stop already!" she said kiddingly. "I can't take it anymore. My cheeks hurt!" She laughed as she rubbed the sides of her face.

The night blurred around Susan and the others. The hour grew late, and the crowd thinned. As was the usual case, the conversation turned to the reason for their celebration—the experiment.

Chuck leaned forward conspiratorially. "Wasn't that incredible, today?!"

LeRonda pushed the empty pizza tin out of her way and leaned forward. "Amazing! I wouldn't have believed it if I hadn't seen it with my own eyes."

"Do you think he was really in there?" Susan said with a serious slur as she tapped the side of her head.

Mick wasn't normally the contemplative type. He preferred facts to theory, but even he had been awe-struck by what he'd seen today. "What will it... I mean, how do you suppose he's going to feel? You know, waking up in another..."

"I never even considered that," Chuck cut in, suddenly sobering up a little.

"I wonder if he'll be aware of being in two places at once? Or if he'll only sense what we program into his new reality?" Susan added.

LeRonda posed the question that was nagging at her. "What if he dies?"

"You mean in the hologram?" Chuck asked to clarify.

"No. What if after we transfer his consciousness from his actual body to the hologram, his real body expires? What does... what do you suppose will happen?" LeRonda paused, then talked in a hushed voice. "What if his soul gets trapped?"

"Come on, guys. How do we even know that there is such a thing as a soul?" Chuck countered.

Susan glared at him. "Only *you* would think that there's no such thing as a soul. Pathetic idiot."

"Look. I believe in what I can see, test or otherwise prove exists through science. Not some religious mumbo jumbo," Chuck declared a little defensively.

LeRonda jumped in with both feet. "Can you disprove it?"

Chuck stared at her defiantly, but remained silent, trying to come up with a valid argument but failing.

"Now, *that* thought is the final buzzkill. My head hurts. I am out of here." Mick rose from his chair. "I'll see you eggheads tomorrow." He staggered away, mumbling to himself about the meaning of life and the possibility of a soul.

"You always ask the hard questions, LeRonda," Susan muttered. "It's too bad Phillip isn't here. I'll wager he could tell us."

"Maybe," she said. "Come on. Let's go home. I'm beat."

"Can I stay at your place tonight, LeRonda?" Susan asked. "I don't feel like going all the way home alone."

"Sure. Come on. I'll call a cab. I'm too drunk to even program the auto-pilot," Le Ronda replied.

Chuck stumbled out the front door of the restaurant. "See you tomorrow," he said as he swayed back and forth, drunkenly, while waiting for them to take off in their cab.

"You want us to drop you off at your place?" LeRonda asked with concern.

"No thanks. I'm all right," he reassured.

"Go home to your wife, and get some sleep, Chuck." LeRonda closed the cab door just as it lifted off.

He stood alone in the lot, pulled out his phone and punched in a phone number from memory. His call was answered on the second ring. "Chuck? Where have you been? I've been sitting here for hours wondering what the hell is going on!"

"Keep your shirt on," Chuck slurred. "I have what you want. Do you have my money?"

"Yes. But the amount…" Nathan hesitated.

"Let's not have that argument again, OK? No pay, no play," Chuck slurred. "I can always find someone else, you know. I'll bet Ace-Net would be interested," he threatened.

"Now, don't be hasty, Chuck. Let's meet and make the exchange. Where are you?"

"At the pizza bar."

"I'll be there in twenty minutes."

"Bring me the money, or the deal's off." Chuck ended the call. He was just about to head back inside when his phone vibrated. He answered the call. "What? Changed your mind already?" He blurted out, expecting Nathan.

There was a moment of silence before a voice Chuck knew all too well spoke. "Chuck. It's me. Rick."

"Oh. H-hi, Rick. I thought you w-were someone else," Chuck stammered.

"Sure. Just wanted to give you a heads-up about tomorrow's test run. I'm going to want everyone at their best."

Rick did his best to keep his tone of voice neutral over the phone.

"Yeah. Sure, boss. Is everything OK? You sound tense," Chuck asked nervously.

"Fine. See you in the morning," Rick answered before ending the call.

The line went silent. Chuck stared at his phone with mixed feelings of dread and foreboding. Shrugging off the gloom, he reminded himself that in less than a half hour, he was going to have more money than he could spend in a lifetime. He could finally give his wife and kids the lifestyle he'd never had growing up. He grinned. Their new home would not come with wheels.

Chuck staggered back into the noise of the bar, smiling. "Hey everyone! The next round is on me!"

Rick set the phone down and wiped away the sweat forming on his brow. He was troubled by the way things had changed in the past few hours. He liked Chuck, but now he was going to have to eliminate him because of one stupid act. Rick slammed his fist on the table in frustration. "Blast! Why'd you do it, you morosophic idiot?!"

Rick fumed for hours until he finally calmed down enough to see that he had no choices left. If he didn't follow protocol, then he'd be just as dead as Chuck was going to be because no matter what he did, Chuck had already sealed his fate by stealing highly classified information.

Rick did what he could to take his mind off Chuck. He knew the next few days were going to be hard ones.

He dialed the windows down to the opaque privacy setting and buried himself in work, planning for the next phase of the experiment.

Rick flicked on his holo-set, not that he wanted to watch anything, but just for the sound of another human voice to help make his office feel less empty and lonely. He paid little attention to the broadcast. To him, it was obviously just a political propaganda speech with cleverly disguised subliminal programming buried in the feed. He recognized some of his own work from his past dissertations on the subject.

Rick smiled to himself, knowing that what he and his team were doing now would make the old ways seem as primitive as cave paintings.

Rick continued working for several more hours until his eyes burned from exhaustion. Reluctantly, he set aside his work and retired to the small studio apartment behind his office. He fell asleep almost immediately.

Chapter 4

Everyone was busy at their consoles getting ready for Saturday's run.

"Hey, Chuck. You look like something the cat dragged in," Susan smirked as Chuck slowly made his way off the elevator.

The others must have been thinking the same thing, because all eyes turned to Rick to gauge his response.

"I guess you guys de-stressed him a little too much?" Rick said with a knowing grin.

Rick watched carefully as Chuck made his way to his station. He saw mild concern in everyone's eyes.

Chuck sat down, ignoring his coworkers, and started running his program.

The team fell into their routine.

"Brainwave activity is holding between 0.5 Hz and 3 Hz. Patient is in a restorative sleep state at delta range."

"Temperature is normal. Heart rate is holding steady at 62 bpm. Respiration is 14. Blood pressure is steady at 121 over 81."

Rick scanned the bio-readings. "Bring the subject up to theta range and prepare for simulation."

Phillip took over. "Patient is entering an induced state of theta and is in a semi-hypnotic state. I am monitoring brainwave activity. All indicators show patient is responsive to external stimuli. Test memory upload initiated," Phillip stated. "Beginning with background history from childhood-teenage years, all false memories have been uploaded successfully."

"What's our status, Chuck?" Rick asked.

"The program is online and all systems are looking good. Awaiting down-stream feed on your mark."

"LeRonda report." Rick prompted.

"Satellites are in geo-synch and waiting on standby. All other backup systems show green across the board. Access to all geo locations is at 100 percent. All photon-wave relay stations are online. We are tapped into every bandwidth of broadcast capability and are ready for activation of quantum projectors in the test cylinder." LeRonda replied.

"All right, everyone. Let's bring Jon in."

"Initializing," LeRonda announced quietly.

No one made a sound. The programmed quantum field swirled around the inside of the cylinder like a mini tornado. Seconds later Jon appeared.

Jon stood there as yet unaware of his surroundings. His blue eyes were closed. The only sign of life was the rhythmic rise and fall of his chest.

"What's our status, Susan?" Rick asked.

"All life signs are normal," she said in a hushed tone.

"Phillip. You're on," Rick directed.

Phillip pressed the key that would activate the speaker. "Can you hear me, Jon?" he asked in a soft voice.

As before, there was no immediate response.

"Jon. If you can hear me, I want you to talk about yourself. Can you do that for me?" Phillip coaxed.

Jon's eyes remained closed. He nodded slightly.

A collective gasp circled the room.

With a shaky finger, Phillip pressed the transmit button. "Tell us when you were born, Jon."

Silence.

"Is he in theta wave Susan?" Rick asked.

Susan scanned her readouts. "Subject's brain activity is holding at theta frequency. All bio-signs are normal."

"Keep urging him to respond, Phillip," Rick encouraged.

"Jon. Can you hear me?"

Jon nodded.

"Can you speak to me, Jon?" Phillip sounded calm, although inside, he felt extremely nervous.

"Yes." Jon's voice sounded raspy, untried—new.

Susan fist-bumped LeRonda with a barely restrained whoop of delight.

"Maintain your stations," Rick ordered.

Phillip waited for the background noise to quiet down before continuing. "Jon. When were you born?"

"I was born in October 1958," Jon responded.

Phillip smiled despite himself. "That's the programmed test reality!" he whispered to the others.

"Keep it going, Phillip. Everyone. Focus on your readouts, and for heaven's sake, make sure the recorders are getting this!"

"Please tell me more about yourself, Jon. About your childhood and family."

Jon

Jon started to speak with a little uncertainly at first, but soon he was speaking in a natural voice, with assurance and confidence.

My Father was a butcher, and my mother was a housewife—whatever that is. Being the son of a butcher has a bearing on this story, but I'm getting ahead of myself.

Growing up was an unfamiliar experience for me. I had to learn to do a variety of things, the least of which was breastfeeding, and then filling my diapers. Not too difficult a challenge at that stage, but still worth a screaming fit from time to time.

Jon paused for a moment before continuing.

Crawling opened up a whole unknown world for me. Mobility gave me access to innumerable places where it seemed I was always forbidden to venture. Go figure. But it wasn't all bad. My desire to explore drove me to greater achievements, and soon enough I was upright on two feet, at least some of the time.

Walking was a bit more complicated, as balance was a concept not easily mastered. I tell you now that there were many a night that I cried myself to sleep after bumping my head on a table leg or doorjamb. Fortunately, my skull was still pliable at that age, so there was no permanent damage, or so I've been told by my neurologist. My psychologist might disagree, although scans show that there's something in my head.

By the time I was three years old, television had become a big part of my learning experience. I saw things that amazed and delighted my growing intellect. If only I could grasp what exactly Lucy was trying to do with Vitameatavegamin, then maybe all the mysteries of the grown-up world would have been clear to me.

The Ricardo's and the Mertz's ability to make my mother laugh puzzled me. But I laughed along with her at their silliness.

I was firmly hooked on TV's reality.

I had not yet figured out the complexities of its operation though, so it was up to mom to turn it on. But when she did, oh boy!

There were men who could fly with silver rocket packs on their backs, and supermen wearing capes who came from other worlds protecting us from bad people who wanted to take away our American way of life—whatever that was.

But if it meant taking away TV, then they were definitely bad.

There was Batman and the Joker, cops and robbers, Indians and singing cowboys who saved the western frontier, spacemen who fought off grotesque monsters from the outer limits, and a princess who was awakened by a kiss. Awesome! Although it would be many more years before I appreciated the kissing thing.

There was a mouse that sang to me from his clubhouse, and ventriloquist's dummies who told us when it was 'Howdy Doody' time.

I remember a rabbit that told me to eat carrots, a sailor who tried to convince me that spinach tasted good, and a guy named Mr. Fudd who taught me about gun safety.

Jon stopped speaking, as if he were searching his memory.

"Is his humor part of his programming, too?" Susan inquired.

"No. He must be feeling part of his own consciousness and personality as part of the feedback loop that we created between the real Jon and his holographic projection. It's absolutely amazing!" Phillip said in awe.

"Shh! He's talking again," Rick commanded, hushing the sideline banter.

Jon

When I was ten, I discovered Star Trek, thanks to my babysitter, who had a forward-thinking mind and a proclivity for the wine bottle in the fridge.

Is it any wonder that I couldn't differentiate between captain Kirk's adventures and Walter Cronkite narrating the Apollo moon shots? As far as I knew, we had already been there, and I didn't get what all the fuss was about. After all, weren't we just going where everyone had gone before?

One thing was obvious to me—everyone had a sidekick. Batman had Robin, captain Kirk had Spock, the lone Ranger had Tonto, Tarzan had Jane—a better choice than Robin, but I didn't start thinking about the implications until I was thirteen.

Jon stopped and tilted his head back as if he were searching his mind for his next thought.

Silence filled the room for several minutes.

Nobody could breathe as tension gripped everyone by the throat.

"What's his status?" Rick whispered.

"Blood pressure is elevated, and respiration is picking up. Readings are still within the normal range, but I'm not liking the spike in readings," Susan whispered back.

"Phillip?" Rick queried.

Phillip scanned his console for any problems. "I'm not sure what's happening or why."

Mary's voice came over the intercom from the medical suite. "Everyone. You need to see what's happening!" she urged.

Chapter 5

All eyes turned to the medical suite. Jon's physical body was writhing around on his bed as if he were struggling with some inner pain. Mary was at his side, trying to keep him from ripping the electrodes and feeder tubes from his body. "Do something!" she yelled.

"His heart rate is rapid. His breathing, blood pressure, and brainwaves are off the charts!" Susan warned. "We're going to lose him if we don't do something, right now!"

"Initiate shut down protocols!" Rick commanded.

LeRonda's hands flew over her keyboard as she closed down one system after another in record time.

The simulation abruptly ended as they took power systems offline. Jon's virtual body deconstructed and vanished in a whirlwind of organic matter. Inside the medical suite, Jon's thrashing subsided.

"All bio readings are returning to normal," Susan sighed. "That was close."

Rick keyed the intercom. "How's our patient, Mary?"

She was too busy to answer him. Several tense minutes passed as she tended to Jon's needs. Finally, she was able to step to the intercom switch. "He seems to have calmed down and his life signs are back to normal." She took a deep breath. "He's sleeping again," she reported, then whipped her head around towards everyone. "What happened?!" she practically shouted.

"I wish I knew," Rick said flatly. "But I'm sure we're going to find out," he consoled. "Take care of hlm."

Mary nodded and went back to her patient.

"Everyone. In my office in five minutes," Rick ordered before exiting the room.

Five minutes later, the team filed into Rick's office and took seats around the conference table.

Rick began the meeting. "All right everyone, let's play back the session and find out what's going on here."

The team sat in silence as they re-watched the session with Jon.

"Any opinions?" Rick inquired.

"To me, it looks like he stopped because he was having trouble remembering something important," Susan offered.

"I agree with Susan," Phillip added. "Notice the way he tilted his head back. That's a definite sign of someone who's trying to recall something from their past. Everybody does that occasionally."

"I agree, Phillip." Rick stated. "But what memory could he possibly be trying to remember? His memories are all programmed by you. Is there something else going on here?"

Phillip steepled his fingers as he pondered the possibilities. "It's reasonable to suspect that some of his own personality has come through, despite the artificial memory implant."

Susan nodded. "That makes sense. You said that the quantum model exhibited a sense of humor that you had not programmed. If it wasn't inserted by you, then where else could it have come from?"

"Perhaps from Jon himself?" LeRonda answered.

"But is that possible?" Chucked added.

Everyone looked at Phillip, waiting for his opinion.

"Considering what we just witnessed, I'd say it's not only possible, but a point of fact; before you ask how, the answer is 'I don't know how,' but it happened." Phillip answered.

"We need to know how to control this situation, or we risk losing our patient," Rick warned. "And *that* is unacceptable…"

Phillip interrupted. "If we knew more about Jon's background, we might be able to identify his problem areas and insert memories to bridge the gaps in the program."

Rick turned to Phillip. "What are you getting at?"

"Jon stopped speaking right at the point in his story when he was talking about all of his TV heroes having sidekicks," Phillip pointed out.

Rick saw where this line of thinking might lead. "Go on," he encouraged.

"Suppose Jon had a childhood friend—a best friend. Someone who he relates to as being *his* sidekick, but the artificial memories I've inserted were missing that key element. That could definitely cause him to have a bout of anxiety. Wouldn't you agree? I think that's exactly what happened to Jon."

"Of course!" Chuck agreed. "If his actual personality is bleeding into the program, then there would be a conflict in the information flow, thus causing confusion over which memories are real or imagined."

Rick leaned back in his chair, deep in thought.

"So, what can we do to bridge the gaps?" LeRonda asked. "We know nothing about Jon except his first name, and we aren't even certain if that's his real name."

"We need more information," Susan said, pointing out the obvious. "There has got to be a file somewhere. After all, he *was* a soldier." She looked at Rick. "Everyone knows the military conducts extensive background checks before they conscript a person into the service," she added. "Where are his records? They must exist somewhere."

Rick didn't answer for several long minutes. "You're right, Susan." Everyone gasped with surprise. "I have a complete dossier on our subject."

"Then, why didn't you tell us before!?" Phillip was outraged. "We had a…" he started to ask, but Rick cut him off.

"No. You *didn't* have a right to know, then. Others had deemed that this information would be disseminated on a 'need to know' basis, only. I agreed with that decision at the time. But after what happened today, the situation has changed. I agree with your assessment of the situation, and if we are to be successful with this project, then it's time for me to be more forthcoming with this crucial information."

Rick entered his security code into his desktop. A soft female voice responded. "Password confirmed. Facial recognition confirmed. System ready."

Rick gave the computer a voice command: "Access the Jon Doe file."

"File accessed," the computer's female voice answered.

"Display file," Rick ordered.

A file popped up on his virtual display. Rick began to read Jon's biographical data aloud. "It says that his family lineage goes back to his great grandfather, who emigrated to this country almost two centuries ago. It seems our subject Jon was named after him. Although his great grandfather's real name was Johann Doezinsky, like most people who entered the United States via Ellis Island, his name was changed to an 'Americanized' version by some poor chap who couldn't spell his last name, or perhaps had a wicked sense of humor. Doezinsky became Doe, meaning our poor soul was born into the world as *Jon Doe*."

"Jon Doe! So, that's his *actual name*? Geez. You weren't kidding about that Ellis Island worker having a wicked sense of humor." Chuck muttered.

Rick continued to scan the report. "It contains Jon's entire life history all the way back to first grade. As with all military files, it also includes a 'self-image' psychological screening. As an induction requirement, they record the candidate talking about his upbringing and education. Perhaps when we examine this recording, we'll find clues that will help us better understand Jon," Rick suggested.

"That sounds like an excellent idea," Phillip agreed. "I've given those tests myself, many times. They reveal a person's self-image along with other personality traits that most of us, when tested in a clinical environment, keep deeply buried. All government employees are required to take those tests, including everyone in this room and me."

"I hope nobody ever watches mine," Susan groaned.

"I'll bet it's a real five-star show!" LeRonda teased. "You could invite all of us over for drinks, fire up the popcorn maker, and we could watch your exciting home movie, together. What could be better?"

"Never happening," Susan declared.

Rick cleared his throat to get the meeting back on point. "Phillip, I'll transfer the data to your console, then I want you to set it up for everyone to view. The rest of you, take five."

"Consider it done." Phillip downloaded the data and prepped it for viewing, while the others stretched their legs and tried to shake off some tension from earlier.

Everyone was back in their seats minutes later.

"The file is ready, Rick. Just give me the word," Phillip said.

"Consider it given."

An image of Jon appeared on the screen, staring back at everyone. He was young, handsome, and full of vitality.

Susan unconsciously turned towards the darkened window and what lay beyond in the medical suite. "Oh my, God," She moaned to herself, thinking of what had become of Jon's body.

Playback of Jon's recording started.

Just for the record, these tests give me the creeps. OK, here goes nothing.

In grammar school, I was taught to read and write. Maybe that's why they called it grammar school, who would have guessed?

My writing utensils were a graphite-filled wooden stick called a 'pencil' and a sheet of wood pulp called 'paper' which always seemed to be the bane of my teacher's existence whenever I handed it in to her with something on it other than drool.

They taught me to print my name, the spelling of which was ill-gotten through a process referred to as 'sounding it out'.

Somehow sounding out the letters and matching those sounds in order to form words didn't necessarily follow any form of logical progression. I mean that 'i' before 'e' except after 'c' spelling rule drove me nuts.

And what's the difference between 'but' and 'butt'? I mean, aside from the obvious function of the latter.

Even so, when I got my grades, I managed to pull a 'D' out of my hat and had become one of the favored 'children who shall not be left behind' and didn't have to repeat the first grade. Yay!

Playground dynamics were a bitch. Sure, I might have sat next to Bart in the first grade, but I moved on, and he didn't. How dare he sit on the swing next to mine? I mean really! Some nerve.

I learned about good sportsmanship in elementary school. It was supposed to be about how you played the game, not about 'winning' or 'losing'. Really?! Then why did coach Dorfman yell so much when we were playing against another team and losing at dodge ball? For that matter, why did the other team celebrate winning with such exuberance?

I knew I was missing some key factor, an elementary point of view no doubt. But like speaking and spelling, English rules just made no sense to me. Oh, well. Mrs. Bouford said it was a 'learning curve'—but it felt more like a tilt-a-whirl to me, and you couldn't get off the tilt-a-whirl until you puked.

When I was young, school was a big part of my education, but the most important lessons seemed to be learned away from the hallowed halls of academia and on the mean streets of my hometown.

To me, there was nothing worse than a fast-moving motorcade of tricycles, mounted by sadistic preschoolers. Where were the super heroes when you needed them?

My home life was simple for the most part. Mom expected me to come straight home from school and do my homework; which I did as fast as humanly possible with no regard for accuracy. It wasn't about getting the answers right—it was about getting it done! The outside world was calling, and I only had until sundown to play. With shaking hands, I would hand my worksheets to mom. 'All done,' I would say with as much assurance as I could muster.

Mom would give them a cursory glance, not actually checking the work. It wasn't until many years later that I realized that my first-grade education may have been greater than the amassed knowledge she gained from her primitive turn-of-the-century world. Progress—go figure.

With scarcely a breath, I awaited the magic words that brought me so much joy, "OK, you can go outside and play, now. But don't wander very far from home."

Given her blessing, I would quickly change out of my school clothes. It was clear to me that school attire was very much like Sunday school dress-up clothing and had to be treated accordingly. I mean, if they weren't considered special, then why did Santa Claus bring me school clothes for Christmas?

Then it was time to dash outside and play with my friends until dinner time. Outside was a wonderful place of magic and wish fulfillment. I could be anything my imagination conjured up. A spaceman, a soldier, a police officer, a firefighter, a doctor. I drove fast cars and flew supersonic aircraft. I could be shot a dozen times and still get up and kill the bad guy. Outside was awesome! The world outside came from my imagination, and I created the rules; therefore, I always won. Perfect!

Supper seemed to be set on some type of universal clock that all the mothers were in tune with, because just when the sun was waning and the mysterious allure of the coming night would draw out the ghosts and other creatures of the darkened world, all the doors on our little street would open and a chorus of calls would echo down the block, "It's supper time!"

Each of us would be called in by our own name, so we had no excuse for not coming in before dark. We were told so many times to not be out after dark that I often wondered what would happen to me if I should find myself out after the twilight. But, alas, I was spared the trauma thanks to my mother's beckoning hail.

The streets would empty of screaming and laughing children and soon the lights would come on behind windows, glowing warm and inviting as the night draped our tiny part of the world.

Each night, it was dinner and then a bath to wash away the filth of play. And, if we were good, we could sit on the sofa with mom and watch TV.

Had I looked outside, I would have seen the bluish electric glow from televisions flickering behind curtains of every house on the block. In my later years, I realized exactly why the TV stations referred to their daily lineup of shows as 'programming'.

Outside our little sanctuary, the world changed each day. I know this because that's what they told us on the nightly news. None of which really meant anything to me, but still I watched, seated on the sofa next to mom, as if I knew what it was all about—good versus evil—I got it. Us against them.

Captain Kirk killed aliens once a week on retro TV, and if I were good, I could stay up past my bedtime to watch him. The world held promise, and I was eager to have that promise kept. Was that so wrong?

The first time I realized I differed from the other kids was when they had a firefighter come to our school to talk to our class. At the time, I was an accomplished student of significant achievement: I had graduated to the next grade. Man, I was on fire! I remember the fireman walking down the aisles between our desks asking each of the kids what they wanted to be when they grew up.

There were lots of firefighters, and a plethora of doctors, police officers, astronauts, soldiers, and airline pilots, and even one kid who wanted to be a teacher! Everyone seemed to know what they wanted to be when they grew up; everyone except me. I had no idea. Sure, all of those other things seemed doable, but deep down inside, I just wasn't sure, not like the other kids seemed to be.

When the man came to me and asked his infamous question of what I wanted to be when I grew up, I answered honestly, "I don't know." What he said next scared me more than all the classic Frankenstein and vampire movies I had seen combined. "Well, you'd better figure it out, kid, before it's too late."

Suddenly a timeline had been thrust in my face. What was considered 'too late' to a fourth grader? My bowels turned to jelly. My mind went blank with panic as the clock in the class room ticked away toward some indefinable future day.

What or who did I want to be? It dumbfounded me. I scarcely heard him finish his rounds, nor did I recall the rest of that class period. Mercifully, the recess bell rang and all of us kids and I ran out to the playground to exhaust as much of our pent-up energy as we could in fifteen fantastic minutes of supervised mayhem.

My world had been forever changed by that single question and the sense of urgency implied therein to decide. Who am I? That was the real question.

Everything was different now. The green grass of the playground field was not as deep, nor was the sky the same vivid blue as it used to be. The swings creaked and rattled. The slide grabbed at my bare flesh and refused to let me plummet to the earth in a speedy fashion, but treated me to a tortured inchworm progression of knees and elbows squeaking all the way to the bottom.

It stumped me. Everything that I'd been taught up to that moment hadn't prepared me for this test. I felt as if all the other kids were reading from a book that I'd somehow missed.

The thing that I realized was that somehow, I felt really different from everyone else. Outwardly, I suppose I looked like all the other kids—I mean I had two feet, two arms, two legs and a face (that could stop a clock). But inwardly, I knew I was different. I didn't want to be different. I wanted to fit in. After all, on retro TV, Mickey Mouse told me I could be a part of the club.

No matter how hard I tried, I couldn't dispel the notion that I was different. It stayed with me, always. There were days when I almost forgot that I wasn't the same as all the others, but inevitably some event would occur or someone would mention my disparity, and then, like a balloon popping, voila! I was back to feeling alone in a crowded world.

Shuffling through life, I sometimes felt invisible, and other times as obvious as the sun. I got into an occasional ruckus, had trouble making real friends, and gradually grew older.

I was a moody, insecure boy who slowly withdrew into my imaginary inner world where I fit in. The years passed with me fallowing in a creeping haze of self-doubt. The summer vacations, which felt like eternity when I was much younger, now seemed to fly by in the blink of an eye.

My Junior high school years were probably the most traumatic for me. I hated gym class, not because of the athletics, but because of those group showers at the end of the period. It felt icky and unnatural, and was made worse by those awful group showers being mandatory. Ugh.

Without realizing it, I withdrew more and more into myself. Then one day. I visited the school library and discovered books! More specifically, stories. There were tales of heroism and valor that drew me into fantastical written worlds and offered me an escape from my real life. I loved it!

I read every chance I got. The library selection was limited and those first couple of years. I was deeply into tales of world war two fighter pilots. I found their exploits amazing, action-filled and often tragic. Their camaraderie and loyalty to each other in the face of adversity really struck a chord inside me. Mostly I suppose that was because I longed to have such friends in my life; although at the time, I certainly didn't realize it on a conscious level.

I was a loner, but it wasn't because I didn't try to make friends. I opened my soul and joined in all the other reindeer games, but somehow, someway, the few people I became close friends with almost always became jealous of me, or envious or hurtful, and we parted ways. I never understood why this always seemed to happen, except that it must've been because I was different.

It puzzled me. I didn't understand why anyone would resent me for just being who I was when all I really wanted to be was more like them. What a conundrum!

Those awkward years of my life passed with agonizing slowness. And now the broadcast TV world had expanded so much that nearly every home in the civilized world received programming via the airwaves. Everyone thought that was wonderful.

Next came high school. For me, it was ten times worse than junior high. Here was a place where the larger world outside the schoolyard influenced the microcosm of the fenced-in society of would-be future adults.

The jocks and the cheerleaders were at the top of the list. Next came the band geeks, followed by aspiring drama actors who were somewhere in the mix, if only by association of being at the sports events. The biology students, the English students, and the geniuses in science class—with their pocket protectors bristling with mechanical pencils and ink pens—followed. The audio-visual nerds, the art masters and the home economics mavens came next, followed by all the average students who fit in so perfectly well. Every one of them had that one thing I still had not achieved: the self-knowledge of who and what they wanted to be when they grew up.

The whole school hierarchy was obviously designed to separate kids into their respective class and train them for the future lives they would step into. For everyone except for me, *that is. There was no class that would help me decide, still no place where I felt that I fit in.*

I was still a loner. At lunch, I would head up to the third-floor balcony to be by myself. From my perch, I would watch all the groups of kids below me in the quad who were mingling and enjoying themselves, and I'd wonder why I felt so different.

It was during these formative years that I discovered science fiction. I became a regular in the school library and almost felt that Mrs. Ito enjoyed my company. I read Jules Verne and Ray Bradbury, Isaac Asimov, and all the other greats from ancient times that I could get my hands on. Through their literature, I explored the universe.

During these years, I spent most of my time reading. And, a lot of that was done in the school principal's office, me being there as punishment because I'd done something disruptive in class. Had the teachers known how much I'd enjoyed those 'reading' breaks, they'd have chosen some other way to punish me.

Somewhere along that cloudy path of youth, I discovered I could make people laugh, and quickly mastered the role as class clown, much to the chagrin of my teachers.

Alas, poor Homer and his odyssey, whose prose I could never choke down. 'Twas a far, far better place to die on the moons of Saturn than on those boring pages of the Iliad.

The principal was a nice old dude who didn't mind my reading habits, unlike my American Lit. teacher who felt it necessary to fail me in her class.

But who was the failure? Was it me because I lacked interest in her class? Or was it my teacher's fault for not inspiring me to learn? We'll never know.

I remember my last day in American Lit. My teacher had moved me to the front of the room to keep a better eye on me—or so she'd thought. If she had ever watched stand-up comedy, she would have realized that 'front and center' was the perfect placement for any performer.

I felt it was my duty to point out the absurdity of the classroom agenda and personally deprive my fellow students from getting their education. My teacher, on the other hand, didn't appreciate my opinion. Amidst the chortles and snickers of the others, she had realized her mistake and quickly sent me to the back of the classroom.

"Are you sending me to Siberia?" I inquired innocently.

I was smug in my knowledge base. Obviously, I had learned something of a geographical nature from one of my classes.

With a sardonic tone and somewhat victorious smile she simply answered, "Yes, I am."

I headed for this distant place of exile, feeling somewhat like Napoleon on his way to Elba. (Oops, a stray bit of history had crept into my head.)

I promptly sat down on a rolling cart, which had no doubt been forgotten in this desolate wasteland by an audio-visual geek.

"The teacher resumed her lesson, her face revealing a satisfied grin now that her classroom's 'disruptor' had been taken care of. If she'd known her adversary better, she might have been filled with trepidation instead, for mere moments later, I was making a racket by wheeling myself across the back of the room.

Her eyes followed me as her oratory died on her lips. "Just what do you think you're doing?!" she napped.

Her loud, angry tone was no doubt intended to cross the frozen tundra of her classroom and pin me to a spot of ice on my *perch. But I was not to be deterred from my quest and immediately responded, "It's cold in Siberia. I'm going to Hawaii!"*

Everyone burst into gales of laughter, and the teacher became painfully aware that she had lost control of the class. At that point, my fate had been sealed. A few minutes later, I found myself comfortably seated in the principal's office, quietly reading in the corner. 'Bliss,' I secretly thought to myself.

Life after high school was just a continuation of my same old fear: "What in the world am I supposed to do with life?" I was angry with the world, and pretty much everything else for that matter. So, I joined the military. I mean, where else do they give you a license to kill, maim, and destroy—except maybe the Department of Motor Vehicles?

So that brings me to the present. Tomorrow, I ship out for paratrooper training. So, to whoever you are watching this. Remember. You made me do it.

Jon leaned forward and touched a button off camera, then the screen went dark.

"Wow," LeRonda exclaimed. "I never would have thought..."

"It all feels different, now," Chuck said with a faraway look in his eyes. "I feel as if I know him."

"Me, too," Susan breathed.

Rick nodded in agreement. "Jon was... *is* a remarkable human being. We can help him become that person again. Phillip. What do you think? Will it be possible to use this additional information to create a better simulation?"

"I can try rewriting his memory implant to more closely reflect his personality. It should help him make the transition to his quantum body."

"How much time will you need?" Rick asked.

"Give me a day or two. There's a lot for me to work on," Phillip mused.

"Tomorrow's Sunday. I know we could all use a couple of days off. Everybody, go home and get some rest. We'll get back to this on Tuesday morning," Rick said.

Chapter 6

Chuck checked his watch as he waved 'goodbye' to his carpool. "7:30 a.m. Not too late for a Saturday night." He walked past his kids' toys lying around the yard—bicycles, a basketball and other childhood accoutrements.

Chuck felt like he was on top of the world thinking about a new home—one without that broken down ancient Chevy pickup truck rotting in the overgrown driveway. He sauntered up to the pile of empty beer cans next to the decrepit couch sitting to the right of his front door and gave the impressive pyramid a nudge with his toe. To his surprise, the pile refused to move.

He grunted out a curse, but then smiled with his secret knowledge. "Nope," he thought. "None of that junk." He fancied a rolling green lawn dotted with shade trees and flower beds. They were going to live in a white clapboard house with plenty of room for all of them. "Yep," he thought. "Life is good!" He opened the door and stepped inside.

"I was hoping you'd show up soon," his wife scolded.

The smile left his face. It was more than her tone of voice that told him his fanciful dream home had just gone up in smoke, it was the briefcase in his wife's hand that he knew he couldn't explain. But he tried to anyway. "Oh, w-well, I can explain," Chuck stammered.

Elizabeth, his wife for the past sixteen years, gave him the look. "Well, I can't wait to hear this," she said sarcastically. "Come on, Chuck! No BS. Why is there a briefcase with five million dollars in our home? Did you open a savings account that I'm not aware of?"

Chuck knew it wouldn't do him any good to bend the truth, so he just sat on the couch and persuaded his wife to join him. "Lizzy, I've... Well, I, ahh, well. I copied my program from work and," he swallowed the lump in his throat and confessed. "I sold it to Vid-Tec."

"Tell me you're joking," she said in an angry tone.

Chuck's silence spoke volumes.

"This is bad. This is really bad, Chuck. Your work is highly classified! Do you know what they're going to do to you, to *us*, if they find out?!"

"Nobody is going to find out. The only person who knows we have the cash is the person who paid me."

"And I suppose you think that makes it all right?" she said exasperated. "Who was it?"

"Nathan Watkins. My old boss at Vid-Tec," Chuck answered.

"What makes you think you can trust him?" she snarled.

"Nathan's going to introduce the data as his own creation and is taking full credit for the tech. He can't come forward and say it isn't his. He'll be fired." Chuck paused, "Besides, it was my code to begin with. I didn't take any of the other people's data."

"Somehow, I don't think the Government would agree with you," she said.

Chuck hung his head down. "I'm sorry. I don't know how to undo this. The truth is, I regretted it the moment I let that crystal drive get away from me. I know this is no excuse, but all I could think of was having a better home for you and the kids. Someplace that wasn't such a dump. The kids would finally get a proper education and we could take a vacation to Bermuda like we've always dreamt about." He looked at her, imploring her to understand his motives. "I did it for us," he said in a small voice.

Elizabeth put her hand on his. "I love you, too, but you know we can't keep this money. Someone will put the pieces together eventually."

"Nathan won't talk. I know it."

"He won't have to. The tech will be the giveaway. As soon as he releases it to the public, the government is going to notice. Don't you think that they'll recognize their own project?" she reasoned.

"Oh," was all he could manage to mutter as the truth of what she was saying sank into his thick skull.

"What can we do? I can't give the money back. It's too late for that," he pleaded.

Elizabeth took pity on her husband. "We'll figure this out together," she sighed.

"Where are the kids?" Chuck asked, noticing for the first time that the house seemed unusually quiet.

"I sent them over to my sister's house so we could talk about *this*," she said as she patted the briefcase. "Maybe if we told Rick what you did, that it was a stupid mistake, maybe he would help?"

"You can't tell *him*! He'd be the first one to turn us in," Chuck argued.

"Maybe he would. We'd better think this through," Elizabeth whispered.

Elizabeth held onto the case a little tighter. She was nervous thinking that it could all be theirs. "Are you *sure* no one else knows about this?"

Chuck pulled her close. Setting aside the case, he hugged her sweetly. "No, I'm not sure. But it's what I'm choosing to believe. What other choice do we have?"

"I guess you're right," she whispered in his ear. "What are we going to do with all this money?"

"We'll keep it our secret for now until we see how this all works out," Chuck whispered.

Sunday 0700 Hours (EST)

The operative pulled out a seat and spun it around so that his muscular forearms rested on the chair back. He could see the disapproval on the face of his superior.

"Can't you just sit in a chair like a normal person, Max?" his boss snapped.

"Yes," Max answered. His eyes were drawn to a blood vessel which throbbed on Aaron's forehead.

"Never mind. What have you learned about our security breach?" Aaron asked.

Max took an almost impertinent amount of time before answering. "The information was difficult to track down, and we are still not one hundred percent positive, but Chuck's cell records show that he spoke with a Mr. Nathan Watkins late Friday night."

"I've heard that name before."

"I'd be more surprised if you hadn't. He's been in the news a lot lately. He works for a company called Vid-Tec—a locally based media conglomerate," Max added.

"Vid-Tec? That's the company responsible for airing Global-Gov's news feeds, if I'm not mistaken," Aaron said with interest.

"More than that, I'm afraid. Nathan just held a news conference on Saturday saying that Vid-Tec was about to unveil a brand-new technology that was going to revolutionize personalized media interaction," Max added.

"What's Nathan's role in all of this?"

"Nathan Watkins is the corporation head of R&D. If he got his hands on our project research material, then I can only imagine what he will do with the information," Max worried.

Aaron leaned back in his chair. "I shouldn't have to tell you how much of an impact this new tech is going to have on the world stage. The implications are frightening." Aaron looked Max straight in the eye. "I'm already being hounded by people In high places who shouldn't be aware of what we've been doing for the past two years. Rick's project was supposed to be a smokescreen to dismiss the idea as being unachievable with current technologies."

"There is still plausible deniability on our end. Vid-Tec is a media company, not a scientific laboratory. Wouldn't their goal be towards media uses rather than what we are doing?" Max asked.

"We can't take that chance. We're not sure just how much data Vid-Tec has received. It could expose the whole program," Aaron said with concern.

Max remained silent.

"This situation needs to be contained," Aaron continued. "I want you to infiltrate Vid-Tec and see what you can find out." The boss's voice left no room for hesitation.

"I'll make the arrangements immediately," Max reassured. "What do you want me to do about the source?"

"Rick has been given an ultimatum to act, but I'm unsure if he has the necessary skills to do what we require when it comes to dealing with one of his team."

Max eyed his boss with a curious mix of respect and disdain. "I don't see why you've got your shorts in a bunch, boss. We are years ahead of Rick and his team."

Aaron glared at him. "That's true for now, and that's all the more reason to keep a tight rein on this technology. I don't want anyone else to have it, especially not those Global-Gov idiots. This country has been, and will continue to be, the predominate power on the globe. Now, get your job done, and clean up this mess!"

"What about the project? After all, Chuck is one of the key programmers. Eliminating him now could be premature," Max remarked.

His boss stared out the window at the monument in the distance. "Perhaps you're right. Let's wait and see what Rick does. He may take care of our problem for us. In the meantime, take care of Vid-Tec. They're the biggest threat to us right now. But monitor Chuck just to make sure he doesn't start selling anymore of our secrets."

"Consider it done." Max rose from his seat and left the room.

Chapter 7

The Cube: Tuesday 0600 Hours

Tuesday morning, the team filed into Rick's office and took their seats.

"I hope everyone enjoyed their time off?" Rick began. "I know I did."

"If you call working for the past forty-eight *hours time off*, then I had a great time," Phillip said sarcastically.

Chuck toyed with his paperwork, apparently deep in thought.

Susan snuck a quick glance at LeRonda and tried not to blush as she remembered their Saturday night tryst.

Mick scanned the security logs for the past couple of days, looking for any anomalous activities. Finding nothing, he waited quietly for the meeting to begin.

LeRonda broke the silence. "I'm ready to get back to the project. Truth is, I had a hard time not thinking about where to go next with the model."

"Me, too." Rick added. He turned to Phillip. "Now, let's get down to business. Phillip. What have you come up with?"

Phillip cleared his throat. "As you recall, Jon's projected holographic thoughts froze at the point where he tried recounting his implanted memories involving a friend or sidekick."

"Right. And we all agreed that maybe something from his past, some boyhood memory, was bleeding through the memory bridge and causing him stress," Le Ronda added.

"That's correct," Phillip stated succinctly.

"So how do we solve this problem?" Rick asked while quietly noticing Chuck's subdued behavior.

"Susan and I worked on an alternative theory of mine yesterday."

"So, that's where you disappeared to," LeRonda prodded.

Susan smiled. "Phillip called me early and said he wanted to discuss his idea."

"Which is?" Rick asked, looking around the table.

Phillip turned to Susan. "Go ahead. It's your code."

"But it was your idea," she said, tossing the lead back to him.

Rick's patience was wearing thin, but he knew not to interrupt, yet. He'd sat through enough meetings to know that one of them would get to the point, eventually.

"We came up with a new scenario for the model. One that introduces Jon to a so-called sidekick," Phillip stated.

Susan took over. "We used the information we just received from Jon's military psych eval to create a more comprehensive background history, one that more closely matches Jon's personality type."

"I get it. By writing in a false memory that better fits his ego, it should be possible for his real mind to better identify with the reality we have projected him into."

"That's the general idea," Phillip said in agreement.

For the first time since the meeting started, Chuck looked interested. "But how are we going to set this up? I mean, we can't expect Jon to live a virtual life solely in his mind, can we?"

"Chuck's got a point," Susan added. "It's one thing to keep Jon talking about his past, with his eyes closed, but what we're talking about goes a lot farther than just memory recollection. We're talking about having him feel as if his holographic self is truly alive and is interacting with other people."

Rick leaned back in his chair. "This adds an additional complication to what we are doing. Sure, all along it's been our goal to insert our quantum hologram into the actual world, but I'm not certain that we're ready for that next step."

"Maybe we don't have to," Mick said.

Everyone turned to look at Mick, surprised that he'd said anything at all. Usually, if it didn't involve security, he just sat quietly throughout the meetings.

"What are you suggesting?" Rick asked curiously.

"The quantum chamber is set up for holographic projections," Mick said.

"Yes, but..." Rick started.

LeRonda chimed in. "I see where you're going with this. We could set up a virtual world inside the quantum chamber that Jon can move through. He would be able to interact with our programmed characters just the same as in real life, but in this case, it would all be controlled from here. That way we could stop the program if he gets into any trouble."

"It's doable," Susan added deep in thought.

"Chuck. Can you modify the program to do what they're suggesting?" Rick asked.

Chuck looked at his teammates. "Yes. It can be done."

"How much time will you need?" Rick queried.

"With LeRonda and the rest of the team helping, I think we can be ready for our first trial run in about four hours," Chuck replied. "It should just be a matter of taking the simulation already prepared by Susan and Phillip and inserting the code into the..."

Rick cut him off. "Spare me the details and get to work."

Chapter 8

The Cube: Tuesday 1340 Hours

"Brainwave activity is holding between 0.5 Hz and 3Hz. Patient is in a restorative sleep state at delta range.

Temperature is 98° F. Heart rate is holding steady at 58 bpm. Respiration is 11. Blood pressure is steady at 118 over 78.

Rick scanned the bio-readings carefully. His next decision could rewrite history or kill the patient. "Bring the subject up to theta range and prepare for simulation."

Susan's fingers danced over her virtual keyboard as she introduced a cocktail of drugs into the subject's bloodstream via computer-controlled injectors.

She watched her monitors closely as the brainwave frequency changed from 0.5-4 Hz to 4-7 Hz. "Subject's brain activity is holding at theta frequency. I am activating aural implants and olfactory stimuli. Visual cortex input and taste stimulators are operational."

"LeRonda. How are we looking?" Rick queried.

"Quantum projectors are online in the test chamber," LeRonda replied.

Phillip took over. "Patient is entering an induced form of theta and is in a semi-hypnotic condition. I am monitoring brainwave activity. All indicators show patient is responsive to external stimuli. Test memory upload initiated. Corresponding memories have all been successfully uploaded," Phillip confirmed.

"What's our status, Chuck?" Rick asked.

"The program is online, and all systems are looking good. Awaiting downstream feed on your mark."

"All right, everyone. This is it. Stay alert. This is a big day for all of us, but most importantly for Jon," Rick said, then paused. "I think I'm not alone when I say how we all feel. Ever since we watched Jon's personnel video, I can't think of him as anything other than a living being in need of our help. He's the very reason that we are doing this project. If we can give him back his life, then all the deaths of those who came before Jon will be vindicated."

"Almost makes it worthwhile," Mick muttered under his breath.

Rick ignored the dismal forecast from Mick and surveyed the gathered team. "Is everybody ready?"

"We are prepped and ready to go," LeRonda answered.

"Everyone. Stay focused," Rick ordered.

"Prepare to start the simulation on my mark. Three, two, one, mark."

Not far away in the quantum chamber, water and air molecules began to swirl and merge as they were redefined on a quantum level. What was insubstantial became solid. The cohesion of atoms took on form and from the void, a man emerged. A spark was ignited and life began anew.

The image was now "live" and capable of complete interaction with the programmed reality of the holographic interface without his being aware that it wasn't real. Jon could be touched, and by the same principle, he could touch and manipulate any virtual matter he came into contact with. The projection was as real as the surroundings they placed him in.

The manipulation of matter at a quantum level really was the miracle of creation.

"OK everyone. Let's wake him up," Rick ordered.

Jon

I wake up. My head feels too small for that lump of coal lodged in my skull.

Note to self: No more Blue-Ribbon beer.

I swing my feet off the bed and hang on to the side for dear life.

My head is spinning. No, the floor is rotating in a very unsettling way.

I can barely make it to the toilet.

It's going to be one of those days.

That long, cold shower felt good. I finally feel alive enough to venture out into the world and actually do something.

Stopping on the steps to my apartment I turn my face towards the sky and close my eyes. I drank in that cool mountain air.

Maybe Jon Denver had something when he sang about the Rocky Mountains.

I feel free—alive—like I haven't felt in a long time.

The sun feels warm on my face. It's refreshing. Odd that it feels as if it's been a long time since I felt the sun or breathed fresh air. Geez, I was outside yesterday. I can't dwell on that too much. It's just one of those special days when the weather is idyllic and makes me feel good to be alive.

Maybe it's because today is the first day of my vacation and I actually have a plan. I am set on doing some backpacking and camping.

I'm off without a care in the world.

I stop at an outfitters' store in town.

The building looks as old as time itself. The glass is tinted with age and the double doors creak as I enter the store. An old cow bell announces my presence. From somewhere in the back a raspy voice calls out, "Can I help you find something, mister?"

Turning towards the sound I see an old man shuffling my way. "I'm planning on doing some camping and need to get some supplies."

"How long are you planning to stay outdoors?" The old guy asks all business.

"I've got two weeks to get lost in the wilderness," I say with a grin.

"Hmmm. Hiking or driving?"

"Hiking."

"Well, you're going to need some outerwear for starters." The old guy leads me through aisles piled high with merchandise that looks like it's from the last century.

"Here we go." He points to a rack of hats and coats. "Grab one that fits."

I buy an old western style oilskin coat with a sheepskin liner, a brown flat-brimmed hat like the one Clint Eastwood wore in one of those old spaghetti westerns that they show on retro TV.

With the old guy's help, I load up with some necessities for camping—a backpack, first aid kit, toilet paper (no pine cones for me), a wicked-looking knife and a compass.

I grab a map of local hiking trails, a bedroll, and a one-man tent. I'm packing enough freeze-dried food to last about ten days if I ration it.

I also grab a collapsible fishing rod and some lures. If I'm lucky, maybe a suicidal fish will latch onto my hook.

On the way to the counter, I snap up a pint of rum—for "medicinal purposes," only. I'm looking around, but can't find any of Lucy's Vitameatavegamin, although they have desiccated liver pills. Yuck.

I walk to the counter where the helpful old dude is ringing up my order. His eyes are bright with youth belying the elderly stoop to his aged body "Looks like you just about got everything you're going to need," he says with a wistful smile. "Was a time I would've liked to have gone with you, I'm too old for that now though."

"You still seem pretty spry for your age," I tell him, just to be polite.

"Thanks," he mumbles. "My idea of the great outdoors is a cold drink and a chair on the patio."

I put on my new hat. "I certainly appreciate your help," I answer as I roll up the rain slicker and shove it, along with the food and drink, into the pack. Securing my new bedroll to the frame, just below the pack, and the canteen of water where I could reach it, I'm ready to go.

"Enjoy your vacation and be careful out there. The forest is beautiful, but it can be deadly too."

"Thanks for the advice." I stick out my hand. "The name's Jon."

He grasps my hand with a firm grip. "My wife calls me Stevarino, and the pleasure's all mine, Jon."

I exit the store, figuring it shouldn't be long before I hit the edge of town. Leaving town, I keep walking. I'm not going to look back.

There isn't much traffic on the old two-lane bypass, and I pretty much have the world to myself.

I find the trailhead a couple of miles outside of town and trek off into the forest. I hike for hours without seeing another soul. For all I know, I am the last man on earth—but I don't mind.

In a peculiar way, it's a familiar feeling, one I've carried with me since childhood. That's me, the loner, on the move.

The sun is disappearing beyond the peaks behind me as I follow a stream down an idyllic canyon. It's filled with wildflowers and glades of cool, green grass dappled amongst the pine beds.

I don't know if I've ever felt as free or alive as I do right at this moment, but I know it's a feeling that I want to hold onto for as long as I can.

The light of day is fading towards darkness, so I think it's about time for me to set up camp.

The summer temperature is cool in the mountains, but very comfortable for hiking.

Tired as I am, I keep going with an almost insatiable curiosity to see what's around each bend in the trail. I suppose I am searching for an Eden-like place to call home for the night.

As I make my way around a curve in the trail, I stop in my tracks to admire the vista that is spread out before me. The canyon that I am following is opening up in front of me. In that geographic split, I can see all the way to the eastern horizon.

I gaze at the full moon almost completely raised above the curvature of the earth as though it's balanced on the brim of the world and framed between two massive pines by the hand of God.

I have found my home for the night.

After having a bite to eat, I clean up a little in the stream. I roll out my sleeping bag. I'm exhausted, but I feel good.

My pack makes a perfect pillow as I lie down on top of my bedroll and fold my arms behind my head. I watch the moon rise higher and higher.

The smell of the pines cleanses my soul. It's kind of hard to describe to someone who's never experienced the great outdoors, but for me, it fills all of my senses to the brim with the almost overwhelming seduction of nature.

I reminisce about my parents and my older brother, long dead now, but they are still alive in my memory. With my eyes half closed, I remember camping with my brother and my dad. The fresh aromas of the pine forest fed those memories, bringing them back to life.

I was just twelve when we pulled our old Chevy station wagon into a camping space at Yellowstone. There was a sense of excitement in the air, of wonder.

That first day, we had hiked up to a lookout point above a waterfall on a narrow rock trail.

As we ascended the trail, a black bear had followed us on our adventure. There was no place for us to go but up. The trail was steep on the uphill side, and the downhill edge dropped precipitously into the river canyon below.

Just ahead of the bear, another couple of hikers soon caught up to us—a husband and wife out for a day's adventure. She found the bear's interest in the hike to be an intrusion into her vacation.

I watched the bear walking up the path towards us, and I felt no actual fear. In fact, the bear just seemed to be out for an afternoon stroll.

The lady felt otherwise. She thought the bear was chasing her for her sack lunch. In a huff, she left it on a rock ledge and scurried past us up the mountain.

My father, brother, and I continued up the mountain, but I couldn't help wanting to sneak a look back. The bear had found the lunch and was helping himself to a sandwich and chips. He looked like someone who had just won the lottery.

I imagined that he's been doing this routine all summer long—intimidating guests in order to get exactly what he wanted, an easy meal. Who says animals are dumb? And, the woman was blonde. Does this constitute a cliché?

Later that night my dad, brother and I sat around a campfire talking with others who were camped nearby. The talk was idle. Mostly about who had done what and what they had seen. I remember how friendly everyone was and how the campground felt like one giant extended family.

I loved that feeling. There was a subtle excitement in the air as well. As I recall, there were signs all around the campsite warning us about the bears that would soon pay a visit.

I wanted to see more bears. I mean, if Yogi and Boo Boo Bear were out there, how dangerous could it be? Besides, if it were really dangerous, then Ranger Smith would be there to protect us.

I knew we were safe because of one simple fact that could not be ignored, we had no picnic basket to raid, just an old Coleman ice chest.

The parade of bears started at around three a.m. I was sleeping in the back of the station wagon next to my dad. My brother was asleep out behind the car, snuggled up in his sleeping bag.

The sound of car horns awakened me blaring from across the campground. I looked out the window and saw car headlights flashing on and off. During all the commotion, I saw what looked like an army of bears invading the campground.

They were into everything. Trash can lids were being slammed to the ground. Every so often I could hear someone yelling, "Get out of there!

I don't think the bears minded it at all. In fact, I think they were rather enjoying the silly humans. They certainly looked well-coordinated in their efforts to gather and forage for food.

With a chuckle, my dad commented on how stupid people were. "Those bears don't care about all of that honking and flashing."

The bears were close now. Four of them cruised past the back of the car on their way to the neighboring camp. They had to step right over my brother to get there.

"Hey dad. What about Tony?" I asked, feeling very concerned for his safety.

"He'll be OK," he answered. But I think it worried my dad, too.

The bears were all around us now. Across the road, I watched as a bear slipped his paws into a slightly open rear window of a station wagon. He pushed that window all the way down and started rummaging around in the back of the car.

After a few minutes, he found something worth eating. He brought his snack over to our car and plopped down in front of us and started to munch.

My dad honked the horn and flashed his lights. I had to suppress my laughter, remembering my dad's earlier comments about "all the stupid people."

The bear was unfazed by the noise and seemed to appreciate the light to better see as he tore open a pound of bacon, enjoying his evening's dinner and entertainment.

Those fond memories make me smile. I close my eyes and can feel myself drifting off to sleep.

Phillip whispered, "This is a good time to end the simulation. We wrote in periods of sleep to better mimic actual life so that the interface would not be rejected on a subconscious level."

"Excellent idea, Phillip. Everyone. Begin your shutdown protocols." Rick glanced around the room with a mixture of pride and relief. "Today's run could not have gone better thanks to all of you and your splendid work," Rick complimented. "Let's call it a day."

He consulted his personal readout. "We will reconvene at 0600 hours tomorrow to review today's simulation. Once again, superb job, everyone."

Rick retired to his office, thinking about the one problem that wasn't as easily remedied—Chuck.

Chapter 9

Vid-Tech Conference Room 3: Earlier in the Day at 0815 Hours

Nathan walked through the security checkpoint. He slid his identification badge through the card reader as he placed his eyes in front of the retinal scanner.

"Morning, Bill," he said absently to the guard.

"Good morning, Mr. Watkins," the guard responded. "How 'bout those Packers? They really blew that last quarter."

"I loved it! Made twenty grand on that game," Nathan boasted. "Want to bet on the next one?"

"No thanks, Mr. Watkins. That's too steep for me."

"Suit yourself."

The guard pulled Nathan's briefcase from the security x-ray. "Here you go, sir. All clear for entry." He handed the case to Nathan.

"Thanks, Bill. Try not to work too hard."

"Who, me? Never," he said with a smile.

Nathan walked swiftly while glancing down at his watch. "Dammit. I'm late for my presentation," he whispered to himself. "I hope one of my aides picks up the ball and starts the program without me," he thought.

He hurried down a gently sloping ramp lined with polished, stainless-steel walls. The floor and ceiling were a deep blue color, and the lighting was subdued, coming from hidden recesses overhead.

He turned left at the first cross corridor and quietly entered a room on the right.

The lights were down, and by the sounds coming from the projection unit, his presentation was already underway.

He slid into the nearest seat, placing his briefcase between his knees.

Nathan focused his attention towards the holo-screen mounted on the briefing room wall.

The lecture was already in progress:

"…meanwhile, technology was progressing at an incredible speed. Television programming became a frontier for advertisers, and they exploited it to the nth degree."

"It wasn't long before the new social media explored the human psyche and the best ways in which to manipulate the target audience."

"Vanity was an excellent advertising angle. Everything from A to Z was dressed up with seductive slogans. But it was more involved than simple ads. We found the ads worked better if we tailored them to go along with the programming."

"Take for example men watching a classic John Wayne Western. Wayne is streaking across the plains on horseback, rifle in hand, fighting off the Indians. We cut to a commercial where a cowboy sits atop his horse smoking a cigarette, while the sun is setting behind him. He takes a big drag as if it's the most satisfying thing he's ever done. Like a proud bull, he blows smoke out of his nostrils and says, 'I'm a Marlboro man. How about you?'"

"Like magic, every young stud who wants to identify with this image goes out and joins the rest of the 'Marlboro men.'"

"This ploy worked for everything and anything," the narrator continues.

"A pretty housewife looks at all the women out in TV land and asks them, 'How do you handle a hungry man? The man handler.' The camera zooms in on a can of extra chunky soup."

"Ersatz housewives were selling detergents and sweet-smelling soaps along with refrigerators and microwave ovens. Scantily clad bikini models invited us to buy sporty cars with the unspoken promise that they'd love to go for an exciting ride with their tops down or the convertible top or maybe both. Commercial television had become a wonderland for mental subliminal manipulation that no one on the receiving end seemed to be aware of at the end of the twentieth century."

The narrator's voice paused for dramatic effect, "Of course, we love it!"

Laughter circled the room.

"In little over two generations, our society has drastically changed. People have become separated from each other. They no longer visit with neighbors or sit on their porches in the evenings and talk about the day, politics, the kids or anything else."

"We've created a society of drones who sit in front of the holo-set, lost to those seated near them, as we broadcast programs beamed directly into their environment. Everybody now has opinions that they gleaned from the holo-tube; opinions that we gave them. We control their attitude about the products they will buy and the politicians they will vote for."

The narrators' voice got louder. "With the advent of cell phones and the overnight explosion of hand-held devices, humanity has embraced a brave new world—a world of technological wonders!"

The narrator glanced around the room.

"But all of this is only the beginning. The next step is no longer a dream, but reality!"

The orator smiled mischievously as he stepped out of the flat screen and into the room.

"We are now at the threshold of a new era."

Gasps of astonishment came from the onlookers.

"Ladies and Gentlemen, it is now within our power to *interact* with our viewers in actual time."

A stunned silence filled the room. Hushed whispers were shared by colleagues as the implications of what they had just witnessed affected their way of thinking.

"This is amazing!" Jan Altman exclaimed. She, the current president of Vid-Tec, was a middle-aged stout woman who had shoulder-length, stringy dark-brown hair, and wore a gray polyester jumpsuit with a white belt and matching flats.

Jan climbed up onstage and gawked at the projected image of the narrator. She felt as though she were standing next to a living human being.

Unconscious of her actions, Jan reached out to touch the holographic image. Her fingertips felt the tactile coarseness of fabric and she jerked her hand back in surprise. "What the…!"

Nathan's holographic image smiled back at Jan.

"Jesus! I can feel his clothes!" Jan exclaimed.

Nathan's hologram turned to the audience. "That's true. Not only can you feel my clothes, but you can smell my cologne and even the fine leather that my shoes are made of. This new technology will enable us to interact with people in ways we have yet to imagine!"

There was a hushed, almost reverent silence in the room.

Jan couldn't contain her awe. Her eyes squinted as she scanned the group until they found the object of her search, the 'real' Nathan. "Nathan. Please come up here and tell us more about this miraculous breakthrough of yours."

Nathan tried not to gloat as he started towards the podium amidst an enthusiastic round of applause from his peers. He stepped up on the stage and stood next to his doppelganger. His own face looked back at him. The effect was a little disturbing. He stepped behind the podium and pressed a button that deactivated the hologram as he looked out at the room full of people. "Maybe we should start with some questions."

A man in the back of the room stood up. "How did you make this possible?"

Nathan didn't recognize him. The man was attired in an expensive black suit and tie. He was ordinary looking with average, unremarkable features. In short, his description would fit just about anyone. And yet Nathan felt an unmistakable aura of menace radiating from the man.

He quashed his feelings and answered. "The overall technical details are complicated and tediously boring, so let me begin with a brief overview of the project. The actual groundwork for this project was the brainchild of several prominent scientists back in the late 1990's. Their job was to create a three-dimensional holographic image that, when projected, could be observed in real time over a wide field of view. The success of their endeavors has given us the basis for all that has followed. Now we can beam images to any location on the planet. We can give those images tactile dimension without the aid of a visual apparatus."

"That's amazing," the inquisitive man in black said without feeling. "You stated at the beginning of your introduction that when a human hand comes in contact with the projected image, the hologram emits ultrasonic sound waves that create the sensation of pressure by ionizing air and water molecules."

"Yes, that's true. But it's more than that," Nathan continued. "These molecules are then reassembled at the atomic level, thus creating a real-time object. Soon, this new technology will allow the restructuring of molecules on site, thereby allowing our projected subject to effectively interact with real-world materials."

"Are you saying that your projected subject can bridge the gap between what's real and what's not?" the man asked.

"Not yet. But the logical progression of this technology would be in that direction," Nathan answered.

"Can you introduce other elements such as taste or the sensations of hot or cold? In short, can your hologram interface with reality to the point of physically altering said reality?"

Nathan was nervous about answering that question, but after considering that each person in the room had to have passed a security screening, he continued. "Again, we're nowhere near that point, yet. In simpler terms, our holographic projection cannot open doors, operate machinery, pick up and use tools, etc. But it's our goal to project an image that can fully interact with the viewer. There would be no difference between a real human being and the holographic version."

He did not know who this man was or how he'd gained access to this meeting, but his presence was more than a little disconcerting.

"Can you create solid matter or mechanical devices? Can you send your hologram to a location with a functional device, say a gun for instance?"

The man's questioning stare gave Nathan pause. "Not at this time. But, in the future, it may be possible to include basic products in our broadcasts, such as a bottle of perfume or a roll of tissue paper—items with a basic molecular structure. I doubt that we'll ever be able to recreate complex mechanical devices with multiple moving parts. But do we really need to?"

Fortunately, Nathan's boss saved him from any further questions.

"I'm afraid that further information regarding this project is tightly controlled," Jan said with a coy smile. "I'm sure everyone in this room understands the importance of what we have accomplished here, and why we don't want our competitors stealing this new technology."

Jan faced Nathan, "Let me be the first to thank Nathan and his team for this marvelous breakthrough."

Jan started clapping and a thunderous round of applause followed by everyone in attendance, all except for the man in black, who had slipped out of the room unnoticed.

The man in black ducked into an alcove as soon as he was outside the meeting room. He removed a sleek phone from his pocket and activated a pre-programmed number. It was answered on the first tone.

"What did you find out?" The voice on the other end of the call asked brusquely.

Max chose his words carefully. "We have a problem. It is exactly what you feared. Vid-Tec has crossed the threshold and now possesses the basic program."

"Damn!" Aaron cursed. "I had hoped that we were wrong, but it seems we have no choice but to eliminate the files and anyone associated with the program."

"Eliminating the program director will not be enough," Max added. "I just witnessed a demonstration of their agenda to a large audience."

"That complicates things," Aaron said, looking up while pondering his next move. "Send a team to Nathan's residence and eliminate him. We must not let this technology get out into the world."

"What about the others?" Max inquired.

There was a moment of silence on the phone. "Let's hope that by removing the head, the body will die. Otherwise, more drastic measures will be necessary."

"I'll take care of it personally," Max said as the phone line went dead.

Chapter 10

Rick's Office: Wednesday 0600 Hours

"I have some thoughts about Jon that I want to run by all of you," Rick said.

"What's on your mind boss?" Susan asked curiously.

"As all of you are aware, this is the farthest we've gone with a test subject. The closest we came with the patient prior to Jon ended rather tragically," he continued.

"That's an understatement," LeRonda moaned.

"My question to all of you is 'why?'" Rick asked. "More specifically, what is it about Jon that's different?"

"Are you referring to his personality?" Chuck asked.

"Not directly," Rick said. "Let's look at the facts objectively. The previous patient was actually in better physical condition than Jon, so theoretically he should have had a higher survivability rating, and yet he died under less strenuous conditions. Can anyone enlighten me as to why?"

"I think I know," Susan answered. "It's very unusual for someone who's been as horribly mutilated as Jon to still be alive. By this point, most people would've lost the will to live."

"Just what are you getting at?" LeRonda asked.

"It's been well documented that people are capable of extraordinary feats when a loved one is involved," Susan added. "Maybe he's hanging on for someone."

"Could this unknown love interest cause a problem in the simulation?" Chuck asked. "Remember what happened in the beginning when he stumbled over a memory of his 'sidekick' friend. What would happen if he should suddenly remember he has or had a woman he loved?"

"He must have had someone special," Susan insisted. "I mean…" she said, blushing. "He's definitely a handsome man, and any woman in her right mind would be lucky to have his attention. I'm speaking objectively, of course."

"Of course," LeRonda teased.

Rick interjected his thoughts. "This is something that should be given serious consideration. A special person in Jon's life could be the reason his soul has not moved on."

"What you are suggesting is entirely possible," Phillip agreed. "There are several studies that have shown that love is a powerful force. Although immeasurable scientifically, history has shown time and time again that love can drive a person to great extremes."

"I've heard of a mother who lifted a car off of her daughter and saved her life, as well as other similar cases," Chuck said.

LeRonda leaned closer. "Assuming that Jon is staying around for this lost love, what if he should realize that the woman he's searching for can't be found?"

"I would think the same thing could occur as before—a break in the reality of his virtual world that could cause him anxiety, or worse," Phillip concluded.

"We'll have to keep an extra close watch on him during the simulation," Rick cautioned. "We've come too far to fail at this point. In the meantime, I'll do a more detailed search through his records and see if I can find out if he had a special someone. She must still be out there somewhere, and possibly be unaware that Jon is still alive, considering the secrecy of his involvement with this project."

"We are swimming in murky water when it comes to a woman's heart," Mick muttered.

Rick ignored the bleak forecast from Mick and surveyed the team. "Are there any more concerns? No? Wow! If I didn't know better, I'd think you were all eager to get back to work," he said with a smile.

LeRonda spoke up. "I haven't been able to sleep since the last simulation—I'm so excited."

"Me as well," Chuck said. "I really want to see what he's going to do next."

"You make it sound as though Jon's calling the shots in our simulation," Rick teased.

"That statement may be more accurate than you think," Phillip said In a serious tone.

"Enlighten me," Rick ordered.

"As you know, the problem was always the merging of two minds—Jon's subconscious mind and the artificially created memories we inserted into his quantum body. Our new program allows for more of Jon's personality to enter the quantum hologram and frees him to act as he normally would under similar circumstances," Phillip explained. "In this way, we've minimized any conflict arising from a program deficiency versus his actual memory of a given situation."

"If I follow you correctly, we are one step closer to achieving our goal of total transference of Jon's consciousness from his dying body into the quantum hologram," Rick substantiated.

A somber silence filled the room as Rick's statement impressed upon each of them the ramifications of the experiment.

"When you put it that way, it sends chills down my spine," Chuck whispered.

"I know how all of you are feeling. I would be a liar if I said that I had no qualms about what we're doing here. But I believe that if souls are real, then Jon's soul must be transferred to his holographic body if we expect him to be a whole person." Rick paused for a moment to gather his thoughts. "If that were me," he said pointing to Jon's partial body in the med-lab, "and there was a way to make me walk again, to be a whole man again, I wouldn't let anything stand in my way, because the only alternative is death."

"Hard to argue with that, Rick," Mick said in agreement.

"Let's get to work, then. Stations, please," Rick ordered.

Susan turned to her console. "Brainwave activity is holding between 0.5 Hz and 3 Hz. Patient is in a restorative sleep state at delta range, moving from delta to theta, now." She scanned her readouts and continued, "Temperature is 98° F. Heart rate is holding steady at 62 bpm. Respiration is 14. Blood pressure is steady at 121 over 81."

LeRonda picked up the thread. "All systems are green across the board. Awaiting activation of quantum projectors, on your mark."

"Let's wake him up," Rick ordered.

Jon

I open my eyes. The moon is up and it's behind me. The forest is lit up with a cool, bluish light that's as bright as daytime on an overcast day.

I'm lying still, not sure what interrupted my sleep. Perhaps the forest sprites are playing a joke on me.

I hear drunken laughter coming from somewhere down in the canyon. The unwanted intrusion into my sanctuary makes me feel violated. I suppose I should've expected it, but I'd been so caught up in the forest's tranquility, that I just hadn't imagined anybody else being around.

The sound of their raucous laughter is drifting up the canyon from some distance away. I close my eyes, trying to block out the noise.

Seconds later, I am startled and wide awake after hearing the sound of gunfire. Behind that echoing shot and the sounds of the noisy campers, I hear something else. It can't sort it out from the other background noises, but now it's clear as the night—it's the whimper of a dog in pain.

My instincts tell me to be on red alert. This group is more sinister than just some happy gathering of people in the woods.

I jump to my feet in a flash. I search through my pack and pull out the knife I purchased for this trip. After slipping the sheath onto my belt, I start down the canyon, wary and alert.

Another gunshot blasts up the canyon, followed by more canine sounds of pain, mixed with growls of frustrated anger.

Feeling a sense of urgency, I break into a quiet run, moving swiftly through the trees like a phantom in the night.

I probably don't have to worry about making noise, judging by the racket of whooping and hollering reaching my ears, but old habits die hard, and some are worth keeping alive.

I see the glow of their campfire from around the next bend, and I begin a stealthy approach.

A few more steps bring me within view of their campsite. There are four of them. They're staggering around a roaring bonfire, passing a bottle of what looks like whiskey or rum between themselves. One of them is waving a large handgun around with no regard for what he's pointing at.

He fires a shot at some vague dark shape lying inert on the far side of their gathering. The echo of the shot is followed by whoops and whistles. "Man, you almost hit him that time!"

"And I wasn't even aiming!" the shooter laughs. "Hey, watch this. I'm gonna shoot from behind my back!"

He whips the gun around, staggers and almost falls down. The gun goes off and comes within an inch of blowing a hole through the foot of the guy next to him.

"You almost shot me, you jackass!" he yells.

His buddies point and laugh at the ashen-white face of their buddy. Then, they all burst out laughing—too drunk or stupid to realize just how dangerous the situation is.

If I had any sense, I would've slipped back to my camp and moved on to greener pastures. But I'm curious to find out what they're taking potshots at. So, I take one step away from the protection of the large pine I was standing behind.

"Hey!" I yell to get their limited-minds' attention.

They don't seem to hear me, so I yell a little louder. "Hey, morons!" That gets their attention. Four pairs of bloodshot eyes, and one gun, blearily turn in my direction.

I let them process what they're seeing—a guy with a knife held down by his side.

"What's up, boys?" I ask.

They take a second, but they're coming around. And by their expressions, they aren't too happy about me interrupting their party.

"Who the hell are you?" the bigshot with the gun mouths off.

My attention is focused on the gun in his hand, which is slowly pointing in my direction.

"I'd be careful if I were you, and put that gun down, slowly.

Something in my voice must have captured his muddled mind, because he stops moving. "Hey, dumbass," he slurs. "Who d'ya think you are showing up outta nowhere and ruinin' our party!"

As the first idiot is mouthing off, the guy on my left moves slowly towards a log. Behind the log, I spot the tips of rifle barrels. I don't need to be versed in Darwin's theory to know my chances for survival depend on what I do next.

I step closer to Jughead, close enough that I can smell the liquor on his breath. In one swift move, I grab the gun with his hand in it, and twist it hard, feeling his trigger finger snap against the guard. He snatches his hand away, screaming in pain.

The revolver feels natural in my hand. It's a long-handled 45 with a 7-1/2 inch barrel. It feels familiar as I spin around and fire at the log.

Wood splinters blow off the top of the log, inches away from the rifles. "Stay where you are, Jethro," I warn with an edge in my voice.

The guy ignores me and reaches for the nearest rifle. These twits just don't seem to comprehend the situation, so I fire another round into the air just over the genius's left shoulder.

He flinches long after the bullet has passed. I know he felt it go by.

"What the...! OK, man!" he screams.

He is sucking in air as if he's drowning. "Just don't shoot at me anymore." The guy rubs his ear as if a piece of it is missing.

I seize the moment. "If you think that was scary, imagine how it's going to feel having a sizzling hot piece of lead punched inside your guts."

He stares at me. The moment of truth has arrived. Can he stare down the muzzle of my gun and take that chance? I can almost hear him asking himself, "Can I beat him?"

I hope I won't need to shoot him. But I'll be damned if I'll let him shoot me.

I keep a steady bead on him. He carefully backs away from the rifles. The four of them step away from the campfire and the guns.

I lower the Colt just a little. "Good. Now we can talk about what you're doing out here and just what you're shooting at over there." I point into the darkness with my new gun.

"Oh, that. That's just an old wolf we captured," one of the other Darwin candidates pipes up. He has a look of triumph on his sweat-glazed face as if he'd just defeated King Kong, thinking that we're all going to be good buddies, now.

"Really?" I said matter-of-factly. "And just what were you going to do to it?" I stated it past tense, but they didn't glean that little factoid. Their fun time is over, but they just haven't realized it, yet.

"We... eh... we..." He looks at his buddies, hoping for help.

"What's it to you, grandpa?" This, coming from the kid with his hands in the air and his tail between his legs.

"Grandpa?" I think to myself. Hmm. Obviously, these clowns are drop-outs. I know the type. So, I don't bother to lecture them on the morals of torturing animals, mostly because I know it would be far above their comprehension, given their single-digit IQs.

"I'll tell you what's going to happen, now. All of you pissants are going to pull your heads out of your butts and you're going to leave everything behind and just go."

The guy who is cradling his broken trigger finger seems to get my drift.

"You can't make us..." he sasses.

I cut in, not letting him finish that sentence. "Is there any part of my statement that you don't understand?"

One of the others is feeling a sense of false bravado, most likely alcohol-induced. But I can't just keep popping off rounds to prove my point. For all I know, my gun could be empty.

I keep that thought to myself and continue. "That's where you're wrong, sonny boy. Why? You're probably asking yourself? Because I've got a gun pointed at your crotch and I'll blow that Vienna sausage right off if you four worthless pieces of shit don't start walking right now!"

Just in case he couldn't process my words, I emphasize the point. "Shooting off your tiny tool will make me an expert shot. Care to try me?" I say with an evil leer.

To their credit, they start walking. I wait for what I know is coming. Sure enough, they only make it about 20 feet before the big guy turns around.

"We'll be back, you mutha, and then we'll see who's gonna be hurtin' who!"

I'm thinking that Einstein was right when he said that the difference between genius and stupidity is that genius has its limits.

"Keep walking, turkey." I'm fairly certain that they'll be back, but I'm guessing that's not going to be until daybreak. And they'll probably bring a few more friends with them to back them up. But I'm not worried. I'll be long gone by then.

I survey their camp. They have little besides the liquor and the guns.

I tuck the pistol in my belt. It's a heavy piece, but I don't want to leave it behind.

The rifles are in a little better condition and probably belong to their dads. There is a Marlin 30/30, an AR15 and a sawed-off 8-gauge with a shortened stock. Very portable and deadly at close range. I decide to hang onto that one for a while. I put a box of shells for the shotgun, and the Colt off to the side.

After emptying the Marlin, I whack it a few times on a tree trunk until the stock breaks and the trigger guard is bent. I do the same thing to the AR, then toss them both into the campfire. The heat will burn, melt, and warp what's left. I know that's going to make them flip out.

I throw the liquor and their backpacks into the fire, too. Might as well go all the way. The fire roars from the new fuel I've added.

I reload the Colt. As it turns out, I was right—it didn't have any rounds left in the cylinder. Good thing the numbskulls didn't try anything stupid. "It's all about attitude," I think to myself.

Satisfied with my work, I turn my attention to their victim. I see the dark form of the wolf lying motionless at the edge of the firelight. It looks dead to me. It's all trussed up like a Christmas goose.

I hate to see the innocent suffer. Doesn't matter whether it's human or animal. I guess I've seen more than enough of one kind or the other. But I'll take the wolf as my companion any day over most of humanity.

I decide that the least I can do is give this poor beast a decent grave, if for no other reason than to keep Poindexter and his hooligans from making a trophy out of it.

As I approach the wolf, I'm surprised to see the rising and falling of his chest. "So, you're not dead, after all," I say out loud.

I move close enough to see his wounds, but stay a short distance away in case he wakes up in a foul mood.

His legs are bound with barbed wire, and the barbs had cut him badly, as he'd no doubt struggled for freedom. The fur on his legs and paws is matted with dried and oozing blood. Seeing this noble animal trussed up boils my blood. For a moment, I contemplate hunting down those four jerks and wrapping them up in barbed wire just to see how they like it.

I move around towards the wolf's head. There's a whitish furrow of bone that almost glows in contrast to its jet-black fur. It runs from front-to-back right between its ears. A bullet that grazed his skull obviously caused the crease. I'm guessing that's the near fatal shot that knocked the poor wolf out.

In a strange way, being unconscious had probably saved its life. At the least, it had postponed the inevitable.

I quickly decide to help the wolf before he awakens from his uninvited rest.

I run back to my camp and hurriedly pack up my gear. When I get back to the wolf, I see that everything is as I'd left it.

I use a multi tool to cut away the barbed wire, and then I clean the leg wounds with water from the creek. They aren't as bad as I had first thought. I figure he would be as good as new in a few days.

The deeper wounds require some extra care, so I dab on some anti-biotic ointment that has pain killer in it to ease his suffering and help speed the healing. I figure if it worked for me, it would probably work for him.

I'm so engrossed in my work that I didn't even notice that the wolf's eyes are open. He has his head lifted just enough so that he can see me tending to his hind leg.

I see movement out of the corner of my eye and turn my head to see what it is. My blood freezes as I am looking directly into the wolf's eyes—the eyes of a predator. Suddenly, I feel very foolish.

I can feel my heartbeat increasing as I gently lay the wolf's leg back down.

He's just lying there watching me with those piercing eyes. I swear I feel like I can hear him talking to me.

"I'm a friend," I say timidly. "I'm cleaning your wounds with medicine, see?" I hold out the tube of medicine for him to see.

He sniffs the end of the tube and then lies back down as if to say, "Yes. I know."

He is unmoving and I don't feel threatened by him. I hope he feels the same way. He certainly acts as if he trusts me. Strange. Perhaps he senses a kindred spirit, a loner like himself.

I stand up slowly. "Easy boy," I say in a calm voice. "I just want to take a look at that crease on top of your head."

He startles me by rolling onto his belly, but he doesn't get up. He just lays still with his head on his paws.

I bend down and gradually reach forward and touch his shoulder. He thumps his tail a couple of times. I take that as him granting me permission to proceed.

I move my hand to his scalp and gently probe the wound. The bullet had skinned the fur off to the bone. But other than the bald spot, he seems no worse for the wear.

"I'd like to put some medicine on that," I tell him, hoping my calm tone of voice will comfort him.

Once again, I place the tube near his nose so he can smell it. He licks my fingers. I take that as his sign of approval and not him tasting his future meal.

I lightly rub the salve into the wound. It must feel good and be soothing because his tail thumps like a lucky dog's.

Feeling happy with my impromptu veterinarian skills, I stand up and step back.

The wolf stands up and shakes the pine needles and dirt off his fur.

He sure is a big guy. I look at him and he looks back at me. His tail makes a lazy arc behind him.

"Now what?" I ask, wondering what's going on in his head.

He sits down and looks up at me with an expectant air about him.

"Well, it appears you want to be friends."

He looks at me as if he knows exactly what I'm saying.

"My name is Jon."

I'd never seen such intelligence in an animal before. This big guy looks smarter than the combined brains of the four dimwits I'd just chased off.

"What shall we call you?" I ask.

He squirms a little, as if he's excited by the prospect. The white looking bullet scar on his head gives me an idea. "I think I'll call you White Scar." I hold out my right hand towards him, palm up. "What do you think?"

He shuffles forward and licks my hand as if to say, "I like it."

I kneel in front of him and place a hand on each side of his neck. My face is an inch away from those big brown eyes and his sloppy tongue.

It feels supernatural, as if I were completing a ritual as old as mankind itself.

"Friends?" I say.

I swear I think I hear him say, "Friends," agreeing to my offer.

Then he surprises me by lifting his right paw until it touches my hand. I take his paw. We seal the bond of friendship with that simple act.

I stand up with a silly grin on my face and a heart swelling inside me to the point of bursting. I have a new friend, a sidekick, just like my entire gang of heroes from my TV youth. Move over Rin Tin Tin, White Scar is in town. "Cool," I thought to myself.

"Well, my new friend. I think it's time we made tracks. We can expect those macho nuts to come back soon and try to regain their manhood."

I figured they must have had a vehicle nearby, and it was likely they might have more weapons. Not a good situation.

White Scar sniffed around the campsite, growling every time he caught a whiff of scent from the hooligans.

"I feel the same way," I reassure him.

I grab the sawed-off eight gauge and stuff it inside my pack, along with the boxes of shells. It fits nicely.

The other guns are now piles of useless junk, melted and twisted in the firepit.

I toss the ammo for the 30/30 and the AR into the fire as well. They would heat up and go off with enough force to blow up something. Good enough. It's time to go.

Starting back up the mountain I want to call White Scar to follow, but I hold back. I keep walking wanting it to be his choice to stay with me.

It wasn't long before I hear him softly padding behind me. He comes up beside me, licks my hand as if asking for my permission to tag along.

"Friends," I said.

He holds his head high and walks beside me with pride.

We make it past my old campsite and continue up the mountain. The moon is sitting right on top of the peak ahead of us.

Behind us, I hear the ammo explode in the campfire.

We hike until the mountainside is in shadow, and the moon has passed beyond the ridgeline.

Hours later I find a nice level spot by the creek and lay my stuff down. I'm tired. I roll out my bag and lay down on top of it, wrapped up in my coat.

White Scar lays down next to me, and in minutes, I drift off to sleep.

"End simulation," Rick ordered.

Chapter 11

Wednesday 2340 Hours

Nathan hovered through the security gate and entered the private community where he lived. Two minutes later, he floated down Waverly Drive and turned into his garage.

The garage door slid silently down behind him, sealing him in his cocoon.

He shut off his air-car and sat, staring out the windshield at a blank wall. The only sound was the popping of hot metal as the car cooled in the air-conditioned space.

Unlike most garages, his was empty, except for his car. He had no need for rakes or hammers or any of the multitudes of tools other people used all the time. Everything was taken care of by the corporation. But as he stared at the blank wall, his thoughts weren't on garden tools, but the new technology that he had promoted.

Chuck had gone way beyond current tech and that by itself was worth worrying about. Nathan wasn't usually shy when it came to making more millions, but he felt that maybe this new "program" wasn't such a good idea.

For that matter, they could program people to believe anything they were told, and they'd never even know they were being manipulated by unseen forces. And that's what was troubling him. In fact, it scared him to his core.

He got out of the car and went into his empty house. He had never married, had no kids or family to speak of, and lived a solitary life with the occasional visit from a lady friend. Tonight was not one of those occasions.

The house was ultra-modern with computerized voice recognition software that allowed him to control every function from the water temperature in the shower to the cooking surface on the stove.

"Illumination," Nathan commanded. The kitchen lights came on as he stepped through the garage door into the house.

He laid his briefcase on the breakfast nook table and grabbed a micro-brewed beer from the fridge.

The kitchen was bright and cheery with white marble cabinetry accented with gold hardware. There was a cooking island in the middle with polished copper pots hanging from brass hooks. The overall effect was clean and sterile. Just the way he liked it.

Opening the bottle, he took a drink of the tastefully expensive brew as he walked into the living room.

"Fire, low flame." The firepit sparked to life with a cozy fire burning low.

"Reduce living room lighting to evening soft." The lights dimmed to a soft glow.

The living room was almost the complete opposite of the sterile kitchen. It resembled an outdoor forest glade, complete with a cascading waterfall that fell from the second story loft into a large pond filled with fish.

A forest of trees surrounded the pond reaching up to the skylight dome thirty feet overhead. The earthen floor was covered with fertile vegetation, ferns, moss and a variety of wild grasses. A decorative flagstone path wound its way to the only furnishings in the room—a very comfortable couch set into a redwood tree trunk.

The fireplace was at the tip of a small island, and in every way looked like a natural rock fire ring left by campers.

Rick sat on the sofa, which sucked him into its comforting embrace, and he stared into the flames.

Normally he would find himself completely relaxed in his quasi-forest setting, but tonight he sat in tense silence. He was worried, and for good reason. This new technology that he'd unveiled today had the potential to be perverted into a terrible weapon if it landed in the wrong hands.

True, it was the next logical step in media programming, but when is too much of a good thing too much for everyone?

"Holo on," he commanded. A virtual projection centered itself in front of the sofa.

"What selection?" a soft female voice responded.

"News. National Network." The announcer's voice immediately began.

"Our presentation of the first historic speech by the new globally appointed presider will start momentarily. Tonight's broadcast is brought to you by Vid-Tec, the world leader in holographic technology."

On screen, the newly appointed presider waved and smiled for the cameras before starting her speech.

"My fellow humans. I'm here tonight to discuss our future and my plans for the rebuilding of our great society. Let us not be deterred by recent events. For the record, let me make one thing

Jason Resnick was the program director for tonight's Vid-Tec broadcast, and he was feeling the stress of his position as he muttered into his headset, "Begin Series 1."

The broadcast went out selectively to the eastern block and most of the African continent. At this stage of the project, the New Confederate States were being targeted. But should this new program prove itself successful, then a massive-media campaign would be launched directed at the minds and hearts of loyalists and confederates alike. It would subject everyone to the Extremely Low Frequency (ELF) programming.

They sent images of people cheering and applauding into the airwaves. But it was not just the subliminal images that made this new technology special—the media had been doing that since the invention of the radio. What made this the next ultimate step was that by inserting emotional feedback at an extremely low frequency, the broadcaster could actually manipulate the way people felt in real time. The new technology built into Ultra High Def (UFD) screens allowed for the controllers to use the screens as a two-way interface. They literally had a window into every household around the globe. At least that was the theory.

Unseen by the public, they absorbed it on a subconscious level via the media. Those who were in control of broadcasting were literally hacking into the public's minds without their knowing it.

"Station 2. Set up for the next feed," Jason ordered.

"I'm on it." The tech cued up the next series of images. His finger hovered over the keyboard, ready to initiate the next phase of the programming as the global presider continued her speech.

"My plan for rebuilding our global community is to first rebuild our society. I will do away with poverty. No one will go to bed hungry! No one will be without the ability to provide for their families and loved ones! Why should one nation have all the luxuries while another nation struggles to find water or food for the masses?"

The feed showed images of hundreds of millions of people worldwide cheering and waving with fervor. It didn't matter that the images were from an era when humanity first went to the moon. All that mattered were the feelings that the viewers were being force fed.

"I will institute new legislation that will guaranty fair distribution of global resources. I will promote the general welfare of our citizens by immediately granting free housing for the poorest of our world. We will provide everyone who is currently on welfare a new home! The cost of this free housing has already been secured by my predecessor. The time has come to realize that we are no longer a continental government, but we

are a world of people moving towards our one true heritage on a global scale!"

Jason pointed his finger towards Bill. "Now!" he ordered.

Bill cued up pictures of children playing and laughing in a park-like setting, while mothers sat on benches in the shade watching them with contented smiles on their faces. It showed men smiling as they worked at a variety of jobs from construction to farming. Everyone on screen was smiling as if life couldn't be better. The feeling was one of total contentment.

"I promise the blessings of emancipation to everyone! Together we will pass on our posterity to our children and future generations to come! We have set aside large tracts of land for entire communities. Schools, hospitals and jobs are going to be provided in a safe and secure environment for all those who want them! As I speak, we have already compiled a list. Those who are lucky enough to be on that first list are going to know exactly how winning the lottery feels!"

More cheering bombarded the airwaves as the tech's under Jason's command went about their jobs with smooth proficiency. They sent a feeling of warmth and gratefulness out with the feed.

"Despite the progress we've made since the revolution, we face a set of core challenges to re-building our world. The rebel nations who oppose our New World Gov have reduced our total economic viability by 15%, but we are still a powerful government

and we will remain so! We can and will continue to build our infrastructure where needed. Our bridges and highways are aging. But with new technologies, we have alternative solutions. This will create jobs for our unemployed. Stimulate our world economy, which has gone out of control!"

"I will rewrite the laws that govern companies and ensure that profit-sharing is rewarded. I will also raise the minimum wage so that every global citizen can have the lifestyle that they deserve."

"We will wipe poverty out within two years. Slums will be a thing of the past as we relocate volunteer families to brand new communities on Global-Gov land. Able-bodied men and women will have jobs and earn incomes that will guarantee their security. I will make it possible for parents to succeed at work and home by updating laws that match how families work. We will fight for equal pay and guarantee paid leave—two changes that are long overdue. And I will provide relief from the high cost of childcare and housing with my planned communities for low-income families. This will ensure people greater retirement and health security! By working together for the betterment of humanity, we can succeed as a global community!"

"The presider raised her hands high and smiled for the world. "We can do this!"

Nathan worried maybe it was already too late. Maybe none of this mattered anymore. After watching that speech, it was obvious to Nathan that eventually someone would discover what he now possessed, and the world would be changed perhaps beyond redemption.

The news continued.

"This just in: Authorities answered a call from concerned neighbors about shots fired. When agents arrived, they discovered a body in a home on Waverly Drive."

That caught Nathan's attention. "Volume up by 10 points."

"A man appears to have committed suicide. Agents have not released the name of the victim. As yet, no motive has been determined. We'll bring you updates on this terrible tragedy as it comes in."

"And now, in national news:"

"The Global senate and congress are once again proposing stricter gun laws with an emphasis on banning all types of personal firearms. Tonight's special commentary is on gun violence and the enforcement of the Global-Gov ban on firearms worldwide. Here's Karen Strom with that report…"

"Holo off," Nathan commanded.

He suddenly had a sick feeling in his gut. What was going on?

Nathan went back to the fridge and grabbed another beer.

He leaned back against the countertop and thought about what he'd just heard. His thoughts were a confused jumble of conflicting ideas, but one thought stood out above all—things were a lot worse than he'd imagined.

"Computer. Show street view." A small screen on the fridge came to life. Cameras in front of the house showed a quiet tree-lined street. There were no police cars or hysterical neighbors on their doorsteps.

"What the hell's going on?" He was thinking about the newscast, and then about the program he'd bought from Chuck. Suddenly, movement in the living room caught his eye. He turned to get a better look and saw the same man from the meeting, the one in the black suit.

"What are you doing here?" Nathan asked angrily.

"Nice place you have here," the man in black said while looking around. "As to why I'm here? Let's just say that I'm cleaning house." He picked up the fireplace poker and looked at it. "Amazing. Please step over here."

"What's the meaning of this?" Nathan asked, but it was becoming crystal clear to him what this was all about.

"Your company bought something from Charles that it shouldn't have. I'm here to make it disappear."

"I don't know what you're talking about," Nathan said, feigning ignorance.

"Oh, but you *do*, Nathan. You know very well what I'm talking about." The man pointed the poker at Nathan, then waived it towards the couch. "Sit over there."

Nathan moved to the sofa and sat down. "How did you get in? This house is entry hardened."

The man smiled. "Let's just say I beamed in."

Nathan stared at the man more closely. "Are you a projection?"

"I'm as real as you are. But I suppose, technically, I'm not here in this room. But you already know that I'm as real as I need to be."

"What do you want from me?" Nathan asked nervously.

"My employers want the download codes for your computer systems inside of Vid-Tec. We want access to all of your data and we want the names of everyone else involved with this project."

"I can't give you that! It would ruin me." Nathan moved as if to stand up.

The man pushed him back down with a sharp jab from the poker. "Sit down. I'd hate to do something we'd both regret."

"And if I give you what you want, what will happen to me?" Nathan's voice grew hoarse.

"You *know* what I'll do if you don't." The man grinned wickedly while turning the steel rod around, admiring it from all angles.

"You killed Charles, didn't you?" Nathan's mind was working overtime trying to find a way out of this mess.

"Not yet," the man said coldly. "Give me the codes." He gestured with the fireplace poker.

Nathan was putting it all together. "That program isn't about selling products, is it? It's about creating virtual assassins."

"Unfortunately for you, that's correct."

Nathan glared at the man in black and saw his impending death in the man's soulless eyes.

"I won't help you. Go screw yourself!" Nathan slowly moved his hand down between the seat cushion where he kept a hidden gun.

"I was hoping it wouldn't come to this." The man raised his hand and swung the poker downward with a ferocious blow to the side of Nathan's head. Nathan slumped over, barely alive.

He groaned and tried to rise, but the pain was too much, and he collapsed.

His assailant stared down at him. "We can't have an unexplained murder on our hands, at least not yet. But before you die, I hope you'll reconsider offering up those codes. Otherwise, we'll have to take more drastic measures to ensure that our program doesn't get into the wrong hands."

Nathan tried to speak, but his head was foggy and his thoughts came floating up from a deep well of pain.

"I see you were reaching for something. Could this be what you were searching for?" The man pulled Nathan's gun from between the cushions.

Nathan was terrified. He knew he was going to die.

The man in black leaned down close to Nathan and stared into his eyes. "This new technology is amazing. See how easily I've killed you in your reality, yet this body I'm using is nothing more than assembled atoms and dust." He stood back up and stared in awe at the bloody bits of hair from Nathan's head that were on the tip of his poker. "Now about those codes?"

Nathan groaned. "Go screw."

"I knew you'd say that." The man's eyes shifted down to Nathan. "Oh, yes. Something left undone. Did I mention how god like this all feels? No? You look terrible. Here. Let me help." He swung one last time, splitting Nathan's skull open at the temple.

Nathan's body shivered with convulsions for a few seconds and then lay still.

The man in black knelt down next to the body and felt for a pulse, nothing.

He placed the gun in Nathan's dead fingers and helped him pull the trigger. Nathan's bloody head exploded with gore.

"A little overkill for sure, but you can never be too careful." He dropped Nathan's hand, then casually walked over to the indoor pond and rinsed the poker in the water. Bits of bone, blood and flesh swirled outward, attracting the denizens of the aquatic decoration which evidently enjoyed their late-night snack.

He replaced the poker in its rack by the fireplace and walked over to the wall where he deactivated the security locks. The CPD team would arrive soon. His part was completed. He looked around one last time, noting the rushing sound of the waterfall and the quasi feel of the recreated outdoor setting. "I may have to get a place like this."

Seconds later, his projected image vanished.

Chapter 12

The Cube: Thursday 0630 Hours

The team sat in their respective seats in Rick's office waiting for the director to finish reading their reports from the previous day's test simulation. "Phillip. I'm really impressed with the way you integrated the sidekick into the simulation. Jon's reaction was so natural."

"I can't take all the credit for that. The entire team had input into that scenario," Phillip commented. "It was our combined effort that helped to overcome the glitch from the first trial, that being Jon's need for an animal companion. Susan came up with the idea that Jon must have had a dog when he was a young boy. He must have been thinking of the dog and wondering where it was. That memory is what caused his anxiety in the first simulation."

"Your logic is sound. Congratulations to all of you for a job well done. By the way, whose idea was it to make the animal companion a wolf?" Rick asked.

Everyone looked at Mick.

"I see," Rick said. "I should have guessed it would have been you."

"It seemed like a good idea at the time," Mick said nonchalantly.

"So where do we go from here?" Rick asked the team.

Phillip voiced his thoughts. "We have a second model encoded for the simulation that would require us moving to the next phase of the testing. But I strongly suggest we continue with the current model with the intention of creating a stronger mental bond between the two principles."

"How do the rest of you feel? Susan?" Rich asked.

"I agree with Phillip," she answered.

"LeRonda?"

"I think Jon is ready for the next phase. We could insert his quantum hologram into a real-world situation and carefully monitor his progress from here without too much risk for Jon."

"How about you, Chuck?" Rick asked.

Chuck squirmed. "LeRonda is right about the tech being sound. We could easily reprogram the simulation for quantum dispersal to remote locations in real time. But I keep thinking about Jon and how we almost lost him that first time just because we didn't know enough about him. If we keep him in the current simulation, it offers us the opportunity for further observation."

"It would be the safest way to proceed for Jon," Phillip agreed. "There is still the unanswered question of why he's hanging on to life—almost obsessively, I might add."

"Have you had any success with Jon's background profile? Anything that might indicate a past relationship?" LeRonda asked Rick.

"Nothing yet, but I'll keep searching." Rick mentally weighed the alternatives. "Very well. If there's nothing else, we will continue with the current simulation and maintain passive observation—for Jon's safety. Let's go to work, people."

Jon

I'm having a pleasurable dream about a woman I'd met in Denver. We are locked in a passionate kiss, but I'm having trouble getting past her bad breath. She runs her sandpaper like tongue up my cheek. It's really ruining the mood for me.

Slowly, I climb up out of my sleep realm to find White Scar licking my face.

"Ugh, boy. What in the world have you been eating?"

Sitting up, I wipe his slobber off my face with my sleeve. Thankfully, he steps back a pace.

That's when I notice his alert stance. He keeps looking back down the mountain while growling under his breath.

I'm up in a flash. I figure it has to be the Mountain Dew boys back for a rematch.

As quick as I can, I gather up my camp and throw on my pack. I want to avoid another confrontation with those boneheads. Mostly because I know how it would end, and I don't want any more blood on my hands, if I can avoid It.

"Come on, boy. Let's get out of here."

I move swiftly, hoping to put some distance between us and them.

White Scar is right beside me, although he keeps looking back every few steps. I don't think he's happy with my decision to make a hasty getaway, but sometimes valor wears a chicken suit. I'm not too happy about it either. Was I really leaving this area to spare their lives, or my own? Self-doubt can be a bitch.

What is that little voice in my mind trying to tell me? Is it just some macho testosterone wanting me to go back and face those idiots? Maybe it's some leftover primeval gene that is urging me to grab up a club and clonk Krug over the head to protect my cave. Whatever the feeling is, it doesn't make me feel very good.

White Scar seems to be having the same internal argument. He looks unhappy about our decision to leave. I understand his angst. He wants revenge, pure and simple.

I force myself to keep going. White Scar forces himself to stay with me. We make it about a hundred yards when I'm stopped by gunfire from down the canyon. I can just make out some angry-sounding yelling echoing up the mountain.

"Sounds like they're not happy with what I did to their stuff." White Scar looks at me and I swear I see a wolfish grin on his face. He seems happy to have made them mad. I know I am.

"Come on." We continue up the mountain for another mile where we come to a cross trail. I pull out my hiking map and study it. If we turn south, the trail traverses the mountains and then gradually winds its way down into the flatlands below. Turning right and going north takes us across the mountains and up into higher territory.

The map shows a lake about ten miles up the mountains. I figure we can stay there for a while. I have enough vacuum-packed food for about a week, maybe longer, if the fishing is good, or more to the point, if I can catch any fish. The lake seems as good a destination as any, so off we go.

White Scar scouts ahead. I lost sight of him on the winding trail. He's been gone so long that I figure he must have gone back to the wild. Maybe he got tired of me. It probably isn't much of an adventure hanging out with a half-century old coward. There's my caveman gene again.

As it turns out, I was wrong about White Scar. He's trotting up to me. And now, he's licking his chops like he'd just had a meal, which he probably had.

"How's the food?" I ask. He just wags his tail and pads along beside me. "Bring any for me?" He looks at me as if to say, "You didn't ask."

"Well, maybe next time," I joke.

We walk onward, neither of us talking much. Me, mostly because I have nothing to say, and him mostly because he can't talk.

We make it to the lake by early afternoon. We're in a bowl-shaped valley with snowcapped peaks in the distance.

The valley is rife with spring blooms. Wildflowers and tall grass fill the valley floor with rainbow colors. The air is warm and smells fresh and sweeter than anything I've ever experienced.

Tall pines back up to the slopes and create a picturesque border, as if God had put all the beauty of his making into one magical place. "Heaven on earth," I sigh.

We hike down a slight incline and stop beside the lake. In the bright sunlight, the lake sparkles like a star-filled night. The lake is about fifty yards across and a little narrower in length. It's the most serene-looking body of water a man could lay his eyes on.

I'm tired. I just want to lie down on the grass and stare up at the sky.

While scouting for a place to set up camp, I notice something at the far end of the valley. I concentrate on what I'm seeing, but it's difficult to tell what it is. There's a vague shape that could be artificial but it's in the shade of the pines and the light could be playing tricks on me. Light, the age-old trickster, I guess I'll have to hike over and explore a little.

As I wind my way around the left side of the lake, birds are singing all around me. The beauty of the place tugs at some primitive part of my brain, conjuring up images of what Eden must have looked like.

I feel good inside—alive. I haven't felt this way in a long time. It's like being a kid again and going outside for the first time after a summer rain. Everything is new and exciting.

Funny, I didn't know that I'd been missing that feeling until this moment when it came flooding back. I stop and drink it all in—the sights, the sounds, the smells, the sky, the lake, and White Scar looking at me as if I've lost my mind.

"Back at you, buddy." He makes me smile.

We're walking again. I'm in a fog of delirium. Man, I have paradise syndrome in a bad way.

Ducking under a tree branch, I look up, the sight that unfolds before me stops me in my tracks. Just when I thought it couldn't get any better, right in front of me is an old log cabin. It appears to be in decent shape. The roof looks solid under a thick layer of pine needles and moss. The front porch is sagging a little, but that just adds character to the old place.

For a minute, I'm wondering if someone actually lives there. I hope not. I'm feeling a little selfish about my valley and I don't want to share it with anyone. As it turns out, there's nothing to worry about.

I climb up the two steps to the porch and gently knock on the door. No answer. I push the door open and step inside.

The place looks like it's been frozen in time. It's a little dusty, but surprisingly in order. As far as I can tell, it looks like the owner stepped out a few months back and could return at any moment.

It feels like I'm trespassing, but my curiosity is pulling me all the way in. The furnishings are minimal, to say the least. There's an old wooden rocker set against the back wall near a potbelly stove that has the historic Sears & Roebuck logo stamped in the cast iron. It's easy to imagine the thing featured in a catalog from the turn of the 19th century.

Next to the stove is a stack of split wood in a hod, along with a couple of lumps of coal. A rickety bed of stretched springs is propped against the far wall.

Obviously, I was not the first person to enjoy the solitude of this mountain retreat. The place has a welcoming feeling.

An open cupboard has a couple of blue lacquered tin plates sitting in it, along with a matching tin cup. The counter is made of a single split tree trunk and has a white porcelain bowl sitting on top that probably served as a sink. Though there's no running water.

On the shelves to my right are dusty cans of food swollen from bacteria. And covering the windows are curtains spun from cobwebs. It's apparent that this place has been vacant for some time. If not for my visit, this cabin would have been vacant until the end of time, I imagined.

"Well, it looks like we found a home," I said to White Scar.

He walks around, sniffing here and there. Finished, he looks at me as if to signal his approval.

Dropping my pack on the floor I go back outside. I can't get over how serene this little valley is. I feel alive in ways I haven't felt since my youth.

Exploring around back for curiosity's sake I discover an old stick-rail corral that's mostly fallen over, deteriorating on the ground.

About twenty feet away from the corral are the remains of an outhouse. Envisioning all the nastiness inside, I reassure myself, "I won't be using that."

Continuing around the far side of the cabin, I'm wondering to myself, "Why would anyone want to live way out here in the middle of nowhere?" Although I can see the attraction because of its location, it can't be much fun holed up in this place all winter long.

There's a small creek running past the far corner of the place. The water is cold and crystal clear.

I bend down to scoop up a handful, tasting the refreshing purity—no chlorine or fluoride in this water.

As I stand up, my eyes follow the little creek up to the top of the slope. There, to my surprise, is the answer to my question. A long time ago, this used to be a miner's cabin.

About 20 yards back, I can see the mouth of the mine set into the face of the slope.

White Scar is sniffing around the entrance a little, but he doesn't seem too interested. I take it as a good sign that Sasquatch isn't living in the empty shaft.

I'm intrigued by the old mine, but decide to wait until tomorrow to do any more exploring.

Turning back to the cabin, I pull the old rocker out onto the porch. Then I sit back with my feet up on the porch rail, admiring the beauty of the surroundings, and take a big swig from the old medicine bottle.

I just sat on the porch for most of the afternoon, listening to the drone of insects, the singing of birds and the soft rustling pines overhead.

Lost in his own dreams, I am comforted by White Scar who's lying beside me sound asleep with a peace of mind that I don't think he's ever experienced living in the wild.

Sitting here contemplating my life, I'm thinking about a lot of things.

White Scar's paws keep twitching back and forth—he must be chasing something in his dream. Whoever said animals don't dream obviously never watched them sleep. Every pet owner has seen their dog growl or cat hiss in their sleep, behaving just the same as people do when they have vivid dreams.

I've been sitting most of the day doing absolutely nothing and feeling no regrets about it. The sun has moved across the sky and is teetering on the western mountain rim, ready to slide down the backside and out of sight. My stomach is growling.

It's supper time, so I decide to try my hand at fishing. I grab my extendable pocket fishing pole thingy and stroll down to the lake.

The last rays of the sun are reflecting off the water, creating sparkling points of reddish orange light. The sun drops behind the mountain, casting the lake into shadow.

White Scar followed me in his meandering way until we reached the lake shore, where he promptly lay down in the nearby grass.

Putting his head down on his paws, he watches me with what I gather is a bemused look in his eyes. It makes me wonder if he knows something about fishing that I don't.

I cast my lure out into the lake and wait.

Sipping on that medicinal rum sure helps pass the time. It goes down smoothly, making me feel as if I should be wearing a plumed pirate hat and standing roguishly with one foot atop a keg. "Arrr!" I said playfully.

An hour later, I catch three decent-sized trout that are now lying on the ground beside me. I'm surprised at my good fortune, and am, of course, grateful.

Picking up my catch, I stroll to the far side of the lake to gut them just in case a bear, or maybe Big Foot, is attracted by the smell. I don't have to worry about what to do with the fish guts— White Scar was quick to take care of those.

I take my haul to a spot near the cabin.

Twilight has come and gone, and the valley is draped with deep shadows as the dark of night is ushered in.

After clearing away some pine needles and leaves, I set a few stones in a circle and in short time have a nice little fire going. There's not much to do but stare into the flames as I cook the fish on a spit of wood.

White Scar and I enjoy the quiet solitude of the evening, talking and nibbling on barbecued fish—I do most of the talking and he does most of the nibbling. I am proud of him for not wolfing down his food or talking with his mouth full. A wolf has to have good manners.

I take another swig of rum. My pirate leg twitches.

White Scar lays nearby, though I don't have to see him to know where he is—his fishy breath is a dead giveaway.

No sign of the Jethro's so I'm thinking they've given up and gone home.

I'm at peace with myself and the world. It's true what they say about "ignorance being bliss."

The moon has yet to rise above the eastern rim of our little valley, but I can see its glow in the sky.

I lay down next to the fire and put my hands behind my head, staring blissfully into the heavens.

There's something missing in my little piece of the galaxy, though it takes me a little while to figure out what that something is. It's someone. The Garden of Eden is a lovely, but lonely, place without a companion. "No disrespect intended, White Scar."

A wisp of a memory floats across my mind. It's of someone special, but then it goes away. Try as I might, the memory is not coming back to me, but the feeling remains. It's a haunting sensation that deeply disturbs me. Why can't I remember her name? I know she's out there somewhere, and I can't shake the feeling that I have to find her.

I pull my jacket around me and gaze to the heavens, thinking of her, until my eyes close.

"End simulation," Rick ordered. "That was close."

"Jon's heart rate and breathing went up a little at the end, but he was nowhere near the danger point," Susan confirmed.

"We can't take the chance that the next time we immerse him in the simulation he'll have a memory conflict. I recommend we hold off until Rick can get us more information about Jon's past," Phillip suggested.

"What if he had a girlfriend, or spouse, but they broke up? Wouldn't that lessen the trauma of the memory?" LeRonda asked.

"Possibly. Of course, it would depend entirely on whether they found closure at the end of their relationship. I wouldn't advise reopening old wounds. That could potentially cause serious problems during the next simulation," Phillip postulated.

"What if we wrote a love interest into the program?" Susan asked.

Phillip gave the question serious consideration. "What if we did that only to find out that he's still in love with the mystery woman?"

"That might be worse," LeRonda warned.

Chapter 13

Rick's Office: Thursday 2148 Hours

Rick had been in his office searching through Jon's records for hours with little to show for it. He was about to give up for the night when he came across some classified files he didn't recognize. Curious, he clicked on the blinking icon to view more.

A new screen opened with a flashing warning at the top of the page—*Classified: Top Secret*. Beneath that were date stamps and time notations, along with a list of penalties for security clearance violations up to and including the death penalty.

"What the devil?" Rick mumbled to himself. He continued reading:

Department of Defense DD form 214

Subsequent status change for service member pending following:

Pentagon mission report for CSC 2/325 Infantry Battalion 82nd Abn. Div.

Aleph Nigeria Campaign 25March 2078

Combat casualty report for SGT Jon Doe

Status: Combat Team: NO SURVIVORS

Data source, Armor recording: Confirmed partial recovery because of high radiation exposure

Rick stared at a blinking curser, following that last bit of information. With a shock of understanding, he realizes that this must be a transcript of the data crystal which was retrieved from Jon's combat armor. Rick knew it would contain the last field combat record of Jon's actions leading up to the massacre of his squad. He would literally see combat from Jon's point of view. Inside his suit of armor, all of Jon's thoughts and spoken words were being recorded with cold machine efficiency. Rick would be able to view them all.

The chilling thought made the hairs on Rick's arms stand on end. The idea of re-living another man's combat experience was both fascinating and strangely macabre, considering he already knew the fatal result for all those involved.

Slowly, almost reverently, Rick clicked on the cursor. The screen changed to a field of view from Jon's helmet cam. Scrolling through the time index, he stopped when the counter reached fifty-nine minutes from zero.

Rick leaned forward with nervous anticipation as the image cleared from static to clarity.

… night in the jungle is never silent. I can see the lieutenant off to my right. No, "see" isn't the right term; I can "sense" him in the blackness.

We are a combat team. Highly trained for night infiltration and covert operations. The others are just as much a part of the darkness as I am.

Somewhere up ahead, the enemy is waiting.

We move as a single entity. Slowly, calculatingly, we advance in silence. Intel has the enemy position located three klicks dead ahead.

My heart rate is normal, or so my body armor bio-feed indicates. I would disagree, if the machine dared to ask. Adrenalin burns through my veins and makes my senses hyper-alert. I feel alive in a way that is primordial. Ten thousand years of human survival instincts surge through my body.

My sense of smell is heightened by the damp earth and the green chlorophyll from blossoming night blooms. The cool night air that I breathe has a flowery scent. But tonight, I am not here to smell the roses. Tonight, I am a hunter, a predator.

Unseen in the jungle canopy above me, a group of primates' howl.

Sensing the others stop, I hold my position. I key the control on my left inner forearm to seal and power up my armor. My visor slides down and locks into position. The world comes alive around me as the suit's systems come online.

Are we compromised? Is the enemy aware that we're nearby? Have the monkeys given us away? Quickly, I check the readout on my passive scanners. The image clarity is excellent. Thermal imaging shows nothing but monkeys in the immediate area.

I wait, scarcely breathing.

"Sgt Doe."

"Sir." I reply through my sub-audible bone mic.

"Flank left of my position and give me a sit-rep."

"On it."

I move off our line, tracking left as ordered. Pushing through the foliage would have been impossible without my augmented armor. Even with the armor it's difficult. The jungle is dense with vines and rot.

It takes months of training to use the armor and months more to learn how to be stealthy while wearing two hundred pounds of augmented kev-steal.

"Lt. I'm three hundred yards out. Scanners show clear."

"Copy. Continue sweep."

I double click my mic, letting him know I understand the order and take a sip of water from my feeder tube.

The night drones with the soft buzzing of insects.

A large python hangs from a tree limb, its head swivels in my direction. It's not a threat, but I still get a shiver of revulsion. I hate snakes.

It's funny how the mind works. I think about her. I can't help it. She was the best thing that ever happened to me, and we had been so happy together, living in ignorance of the world and its problems. At least that's how it had been up to the moment the message arrived, saying that I'd been summoned to serve under the Conscription Act of 2087.

The morning I'd left still made me feel terrible inside. Both of us cried. I promised I'd come back and that we'd never be apart again. I can still smell her perfume.

"Stay alert people." The Lt's voice snaps me back to the present. Chastising myself for daydreaming, I notice the others are on the move. I take one more step...

Static fills the screen for a few moments, then clears again. The scenery has shifted slightly.

…I take another step, unsure of what to expect. My senses are hyper-alert. Thankfully, the chattering of the monkeys has subsided, and once again the jungle is a mysterious place.

Our mission tonight is simple—find the enemy and engage.

Sometimes it's the simplest things that prove the most difficult. We've been on patrol for 12 hours and so far, everything has been routine. I'm trying hard to keep my thoughts focused, but it's funny what the mind will do to fill the time. I keep thinking about Mary and the last time I held her in my arms. I can still feel her lips on mine—sort of.

The Lt's voice comes over my headset and cuts into my thoughts.

"Movement up ahead," he whispers.

The rest of my squad appears as green dots on my heads-up display. The bottom right of the display shows my suit's power status, air and water levels, outside temperature and air quality.

I glance at the left side of the screen and get a reading on my biometrics and those of my squad. Dead center shows me weapons status and ammo levels.

The armor has changed me. I'm no longer a man. With my augmented strength, I can tear a steel beam in half. My visor allows me to see in the dark in several wave lengths. I am a machine designed to kill.

My custom fit armor carries more firepower than an infantry platoon from the turn of the last century. The fighting suit doesn't feel pain. It doesn't know mercy or care about the operator.

They have designed it for a singular purpose, to help me kill, and it can keep me alive for a week at a time. It is a marvel of technology that is virtually indestructible. I hate it.

Red dots have appeared at the top of my display. "I have contact. Bogies at my twelve, coming in."

"Roger that. I've got 'em, too."

The others call in until we all have the enemy position locked in. There are a lot of them—I count over a hundred before my display turns them into a red blob.

"D 3 and D 2. Take left flank. The rest of you home in on my mark."

I chin the freq. "D 2 on the bounce."

The others call in one at a time.

The Lt. is all business. "Stay frosty, people."

I absently note that my pulse has risen a few points as I move to a flanking position with D 3.

The muzzle of my weapon leads the way.

Outside of my suit, the world seems like an alien place. Of course, it's what my instructors referred to as, "disconnect syndrome." Inside the armor, a man feels isolated, disconnected from the actual world with a feeling of separation that could make you careless. It happens to everyone who wears the armor. And if you let it control you, it could get you killed.

The shrinks told us all about the reasons for it in training, and the armorers showed us all the ways it could get a man destroyed.

"D 2, status," The Lt. whispers.

"In position."

I adjust the input on my visor to Amp 2 so I can see a little better in the dark. My screen magnifies everything outside. "The enemy is one click away and closing. I'm counting a hundred men, maybe more."

The Lt.'s voice came through loud and clear, "HQ sure screwed the pooch on this one. Shit! We've run into a heavy unit—bad news. These guys wield enough fire power to burn through our armor."

"D 5. Are you seeing this?"

"Scanning now. I'm not reading any armored transport or artillery."

"Copy. Move to within a half click."

Delta 2 is moving out to my left.

On my heads-up, I can see that the rest of the squad is moving up on my right flank. If we can get them in a crossfire, we stood a chance of chewing them.

"D 5 set your mortar on that high ground."

"Copy."

I watched D 5 move on my display. We were thirty feet apart, lined up in a shallow creek facing the enemy.

"In position. Ready to fire."

"Sgt. Doe, are you ready?"

This was it. Moment of truth. "In position and ready to fire."

I wonder if I'll live to regret this moment as a soft thump registers on my audio input. My battle comp identifies it as a mortar round. Seconds later there's an explosion.

My audio filter cut in a thousandth of a second too late. My ears hurt.

"Incoming!"

A blinding flash. The automatic dampener cuts in as I'm blown onto my back.

Radiation warnings are flashing on my visor.

Delta 3's vitals go offline.

"D 3 respond."

Kneeling, I open fire. My plasma rifle chews through the jungle and then through human flesh. I can hear their screams as my energy beam cuts through the enemy's position.

To my right, I see the Lt. giving them hell. I can see the beams from his group chewing on their left flank.

Movement on my visor gives me a glimpse of a soft ball size object arcing down to my right. Another micro-nuke. The blast picks me up like a rag doll and flips me through the air. Without my armor I'd be red vapor.

That micro-nuke hit close; my readout shows a 30% power drop. The radiation is spiking on my sensor, but my armor protects me.

Rolling onto my back, I launch a salvo of five plasma grenades back at the bastards.

As soon as I hear the first explosion, I rise enough to get a field of fire. The tip of my plasma rifle glows cherry red as I cook everyone I can see.

The Lt. is taking some serious fire. D 5 and D 6 are hit. Out of the corner of my eye, I see their bio's go dark.

We've lost half our squad in just a few minutes.

I let loose another salvo of plasma grenades. My battle comp shows I have one salvo left.

They say you can't feel anything through the armor. Bullshit! I can feel the concussions from their blasts. I'm up and running as soon as they hit.

Incoming fire comes my way almost immediately.

Taking a headlong dive into a blast crater, I roll into a firing position, I cut loose with everything I have. My beam slices through a group of the enemy coming my way. There isn't much left of them now. But I'm still taking fire from way too many directions.

I move again, but I don't get far.

Rounds are clattering off my left shoulder. The kinetic force spins me off my feet. My armor is holding up. I'm not.

My visor shows thirty enemy troops coming my way about 200 meters out. I also see that the Lt. and I are the only ones left.

He must have read my mind. "Pull back, Jon!"

"I'm moving!"

Another blast rocks the earth from the Lt.'s direction. His light blinks out. Shit!

Everything slowed down. I'm outside of my mind, watching everything happen in slow motion. I launch my last salvo of plasma grenades.

I'm moving. No! Another micro-nuke just sailed over my head. I can see it floating past.

It's funny what the mind does in these situations. The micro-nuke reminds me of playing softball when I was a kid.

I watch it hit. The intense light overloads my visor.

My battle comp is flashing red warning lights on every system. I think my armor has been melted by the extreme heat. All power is offline. My worst nightmare has come true. I'm trapped inside my armor.

It's funny what the mind will do, I can see Mary's face and feel her soft, warm lips on mine. Mary…

The screen goes dark.

Rick pushed back from his desk, running his hands through his hair. His palms were clammy, and he could feel his heart thumping wildly behind his ribs. "Jeez!" he shouted as he stumbled over to the watercooler. A couple of sips of cool water later, he was feeling a little more like himself.

Jon's battle was the most intense thing Rick had ever experienced. He could still feel Jon's fear in his last moments. Rick also confirmed something else that he'd only suspected before—the reason that Jon was hanging on to life was his love for a woman named Mary.

Chapter 14

Colorado Police Headquarters: Friday 0300 Hours

Agent Doherty walked over to the coffee machine and poured himself another cup. It was turning out to be a horrible day, and the sun hadn't come up yet.

He took a sip and scrunched up his face. "Ugh! This stuff could strip paint." He stood behind his partner's shoulder. "What have you got, Spinoza?"

"The lab results came in on the Waverly Drive stiff," Spinoza informed. "Looks like your suspicions were right on target. The bullet to the brain was delivered post mortem. The Medical Examiner said that the guy…" Spinoza checked the paperwork. "…one Nathan Watkins, formerly employed by Vid-Tec, was bludgeoned to death. The GSW was apparently an attempt to cover up the actual crime."

"So, Nathan didn't commit suicide—he was murdered. Better send the crime scene investigators back to the house and see what they can come up with," Doherty ordered.

"I've been thinking about another thing that doesn't add up with this case," Spinoza continued.

"What's that?"

"I was checking timelines, and the news media broadcast the initial report *before* we were notified," Spinoza reported.

Doherty looked at his partner. "Is that so? We'd better send an agent over to the news station and find out how and when they got their information."

"What else have we got?" Doherty asked.

"Same old garbage. An old guy called in yesterday saying something about a cat disappearing from his house," Spinoza said with a smirk.

"Why do we get all the lobotomies?" Doherty smiled.

"It gets better. The guy claims the cat left his fur behind when he disappeared." Spinoza smiled knowingly while twirling his finger at the side of his head. "This guy sounds like he's one day away from the vats."

"Anything else?" Doherty asked slightly exasperated.

"Let's see. Next on today's 'to do' menu is a guy who must have had one heck of a party last night and ended up kissing the side of Quarry hill at a hundred and fifty K's. Not much left of the victim," Spinoza said.

"Let the locals take care of it," Doherty said disinterested.

"They flagged it for us to handle. Turns out the victim was Bill Honely, Assistant Director of R&D at Vid-Tec."

"A Vid-Tec wiz; like our victim Nathan?" Doherty asked curiously.

"One and the same," Spinoza answered.

"Maybe we should look into that. It seems a lot of Vid-Tec employees have been meeting their maker lately," Doherty quipped.

"That's one miraculous coincidence," Spinoza said. "I'll get the cruiser warmed up and meet you out front."

"I'm right behind you." Doherty walked over to the sink next to the coffee pot and poured out his cup. He gave it a cursory rinse, grabbed his hat and coat and went out front to find Spinoza waiting for him.

"Let's make some time, Spinoza. I want to get there as soon as possible before the locals screw up the scene."

"I'm on it."

Spinoza flipped on the light bar and punched the accelerator. The cruiser jumped off the pavement and flew off towards the rising sun.

Doherty watched the glow on the eastern horizon as he thought about visiting Vid-Tec to see what he could find out. "Has our new replacement checked in lately?"

"Yesterday, we got a message from the higher-ups that he has been temporarily reassigned," Spinoza said matter-of-factly.

Doherty snorted. "He hasn't been *assigned* to us, yet. How can he be *reassigned*?"

"That's the genius of bureaucracy," Spinoza said with a smirk.

In silence, they flew to the air-car wreckage.

Twenty minutes later, they were looking down on the wreck site as they were circling for a place to land.

"Not much left," Spinoza said.

"Looks bad," Doherty agreed. "The freezer techs are going to have a hard time separating Mr. Honely from the car."

"Hope they brought a spatula," Spinoza said sarcastically.

Doherty didn't bother to comment. Sometimes his partner's sense of humor lacked one key factor—humor.

An hour later, they were completed with their examination of the wreck. The black box had been completely destroyed in the crash, which was unusual but not unheard of, so the only thing they knew for certain was that Bill Honely's life had ended rather abruptly.

"That sure was a waste of time," Spinoza said as he climbed into their cruiser and pressed the button that would seal the door.

Doherty slid in the other side. "Yeah. Radio in and order an autopsy."

"Are you kidding?" Spinoza answered. "There are barely any pieces big enough to scan."

"I have a hunch that things aren't what they appear to be," Doherty said.

"You're the boss," Spinoza said before checking in with dispatch. "Where to next?"

Doherty glanced over. "Let's check out Vid-Tec. I'm curious to find out why they're having such a high employee turnover rate."

Spinoza lifted off and fed the coordinates into the nav-comp.

Chapter 15

The Cube: Friday 0600 Hours

As usual, the team was already assembled and were busy preparing for the morning briefing.

"Before we begin today's simulation, I want to share some recent information I gathered last night. I'm sure it will shed some light on why Jon is still with us," Rick affirmed. "Jon *did* have a love interest, and sadly his last thought was of her."

"I knew it," Susan boasted. "Love can conquer all obstacles."

Phillip agreed. "You may be right this time, but we have bigger problems to deal with before we can assure ourselves that Jon's psyche can handle what's coming next."

"Enlighten us," Rick said dryly.

"I recommend we continue the current simulation with Jon and White Scar in order to help Jon feel a sense of security and stability within the simulation," Phillip recommended. "A sudden shift in his surroundings, without the continuance of familiar bonds, could shatter the illusion of realism and cause traumatic failure."

"When we shift from this simulation to the next phase involving real world interaction, the familiarity of having White Scar at his side will help ease his transition," LeRonda added.

"That's it exactly," Phillip confirmed. "It'll also be helpful for him to still possess familiar items that he collected in his current scenario."

"Such as?" Chuck asked.

"Well, the weapons for one," Susan suggested. "His reliance on them in potential life-threatening situations could give him a sense of survivability."

"Excellent observation, Susan." Rick complimented. "And since his survival is our goal, we should make certain he has what he needs both physically and mentally."

"What are we going to do about his lost love?" LeRonda asked.

"I guess we'll have to cross that bridge when we come to it," Rick replied. "In the meantime, let's start today's run. Stations, please."

"Brainwave activity is within the norms. I am bringing the subject up from induced delta to theta range. Blood pressure is normal. Respiration is normal; heart rate is normal. Activating aural implants and olfactory stimuli. Visual cortex input and oral stimulators are operational. The subject is ready and waiting," Susan reported.

"All monitors show clear. We've got the whole place to ourselves," Mick replied.

"Quantum projectors are online. Satellites are in geo-synch and waiting on standby. All other backup systems show green across the board. Access to all geo locations is 100%. All beam towers and photon relay stations are online. We are tapped in to every bandwidth of broadcast capability and are ready for initialization at your command," LeRonda stated.

"Program is running at 100%," Chuck said.

"Subject is aware and functioning. I am preparing the transition from induced delta to theta at your command," Phillip reported.

Rick gave the last command and set the crystal into its cradle. "The cradle of life," he mused to himself.

Not far away, in the test chamber, water and air molecules began to swirl and merge as they were redefined on a quantum level. What were insubstantial motes of dust had become solid. The cohesion of atoms took on form, and from the void, a man emerged. A spark was ignited, and life began anew.

Jon

The next morning, I wake up next to the burned-out fire. I'm feeling stiff and cold.

White Scar is nowhere in sight.

Getting up I stretch out the kinks in my back. Pine needles are no substitute for a mattress.

The damp morning air is crisp and invigorating. Clouds rolled in during the night and I can almost taste the impending rain.

I carry my fishing rod down to the lake not really thinking about any one thing in particular.

My little valley is serene. It wouldn't have surprised me to see retro TV's Andy, Opie and Barney holding homemade fishing poles, sitting on the other side of the lake.

I stand at the water's edge, toss in my lure, and hope for a lucky catch. The glasslike surface of the lake ripples outward in all directions until tiny wavelets reach the shore.

It's silent. The forest seems to be holding its breath in anticipation of the coming storm.

The fish are obliging and suddenly, my breakfast is wriggling on the hook.

White Scar is still nowhere in sight, but I figure he'll show up as soon as I start cooking...

No such luck. I guess he's still busy doing whatever wolves do, so I'm going to try not to worry.

Somehow, the thought of him leaving me for the call of the wild makes me feel a little lonely. What fun is paradise if you don't have a friend to share it with, even if it's a smelly old wolf?

The fish is done so I stoke the fire back to life to ward off the chill.

It isn't long before the first drops of rain fall.

Finished with my breakfast I move up onto the porch and sit in the old rocker, watching the rain come down harder.

There's something about sitting outside under a porch during a rainstorm. Watching it fall on the leaves of a tree and listening to its steady beat on the roof is therapeutic. Of course, being dry is also a good thing.

Everything in the distance has a blurry quality that coaxes my mind into a trancelike state. I feel myself drifting off. If I had a warm bed, I'd climb into it and snuggle down for a good sleep. But I don't have one, so I sit and watch the rain.

In the midst of my daydreaming, I'm jolted out of my trance by a dark shape entering the valley from the trailhead. I recognize White Scar's sleek form despite the pounding rain. A part of me is relieved that he's back.

Here he comes from around a tree. I watch as he climbs up onto the porch. His fur is plastered down with rainwater. He's giving me a silent look that says, "I'm back" and he promptly lies down and puts his head on his paws.

"Rough night?" I ask.

His body is still, and only his eyes moved at my query as if to say, "That's an understatement."

I lean the back of the rocker against the wall, put my feet up on the rail, and close my eyes. It feels good to relax. I have nowhere I have to be and nothing I have to do.

As I'm dozing off, I'm thinking of my mystery woman.

"Begin shutdown sequence," Rick ordered. "So far, so good, everyone. Let's wrap it up until tomorrow," he said before pausing. "Chuck. Come to my office when you're done."

Rick sat behind his desk and stared at the wall, thinking. He'd gotten another disturbing call the previous night, urging him to eliminate Chuck. But Rick was beginning to see that there might be another way to deal with Chuck. It all depended on what Chuck did next.

"You wanted to see me, boss?" Chuck asked as he entered the office.

Rick noticed Chuck had dark circles under his eyes. "You OK? Looks like I'm working you too hard."

"No—I mean—yes, I'm fine," Chuck stammered.

Rick stood up and paced the room, "There's something I've been meaning to talk to you about. Sit down." Rick began as he locked the door. "There's no easy way to say this so I'm just going to ask, It seems a data file has been copied. I was curious if you knew anything about that?" Rick stopped and looked at Chuck, trying to read his reaction.

Chuck hung his head in shame. "My wife said I should tell you, but I was too afraid."

"Tell me what?" Rick coaxed in a quiet voice.

Chuck took a shuddering breath, gathering up his courage, "I made a copy of my program language."

"Oh? Go on."

"I sold it to my old boss at Vid-Tec. I'm really sorry, Rick. I didn't think it would do any harm. After all, it was my program. I swear I didn't compromise anybody else's data..." Chuck was almost to the point of tears.

"I see," Rick said. "There's something you should know. Your old boss, Nathan, was found dead recently."

"Dead?" Chuck faltered. "But how? I mean, what happened?"

"Initially it was reported as a suicide."

"Suicide? That makes little sense." Chuck was becoming scared.

"I have good reason to believe that they murdered him," Rick said.

"Oh, my God! The government did it," Chuck sputtered. "This is all my fault! I regretted it as soon as I did it, but I couldn't figure out how to fix my mistake." Chuck sobbed. "They're going to kill my family, aren't they?"

"Who else knows about this?" Rick asked.

"Just my wife. I've told no one else," Chuck said between sobs.

"What about your wife? Has she told anyone—her sister, family, anyone?" Rick asked sternly.

Chuck sniffled. "No. We swore each other to secrecy."

Rick paced the room, deep in thought. Chuck had screwed up big time, but Rick felt he didn't deserve to die for a mistake in judgment, and neither did his wife and kids. "How much?" Rick asked.

Chuck was taken aback. "What?"

"How much did you get?" Rick pressed.

"Five million."

"That should set you up with a new life," Rick mumbled. "You want to get out of this mess with your skin intact, then you'd better do exactly as I say, Chuck. You won't get any second chance. Do I make myself clear?" Rick's eyes bored into Chuck.

Chuck swallowed the lump in his throat. "I understand," he said with his head turned down in shame.

"Good. Here's what we are going to do."

With growing hope, Chuck sat and listened for the next several hours.

Chapter 16

Vid-Tec: Friday 0830 Hours

Spinoza descended into the Vid-Tec parking lot a half hour later. He circled around until he found a visitor's spot near the front.

The surrounding grounds were perfectly landscaped with rolling hills of manicured lawn and tall trees enclosing a shady pond complete with a rock waterfall.

Vid-Tec's 12-story modern office building was striking. Its mirrored-cylindrical walls reflected the man-made scenery that encompassed it.

"No wonder my holo bill keeps going up every month," Spinoza quipped. "Look at this place!"

"I thought it was because of all the porn you watch," Doherty taunted.

"Did you just make a joke? Now I know I've entered the seventh level of hell," Spinoza poked back.

The car settled down with a soft thud.

"Wait here," Doherty said as he climbed out of the cruiser.

Doherty headed to the entrance crossing over an arched bridge that spanned a meandering creek. He felt like he was approaching a modern version of a medieval castle complete with moat. He had no doubts that inside the glass doors would be a security post, and he wouldn't have been surprised to see the guards wearing shiny suits of armor.

The mirrored doors opened automatically as he approached, and he stepped into a softly lit atrium.

The security checkpoint was straight ahead. He started towards it when a woman seated behind a curved desk on the left asked, "Can I help you?"

She was a pretty brunette woman in her mid-thirties with a corporate dress and conservative, expertly applied makeup.

His first impression of her was that she was very professional. Twenty years ago, he might have flirted with her, but today, he was all business and short on patience.

"Yes. I'd like to see the person in charge of human resources," Doherty said.

"May I ask what this is about?" she inquired.

"It's confidential."

"Of course. Let me get someone who can help you. If you'll just have a seat over there, this will only take a few minutes."

Doherty stood his ground. He didn't mind using a little intimidation to get what he wanted. Right now, it was answers he needed.

He watched the security guards from behind his sunglasses. They seemed confident as they stood idly by their station gazing back at him.

A moment later, the lady with no title hung up the phone. "Mrs. Bordeaux will be down in a moment to speak with you."

"A moment? More like 10 minutes," Doherty thought impatiently, but he stayed planted to his spot.

The secretary behind the desk tried to ignore him, but as the minutes ticked away. Doherty could tell she was having a hard time keeping the professional smile plastered on her face.

A long couple of minutes later, he heard high heels clacking on the marble floor from the direction of the elevators, just beyond the security station.

The guards shifted around a bit as if uncomfortable. Then a middle-aged woman in business attire appeared. With an impatient expression on her face, she stepped past the guards and headed for Doherty. It was obvious to Doherty that she wasn't used to having her day interrupted by menial distractions, and the only reason she'd come down was that he was a CPD agent.

She marched up to him and extended her hand. "Good morning, agent..." Her eyes slid down to his name plate. "...Doherty. I'm Peggy Bordeaux, head of Human Resources. How can I help you, today?"

He returned her cool and firm handshake.

"My visit concerns two of your employees." He pulled out his notebook and made a show of searching for the names as if he were a shade over-the-hill when it came to remembering details. It was a tactic he'd learned long ago, and it had a way of making people underestimate him.

"Let's see. Oh. Here they are—Mr. Nathan Watkins and Mr. Bill Honely. I understand they work here?"

"Yes. In fact, they both work here in research and development. Nathan was senior director and Bill is his assistant." She gazed over the top of her glasses at the agent. "Unfortunately, Nathan committed suicide recently, as I'm sure you must be aware of. We are all terribly saddened by this tragedy. I'm not sure where Bill is today. It seems he hasn't reported for work, yet. I can make some calls and see what I can find out."

"That won't be necessary. I know where he is," Doherty said.

"I don't understand?"

"Perhaps we should speak someplace more private. I'm afraid I have some bad news, and I also have some questions," Doherty stated matter-of-factly.

Peggy stared at Doherty for a couple of long seconds. "We can talk over here." She led him to an unobtrusive door just past the receptionist's desk. Inside the room, there were several chairs neatly spaced around a glass coffee table. A large picture window gave the illusion that the room was much bigger than it really was.

"Please make yourself comfortable. Would you like a cup of coffee or perhaps something else to drink?"

"No, thank you." He remained standing while she sat down across from him, smoothing her skirt.

"What exactly did Nathan do for your company, Mrs. Bordeaux?" Doherty still held his notebook in his hand and thumbed through the pages as if looking at written notes. In truth, the pages were blank.

"Maybe we should start with why you're here," Peggy said curtly.

Doherty let his eyes slide up from the pages and gazed at her over the rim of his sunglasses. "It seems Bill was killed in an air-car accident sometime last night." He watched her closely and studied her reaction. Shocking news usually had an effect on people that could be revealing in a lot of ways. Peggy was a cool customer and hid her reaction well.

"I see," she commented. "Are you sure?"

"Reasonably sure. However, to be certain, an autopsy will be conducted on the remains."

"That's most disturbing. And we at Vid-Tec are deeply saddened by this horrific event. But I don't see how we can be of any help to you." She wore a mask of professional neutrality on her face. No doubt honed from years of practice as head of Human Resources.

Doherty couldn't help but wonder if she wore that same expression when she was in bed performing her nightly duties with her husband.

"Mrs. Bordeaux. If you would…"

She cut him off in mid-sentence. "Agent Doherty. Let me be perfectly clear. Any further questions will be deferred to our Legal Department. I am not authorized to discuss our employees' job duties with non-corporate individuals, no matter who they might be. What we do at Vid-Tec is highly confidential, and we are always on guard against technical espionage." Her tone softened slightly. "I hope you understand." She smiled, but there was no warmth in her eyes.

Doherty closed his notebook and looked hard at her for a moment. "I did not know that airing re-runs of archaic TV shows required such secrecy."

"Now wait a…" she huffed.

This time, he cut her off. "Should my investigation lead back to your company, I can assure you that we will be having this conversation again—in *my* office, if necessary." He turned on his heels and left the building.

Doherty sat in the cruiser with Spinoza and stared at the building while he cooled off in the AC. There was something more going on here. He knew it in his gut. Why would a holo-broadcast company need to be worried about technical espionage, seriously. Were they that worried about 150-year-old episodes of "I Love Lucy" being pirated by another provider?

"Let's go, Spinoza. This place stinks like dead carp."

They headed back to the station house. "What do you suppose their R&D Department is working on that would've resulted in two deaths?" Doherty postulated.

"I haven't got a clue," Spinoza replied.

"That's comforting, at least I know you haven't gone over the edge," Doherty smiled.

"Two jokes in one day! What have you done with my partner?" Spinoza ribbed.

Peggy watched the agent get in his cruiser and slowly lift off. She had a bad feeling inside that had more to do with Nathan's death than she'd let on. News of Bill's fatal car crash had added to her worried mind.

She plucked a phone out of her pocket and called someone on speed dial. The line was answered almost immediately. "Jan, it's Peggy. I think we have a problem." She listened for a moment. "I'll be right up," she said.

Chapter 17

The Cube: Monday 0600 Hours

"Brainwave activity is within normal range. I am bringing the subject up from induced delta to theta range. Blood pressure is normal. Respiration is normal; heart rate is normal. Activating aural implants and olfactory stimuli." Susan went through her checklist with practiced proficiency. "Visual cortex input and oral stimulators are operational. The subject is ready and waiting," Susan reported.

"All security precautions are in place," Mick reported.

LeRonda flowed into the mix. "Quantum projectors are online. Satellites are in geo-synch and waiting on standby. All other backup systems show *green* across the board. Access to all geo locations is 100%. All photon towers and microwave relay stations are online. We are tapped into every bandwidth of broadcast capability, and are ready for initialization at your command," LeRonda stated.

"Program is running at 100%," Chuck said.

"Subject is aware and functioning. I am preparing the transition from induced delta to theta at your command," Phillip informed.

Rick gave the final command and set the crystal into its cradle. "Here we go again," he mused to himself.

In the quantum chamber, water and air molecules began to swirl and merge as they are redefined on a quantum level. Insubstantial motes of dust became solid. The cohesion of atoms took on form, and from the void, a man emerged. A spark is ignited and life began anew.

Jon

I'm awake. It feels like it's been several hours since I drifted off to sleep.

The heavy rain has letup and is now a gentle shower.

White Scar is nowhere in sight, again. The spot where he'd been sleeping is dry. He'll probably be gone for a while.

I decide to do a little exploring. That old mineshaft has been tugging at my curiosity. Heading inside the cabin, I grab the flashlight out of my pack. Almost as an afterthought, I tuck the forty-five in my belt. Donning my hat and slicker, I'm ready to go.

I walk around the back of the cabin, go past the old corral and make my way to the creek. Following the creek takes me up a 30-foot slope to the mine entrance.

The entrance looks like they blasted it out of solid granite. A steady stream of water flows out of the opening. Looking in, I can see the framework of heavy timbers square set into the rock to support the roof of the shaft. Tacked to a timber above it is a sign with letters burned into the wood that says, "Dawn Mine." Appropriate name.

I shine my light down the tunnel. The beam doesn't get very far before being swallowed by extreme darkness.

Taking a tentative step forward, I notice there's no sign of habitation, no bones or scat—just clear water running down the center of the floor.

I figure the old miner must have unearthed a spring somewhere deep inside the mountain.

The air feels cool and fresh, I suspect there's another opening or airshaft somewhere back there in the darkness.

Bravely I venture forth where someone had been before.

I scrutinize the timbers and notice their roughhewn texture. I'm worried that they might have been weakened by dry rot, but I'm relieved to discover that they're age-hardened, as strong as steel.

Continuing deeper into the mine, I discover the shaft opens out into a large chamber.

I examine the interior with my flashlight. There are kegs of nails the size of spikes, along with several picks, shovels, hammers, chisels of various sizes and several oil lanterns.

This place must have been the staging area for the rest of the dig.

The shaft goes up higher than my flashlight can illuminate. But what I can see looks like a tapered split, with cross beams holding the walls apart.

There is another shaft that turns left and another heading straight ahead of me.

I can hear falling water coming from somewhere ahead.

There is a pool of water on the right. I move closer, fascinated by its crystal clearness.

Shining my beam into its depths, I am surprised to see that it isn't a pool, but a flooded shaft that drops deep into the mountain. I can see cross-members with cables dangling eerily down into the depths as far as my light can reach.

There is perhaps a foot of clearance between that hole and the mine wall.

I move carefully past the pit and follow the small stream that filled those underground shafts until it eventually runs outside the front of the mine.

Gold flakes sparkle in the water. A person could probably make a decent living just panning for gold.

Following a sharp bend in the shaft, I find the stream's source.

A shaft had been dug in the mine's roof that runs upwards at a 40° angle. From that shaft, water rains down like a curtain.

I point my light up the shaft. I am surprised to see that about 20 feet back, it's blocked by an immense boulder. The water is flowing from an unknown source through a crack underneath that giant plug,

Ducking under the waterfall, I enter a shaft that runs straight back into the mountain for as far as I can see. The air in this shaft is dank and the shaft walls are lined with a milky white layer of mineral deposits. It has a low ceiling and gives me a creepy sense of claustrophobia.

This shaft looks dangerous, so I turn back toward the main chamber. I know I'll feel much better once I get back into that wide-open area.

Curious, I poke around in the stacks of supplies and decide to see if any of the oil lanterns still have fuel in them. I'm in luck. Two of them are nearly full. On top of an old crate next to them is a box of stick matches. How convenient.

I pick out a few matches and try lighting one. The end just crumbles off. The matches must've been ruined by the dampness. I'll have to bring new ones or a lighter when I return.

Doing more exploring intrigues me. I find the old mine to be an interesting adventure. And, just maybe, I'm already getting a little gold fever.

I am also curious about the fate of the miner. Perhaps he'd struck it big, loaded up his burro and walked out of the mountains a rich man. But I doubted that was the case.

Looking at my watch, I'm surprised to see that three hours have already flown past. I'd have sworn it had only been five minutes.

Heading back outside; I see the rain is pouring down again. The storm has evidently grown in fury while I was exploring. From the look of the sky, it will probably keep falling for a while. The wind is whipping through the treetops and the soggy ground is littered with small branches and leaves.

I scramble down the slope and go around to the front of the cabin. I'm disappointed that White Scar isn't there.

Gazing towards the lake, I see his dark silhouette through the distortion of the rain. He seems to be staring towards the end of the valley where we hiked the day before. I can't tell for certain, but he looks agitated.

"White Scar!" I shout over the pounding rain. "What are you doing, boy?"

His head turns my way, and he gives me a halfhearted wag of his tail before turning back towards the trailhead.

Tugging my hat down against the wind, I venture in his direction. I have my eyes glued to the ground as I negotiate my way over all the tripping hazards. When I look up again, White Scar has vanished.

"For god's sake, where did he go?"

I continue down to the water's edge, all the while scanning the woods for him.

The lake is roiling with wind-whipped waves. I am just about to turn back to the cabin when I see movement at the extreme range of my limited visibility. The pouring rain makes it hard to see anything clearly.

From under the brim of my hat, I stare out at the trailhead. My blood turns cold as I see several men enter my valley.

Ducking down, I continue to watch. Four men and all of them are armed with rifles. They are indistinct blurs behind the curtain of rain, but I feel certain that it has to be the hoedown boys from the campfire. Not good.

I'm pretty sure they aren't hunting wild boar, although I was once called a bore by my ex-wife.

Staying low, I move slowly towards the trees. I know that fast movement will catch their eye, so I'm being extra careful not to draw their unwanted attention.

As soon as I make it to the cover of the trees, I move a little faster.

I have to know for sure who these guys are and what they want.

White Scar is about 50 feet ahead of me. Apparently, he had the same idea. Great minds think alike.

I observe the men through a gap in the trees. They have stopped in the open meadow at the base of the trail, and it looks as though they are setting up a camp for the night.

Watching while they set up two dome tents and try to get a fire going in the downpour is pure entertainment. Geniuses. They might as well try to strike a match underwater. My estimate of their group intellect went down another peg. But even idiots with guns can be dangerous, so I keep my distance.

They finally give up, and all of them pile into the biggest tent—probably for group therapy, I snicker to myself.

The tent soon glows from within, possibly lit by a battery-powered lamp.

White Scar has got to be somewhere nearby. Though I look around and can't see him, I can smell his fishy breath.

I didn't dare call out to him. It makes me feel better knowing that I'm not alone.

Waiting there in the pouring rain feels like an eternity, but it probably hasn't been more than an hour.

I want to know what these guys' intentions are. So, I cautiously make my way towards their camp.

Luckily for me, the loud beating of the rain on their tent masks any outside noises I might make.

Stopping a pace away from the back of the dome, I kneel to listen.

"Come on, Zack. Pass the bottle."

"Quit your bellyaching, snot face."

I could hear laughter from the others.

"Hey, Terry. What're we gonna do when we catch that guy?"

"The same thing we did to that wolf!" Terry said, followed by a belch. "We're gonna kill him, dead!"

I was pretty sure that "kill" and "dead" were the same thing. Maybe they'd had the benefit of a first-grade education.

The others all joined in with raucous laughter.

Apparently, there's a lot of mutual support-group type stuff going on in their nylon domicile.

I've heard enough. Backing away slowly, I retreat into the woods.

I have some serious thinking to do. When I get back to the cabin, I decide to sit in the rocker and contemplate what I'm going to do next.

I'm not thrilled by my choices. I can take the 8 gauge and turn them into hamburger in their tent—not my first choice. That seems a little extreme—at least at this moment. Later, I may feel differently.

I can hear White Scar sniffing around in the darkness, just out of sight.

"You should've left when you had the chance," I tell him.

Maybe I could discourage them in some way that would make them want to give up and go home.

An inkling of an idea tickles my brain. Getting up, I head to the mine to gather some supplies and tools. I have a lot to do before morning.

The rain stops around midnight, and before long, the stars peek through the last wisps of cloud cover.

The next morning, the sun is peeking over the rim of my little valley just as I am finishing with the first part of my plan. If not for the four amigos, it would've been a picturesque day in paradise.

White Scar keeps pace with me through the woods on our way back to the cabin.

Going inside, I grab my gear. Then we hike up to the mine.

I have a suspicion about the vertical shaft. And if it pans out, I'll have a good vantage point overlooking the valley.

Spotting a narrow path cut into the rock-face I follow it up the side of the mountain. White Scar is trailing along behind me.

The trail switches back and forth until it reaches a point where it turns around an outcropping behind which is an opening into the mountain.

I duck inside and stop while my eyes adjust to the darkness.

The cave is actually another shaft that snakes its way back into the darkness. About five yards in is an opening in the tunnel floor that goes straight down.

I suspected that this vertical shaft must drop right into the glory hole down below.

It was a good thing I stopped when I did. Half-blinded by the sun, I would've walked right into that open shaft and fallen to my death.

White Scar is refusing to enter the mine. He decides he'd rather curl up in the shade behind the outcropping. With his head resting on his front paws, he follows my every movement with his eyes. Apparently, my activities are just a little more exciting than outright sleep.

I set my pack down just inside the entrance and lay the eight gauge on top of it.

Moving back to the edge of the mountain, I have an unobstructed view of the valley, and I wait. It shouldn't be long, now.

Zack woke up with a throbbing headache and a mouth that felt as though he'd eaten a bag of cotton.

He feels weighed down. His legs are pinned. Bleary-eyed, he raises his head enough to see that Earl is lying across his shins.

"Get off me, you moron!" He kicks his legs trying to dislodge Earl.

Earl groans. "All right. Don't get your panties in a wad." Earl sits up and immediately regrets it. His skull is pounding like a bass drum.

Zack crawls out of the tent. After a couple of tries, he stands up and shuffles off a dozen paces to relieve himself.

Earl staggers out of the tent and squints in the morning sunlight. "Geez, that light is bright." He puts his hands over his eyes, trying to block the glare.

Awakened by the noise, Zeke and Terry come out of their tent, not faring much better. Hungover, they mope around in a semi daze for a short while until food sounds like a good idea.

"Man, I'm hungry," Zeke complains. "Where's my pack?"

"You're always hungry," Zack grumbles.

"Try looking in the tent, you jackass," Terry grumbles.

Zeke fumbles with the supply tent's zipper, finally getting it open. He pokes his head inside. "What the…? It's empty!"

"What in the world are you talking about?" Terry groans. He jerks Zeke out of the way and thrusts his head into the opening. "Dammit! Where's all our stuff?!"

Terry glares at the others, trying to figure out which idiot brother thought this would be a witty joke. His broken finger throbs in its splint. "Funny. Ha, ha, not! Which one of you dimwits thought this was gonna be funny?"

Nobody says a word. Then Terry scrunches up his face and comes to a miraculous conclusion: "We were robbed!"

"Robbed?" Zack mumbles. "Out here? Ain't nobody out here but us."

"You twit!" Terry screams. "It's that old dude! He's gotta be out here somewheres." Terry looks around.

I'm watching the circus, trying not to laugh at the stupidity of the local yokels. I can just make out their inane banter and answer them. "Yeah. It was me! Ignorant fools."

Then, I shout to get their attention, "I took all of your guns and food. Now, what are you going to do about it?" I hope they'll just scurry back down the mountain and leave me and White Scar alone. But somehow, I doubt it.

I add, "The difference between stupidity and you fools is there is none!"

Terry turns and looks in my direction. "We's comin' for you, old man! And when we find you, we're gonna make you sorry for everything you done! You hear me, old man!" Broken finger yells. They run in my direction.

Well, there goes my plan right out the window. Now what? I can't just shoot them, even though I'm certain the world would be a better place without them.

I'm thinking it over when White Scar decides for me. He growls deeply as he watches the boys getting closer. It's the most intimidating sound I've ever heard an animal make. It makes me glad that he's on my side.

Suddenly it occurs to me that White Scar probably has no compunction about shredding up every one of those dirt bags after what they'd done to him.

I can sense the barely restrained fury radiating from White Scar. I carefully place my hand on his shoulder. "Easy boy. They'll leave a nasty taste in your mouth."

One thing I know for sure, I wouldn't shoot White Scar to save those boys.

I move out of the shade to the edge of the mountain so they can see me. "Hey!" I shout.

They stop their approach and look up.

"Yeah. It's me! Can you guess who's up here with me? No? Well, let me clue you in. Remember that wolf you were torturing the other night? He and I are best friends, now!"

"So, what?" Terry shouts back. "We'll kill him, too!"

"Idiots," I think to myself, then shout back, "With what? Your looks!" That stopped them. "Why don't you just go home before something terrible happens to you?" I say, trying to reason with unreasonable minds.

Zack, Zeke, and Earl are already backing away. Evidently, the stupid gene has only infected the oldest brother.

White Scar gets up and moves from the shadows and is standing next to me. God, he's big and menacing.

I try one last time. "Look. If this man-eating wolf decides to eat you for lunch, I won't be able to stop him. And, I'm not really certain I'd even try. So, go home!"

Terry is on the fence. Luckily, his brothers pull him back over. "Come on, Terry! We can't take on no wolf without our guns! Let's git while we can!"

I let out the breath I'd been holding as I watch them scurry away down the trail. They don't even bother packing up what's left of their supplies. This time, there's no smart-mouthing taunt from Terry. Now, I believe in minor miracles. "Wow. That was close, huh boy?"

White Scar has stopped growling, but by the look in his eyes, I can tell he's still upset.

I rub his head. "Come on. I'll buy you a fish dinner. It'll be better for you than that redneck junk food. Besides. The buttons would've stuck between your teeth."

He wags his tail halfheartedly.

Every super hero has a super power. My sense of humor had saved the day, with the help of my faithful sidekick White Scar, the wolf.

We lounge and feast on fish most of the day. And I work on finishing the medicinal rum. I'm enjoying the warm buzz and feel comfortable.

Later that night, I sit on the porch with White Scar, contemplating the meaning of life as the stars rotate across the heavens. "I think tomorrow I should head home, White Scar. How about it? Want to tag along?" I'm worried he won't want to come, but I try hard not to let it show.

White Scar lay there unmoving for a long time. I guess he's thinking it over. "No pressure, buddy."

Just as I am nodding off, I feel him lick my hand. I smile as I drift off to sleep.

Friends.

"End simulation," Rick said. "I know it's been a long day, but I need everyone in my office for a post simulation briefing as soon as you're done with your shutdown protocols.

Everyone gathered in Rick's office. "I want to commend each of you for a job well done. Phillip, what are your thoughts about continuing to the next phase of the test?" Rick asked.

"I'm very pleased with the outcome of the simulation," Phillip stated. "All of our criteria have shown perfect results."

"Jon was able to bond with White Scar very naturally," Susan added.

LeRonda spoke next. "With the wolf there beside him as a grounding point for reality, his transition to the next phase will feel normal."

Chuck cleared his throat. "Correct me if I'm wrong, but did Jon change the parameters of the simulation towards the end?"

"What do you mean?" Rick asked.

"Well. The original scenario actually ended more gruesomely," Chuck said.

"I think what he's trying to say is we had originally programmed the wolf to behave more aggressively." LeRonda looked at Rick.

"So, what happened?" Rick wanted to know.

Phillip cleared his throat. "It would appear that Jon's personality is getting stronger in the quantum projection. And in doing so, he's influencing the other projections to some degree."

"Are you saying what I think you're saying?" Rick queried.

"Jon's quantum projection is accepting the reality of his new matrix," Phillip theorized. "It is my belief that his consciousness has transferred from his actual body to the projection without external stimuli."

"If that's the case, we may be closer than we thought to a complete transfer of all mental properties, including perhaps his soul, to the new body," Susan hypothesized.

"I wouldn't go that far," Phillip wavered.

"How far would you go?" LeRonda prodded.

"All right, people. Let's not get ahead of ourselves. We've still got a long way to go," Rick said. "Everyone. Go home and get some rest. Tomorrow, we start the next phase of the experiment, and I'll need all of you to be sharp." Rick dismissed the team.

"I should program the wolf to eat you, Phillip," LeRonda's voice faded away as she exited the room amidst laughter from her teammates.

Chapter 18

Medical Suite: Monday 2340 Hours

Mary checked Jon's IV and decided it was time for a new one. When she finished with that, she checked his bandages and his vitals. Everything looked good. But her patient still floated between unconsciousness and reality.

She'd seen it before in the other test subjects. No number of drugs could keep the subject unconscious forever. The test itself required some level of conscious thought in order for the subject to "live" while the program was running.

She uttered a silent prayer that he would come back to her. But the consequences of his awakening might be more than she could take.

Would he want to live knowing that he could never be more than a hunk of meat connected to a machine? Could she do that to him?

There had to be a way for them to be together again. As she worried about the answers, a vague solution formed in her mind. Was it possible?

She ran a cool cloth over his face. He shifted slightly. Perhaps it was a reaction to her ministrations. Time would tell. She adjusted his sheets and thought about what the future might bring.

"Sleep, my love. I'm near."

Jon Dreams of His Past

Well, the school years are dragging along in the usual way. And then, one day, they're over—done, complete, finished. I am handed a piece of paper, all rolled up in a scroll for dramatic effect. I am sent out into the world, fully educated by the system, ready to take my place in society.

There is only one problem with that—I am a square peg and the world is full of round holes.

Luckily for me, the retro TV programs show me what I am expected to do with my life—get a wife, have two kids, buy a car, buy a house, maybe adopt a dog or cat, place a fishbowl on the counter and, of course, get a good job to pay for everything.

So, I stumble through the programming—I get married to a woman with the face of a cherub; she pushes out a couple of kids; we buy a car, a Gremlin II. If that piece of junk is the best the old US of A can do, then no wonder people stopped buying American cars; we rent an apartment; and I take whatever job comes my way while she stays at home watching soap operas.

Through it all, I still have one fundamental flaw nagging at the back of my mind—I still feel different inside. It's as if I am just going through the motions in order to blend in with everyone else.

I believe that's when my carefully conjured illusion dissolves, slowly—My wife isn't behaving like retro TV's "Leave It to Beaver's" perfect mom, June Cleaver; our kids act nothing like June's kids, Wally and Beaver; and I can't hold a candle to Ward, June's calm and collected dad, who always has all the answers.

My life is more in line with the dysfunctional "Simpsons" cartoon family, along with neighbors like "Married with Children's" misfit parental figures, Al and Peg Bundy.

The harder I try to maintain the media's idea of a dream family, the worse things get. Until the day that I discover retro TV's "The Sonny & Cher Comedy Hour." I see how they regularly tear into each other, man! What a scene that is. The recap at the end of their show quickly turns into a comedic form of spousal abuse for all of TV land to enjoy.

It's not long after Sonny and Cher go off the air that the supposedly happy couple goes off on each other in front of a divorce judge. Yes. TV shows me the way. I mean, if Sonny and Cher can split up, why can't I?

I finally divorce my wife, AKA, the daughter of Satan. Thank heaven. She's ticked off by that move and promptly "runs home to mama" with our two spawn in tow, telling tales of horror and mayhem to anyone and everyone who'll listen.

I am immediately ostracized by the mobile-home community where her family lives. They even replace the yellow ribbon on the old oak tree (a la Tony Orlando and Dawn's nostalgic hit) outside the house with a sign that says, "Keep out, heathen bastard!" I assume it's meant for me. Not that I'd ever try to go past the fifth gate of hell.

Our kids eventually adopt their insane mother's attitude towards me, and my relationship with the kids deteriorates to the point of being nonexistent.

I miss my kids from time to time, but not so much that I am willing to be emotionally abused by them. Alas, poor Yorik...

But the world provides my ex and our kids payback for their sins. I am sitting on my couch and watching a breaking news story about a tornado that had torn the roof off of their trailer.

I'm a little worried about the kids, but my fears are put to rest when I see all three of them being interviewed on the nightly news.

I guess that retro TV Chiffon margarine commercial is right where Mother Nature says, "It's not nice to fool Mother Nature," and then waves her hands and blasts whoever just fooled her with a violent act of nature.

On the newscast, one kid is going on and on about the injustice of the tornado hitting their trailer, and I burst into fits of hysterical laughter saying to myself, "Karma's a bitch."

A steady beeping noise is intruding into my dream. I am trying to tune it out. I'm not ready to wake up yet. Hmm, it's beginning to dawn on me that everything might not be what it seems. Is this just a dream?

Rick leaned back from the desk, exhausted after another long day. He'd just finished what he hoped would be the solution for saving Chuck and his family.

He stood up, rubbing his lower back. The bed in the backroom was giving him a backache. Tonight, he decided to go home for a change.

He grabbed his coat and stepped into the main operations center. The room was empty, and the only sound was the soft beeping of the life-support chamber.

Rick could see Mary busily tending to her patient. He enjoyed the view, seeing her bent over, rubbing a warm washcloth across the patient's forehead.

Rick walked slowly to the glass wall and gently tapped on its surface.

Startled, Mary turned around.

Rick smiled and mouthed "Sorry" with a sheepish look on his face.

Mary nodded and held up her index finger. She finished what she was doing and entered the airlock from the inside. It cycled through, and she stepped outside. The odor of Betadine solution followed.

She unsealed her helmet and set it aside for the moment. "Is there something you need, Rick?"

The room smelled of antiseptics and Mary's perfume.

"Hi, Mary," Rick said, being polite. "It was nothing important—I was just on my way out and thought you might like to join me for a bite to eat?" He'd asked her out a few times, but she had yet to accept his advances with anything more than polite refusals.

She glanced up. "Oh. Thanks, Rick..." She turned back to check on her patient. "...but, I still have lots to do tonight and Jackie hasn't shown up yet. Perhaps another time."

Rick laid his hand on the window and gazed in at Jon. "How's he doing?"

"As well as expected, I suppose." Her voice sounded tired, but her eyes held a glint of something she seemed to be hiding.

Rick's thoughts inevitably wrapped around the moral implications of what they were doing. There was little doubt that the man in the bubble would die without constant life support. In his opinion, there weren't enough remains in that chamber to make up a human being.

Rick panned the entire room, noting all the systems that were functioning properly.

"Poor bastard." He turned to Mary. "Don't worry, Mary. We're making tremendous progress with the simulation, and perhaps one day soon, we can give Jon a new life."

Rick thought he saw Mary's eyes mist over, but she turned her face away from him while putting her helmet back on.

"I hope so," she whispered.

"Well, I'm done for the day," Rick said with an uncharacteristic sigh. He turned away feeling like it'd been a long day.

"Have a good night," Mary said.

"You, too." Rick left for home. He ignored the little voice that was nagging at him because he was too exhausted to care.

Mary re-entered the chamber where she continued to care for her patient. Had anyone noticed, they'd say that she performed her tasks with tender-loving care.

Chapter 19

The Puppet Contingency, Phase Two

The Cube: Friday 0646 Hours

Rick and the team were studying Jon's military files extensively.

Phillip read the report. "The records show that when Jon was young, he had a pet dog named George. For 12 years, the two of them were inseparable until the dog passed away from old age."

"He also had an older brother who died at a young age in some sort of accident. Losing both his childhood pet and his brother were fundamental in changing Jon's emotional ties to others. He stopped allowing himself to become close to anyone or anything for fear of losing them and then suffering."

"That's so sad," Susan empathized. "No wonder he was a loner most of his life."

"There's more," Phillip said. "The psychologist made a notation in Jon's file."

Jon is highly intelligent, but the motivation for his assigned duty is below the curve. Simply put, he wants to be with his fiancée, not in the military. I suspect he has a deep-seated resentment towards the governmental authority that placed him in the service. Jon blames the military for his relationship breaking up. His repressed anger is apparent. He has trouble relating to others on a personal level, but has instead focused his angst towards anyone who is his enemy, assigned or real.

He has hospitalized several soldiers during training exercises with his innate abilities and his underlying need to destroy his enemies. For the record, I'm happy he's on our side. Further, his psych eval has shown a strong emotional tie to his boyhood dog, and it is, therefore, my recommendation that he is assigned to a canine unit. A strong inter-service bond with a canine partner will reduce his thoughts of separation from his fiancée and should ease his feelings of loneliness.

"No wonder he's having trouble letting go!" LeRonda insisted. "He's got unresolved issues with his love life."

"They must have had a fight before he left," Susan suggested. "How terrible for them."

Rick nodded sympathetically. "Keep reading, Phillip. See if there's more that can help us."

Phillip continued reading aloud.

Jon refused canine duty. Instead, he volunteered for paratrooper duty, and was accepted. He scored top in his training courses in all areas including marksmanship, hand-to-hand combat, athletics and gymnastics.

Based on his training evaluation, he was given a much-coveted assignment to an air-mobile infantry armor unit and was trained in the use of the high-tech combat armor. His gymnastic abilities were an asset, and he took to the powered armor like a second skin.

"I've read about those guys. They are badass!" Chuck said with awe. "Only 5% of those who volunteer actually complete the training! And the percentage is even smaller for those who can master the powered-armor suits."

"Why did he get caught up in that, and how in the world did he end up there?" Mick gestured towards the med-lab.

"It must have been terrible. Let's not forget that his entire unit was wiped out." Rick tried to get the memory of Jon's combat footage out of his mind. He had not told the others about that recording and had deliberately hidden the files. "Is there any more information that might help us?"

Phillip took a few minutes to scan through the material. "This is interesting." He looked up and met Rick's inquiring look. "There's a brief note from the psych officer. It says that his fiancée was a woman named Mary Dawson, a doctor of internal medicine."

Phillip turned his eyes towards the medical suite. "Is it possible?" he whispered.

"Mary? Our Mary?" Susan queried.

Rick interrupted before everyone could react to the unexpected news. "Let's not run off the rails, here. We know nothing for certain. It could just be a bizarre coincidence, even though I highly doubt it."

"Why don't we just ask her?" LeRonda posed.

"Now, there's a conversation starter," Mick said sarcastically.

Rick leaned forward and pressed the intercom. "Mary, when you have a moment, please drop by my office?"

He watched through the window as she responded with a wave of her outstretched hand, showing she'd be there in five minutes.

Rick turned his attention back to the group. "The rest of you, go to your stations and begin your startup sequences. This will be difficult enough without all of you making her feel like it's an inquisition."

Her five-minute estimate turned out to be a fifteen-minute wait. Rick didn't mind the delay. He knew her job was difficult. And considering the recent information, if true, it had to be emotionally trying as well.

Rick was sitting in his office, shuffling through a stack of paperwork. He hated paperwork, especially since computers were supposed to eliminate the need. Somehow it seemed to be the reverse. His printer was constantly spitting out forms for him to sign in triplicate—mostly bureaucratic nonsense.

Rick was so engrossed in his work that he didn't hear the door open, nor did he notice the person who had entered his space. His first inkling that he wasn't alone was the faint smell of perfume that intruded upon his thoughts.

He glanced up to see Mary standing near the door.

"Oh. Hello, Mary. Please forgive me. I didn't hear you come in," Rick said apologetically.

"If this is a bad time, I can come back," Mary said, somewhat embarrassed.

"No. Of course not. Please, pull up a chair. Any excuse to get away from this mountain of paperwork is welcome. Can I get you a cup of coffee or a bottle of water?"

"Nothing, thanks."

Rick smiled pleasantly at her as he tilted back in his chair. He could tell by the anxious expression on Mary's face that she was worried that her summons wasn't a social call.

Mary noticed Rick's sidelong glance towards the medical chamber and its special patient within. "This is about Jon, isn't it?" Mary said softly.

"Yes," Rick confirmed. "I can't help thinking about what we're putting him through. I mean, what if he somehow knows that he's a lab experiment?"

Mary looked at the man inside the chamber. Truth was that she had often had the same misgivings about the project.

Rick was uncomfortable. He truthfully didn't quite know how to broach Mary's relationship with Jon.

Nervous, he stood up and paced closer to the window overlooking the medical suite. He placed his hands behind his back and stared down at Jon's seemingly lifeless body. The machines surrounding Jon blinked as if to say, "He's doing fine."

Jon's mind still lived, but does that make up life? Is that enough?

Rick looked at Mary's troubled reflection in the glass. "I suppose we give him life inside the program—a life that he can no longer live on his own."

Mary chose her next words carefully. "But is it the life he would've chosen had I have given him the choice? Or is he just a puppet, performing for our own amusement?"

Rick stared down at Jon. "I honestly don't know," he whispered. He turned towards Mary and reached for Jon's military file.

Mary recognized the folder. "I guess you know?" she said in a low voice.

"I wasn't sure. None of us were. So, it's true, then? You were... or rather, are Jon's fiancée?"

"Yes." Tears welled up in Mary's eyes.

Rick handed her a box of tissues and sat silently, waiting for her to find some measure of composure.

"Can you tell me what happened?" he asked with genuine concern.

Mary fidgeted in her seat, unable to voice her unease. She liked Rick as a person. He was a descent boss, but what he was asking went way beyond the scope of work. Her relationship with Jon was deeply personal, and she wasn't completely certain just how far she could trust Rick.

Mary sat quietly for several minutes, lost inside the memories of the past. "It was his last night at home. The next day, he was scheduled to ship out." Mary dabbed her eyes as they teared up. "I couldn't bear to let him go. I pleaded with him to stay. I thought we could just run away together and start a new life. No one would know. He said he wanted to be with me, but that he couldn't live in hiding. Well, he was right, of course. But in my pain, I refused to understand. I said some things I shouldn't have." She wiped her eyes. "I told him that if he loved me, he wouldn't go. He tried to help me understand, but I was hurt and was being stubborn. We argued." She cried openly. "I told him I never wanted to see him again." She looked imploringly at Rick. "I didn't mean it! That was the last time we spoke—the last time I saw him as he was leaving our apartment." Mary's shoulders shook as she wept tears of grief and guilt.

Rick sat, quietly waiting.

"I wrote to him every day, but I never got a response. I don't even know if he got my letters. Then, about 6 months later, a letter came in the mail. I was so excited, but it wasn't from Jon. It was from the Department of Defense."

"I can still remember the cold sterility of the words telling me that Jon had been killed in combat." Mary wiped her eyes. "They didn't even tell me how or why."

"I made phone calls to find out more information, but I got nowhere. Those heartless bastards wouldn't even let me set up a funeral for his remains. Then a colleague of mine pulled me aside one day and told me he'd heard rumors about wounded veterans being transferred to a secret project. I don't know *how* he came by that information, but he said that he saw a list of names—and Jon's was one of them."

"He referred me to a friend who was working at the Veterans Administration. I pleaded, begged and finally threatened to go public if they didn't let me see Jon. Finally, one of the psych officers relented. But not because of my threats, but they believed that my presence near Jon might help him with the project. That's how I ended up here."

"It must be very difficult for you to see Jon as he is now," Rick mumbled.

Her eyes welled up with tears again. "At least I'm with him. I wouldn't want it any other way."

Rick went around the table and gently placed his hands on her shoulders to comfort her. "Try not to worry. I promise— I'll bring Jon back. I swear it," he assured Mary.

Chapter **20**

The Cube: Friday 0830 Hours

Rick pulled his gaze away from Jon and addressed the team. "All right, everyone. Focus on your jobs. We don't want any mistakes. Remember, Jon's life is waiting for him. And it's up to us to make it happen."

Rick walked to the safe that held the key to the project. Rick inserted the crystal into its robotic cradle and watched as it swung into position beneath an array of lasers.

Susan felt nervous as she began speaking for the record. "Brainwave activity is at 0.5-4 Hz and holding on delta frequency. Temperature is normal. Heart rate is holding steady at 45 bpm. Respiration is normal. Blood pressure is steady at 118 over 78."

Rick studied the bio-readings carefully. His next decision was going to change the definition of reality. "Bring the subject up to theta range and prepare for simulation."

Susan's fingers danced over her virtual keyboard. She watched her monitors closely as the brainwave frequency changed from 0.5-4 Hz to 4-7 Hz. "Subject's brain activity is holding at theta frequency. I am activating aural implants and olfactory stimuli. Visual cortex input and taste simulators are operational. The subject is ready and waiting."

"Phillip. Status, please."

"Patient is entering an induced state of subjective consciousness. I am monitoring brainwave activity. All indicators show patient is responsive to external stimuli.

"Memory upload started," Phillip reported. "Background history, job history, and personal history are all inserted. Brainwave activity shows positive acceptance of inserted memories."

"What's our status, Chuck?" Rick asked.

"The program is online and all systems are looking good," Chuck responded.

"Initiate security protocols, Mick," Rick ordered.

Mick's hands manipulated virtual controls as he locked out the elevator and shut down all incoming communications. Only the highly encrypted satellite uplink remained open. "All security procedures are activated," Mick stated. "The cube is locked down."

"Anyone topside?" Rick asked.

Mick studied numerous security feeds from all points of entry into the vacant hanger that concealed the elevator entrance. "All monitors show clear. We've got the whole place to ourselves," Mick replied.

"What's our security status at the remote site?" Rick knew it could be disastrous if someone accidentally entered the room where the quantum hologram generator had been installed.

Mick changed his feed to the site. "The building is secure. All indicators show *green* and uncompromised."

"Excellent work, Mick. LeRonda. How are we looking?" Rick queried.

"Quantum projectors are online. Satellites are in geo-synch and waiting on standby. All other backup systems show *green* across the board. Access to all geo locations is at 100%. All photon towers and quantum relay stations are online. We are tapped into every bandwidth of broadcast capability and are ready for initialization at your command," LeRonda replied.

Rick surveyed the room. Like a beaming father, he felt a touch of pride. Perhaps it was the significance of this historic moment—but no matter the reason, Rick couldn't think of a better group of people to work with on this project. If successful, then their patient would have a new lease on life.

Since Rick's meeting with Mary, he struggled to think of Jon as just their "test subject" as he once had.

Rick let out a breath and quietly chastised the butterflies in his stomach. "Start program on my mark—five, four, three, two, one, begin."

"Let the paradigm bring life," Rick whispered under his breath.

A blue glow appeared as the lasers powered up. Beams of pure light lanced down into the crystal. In ever expanding numbers, the crystal blue light refracted inside the artificially made facets of the prism until they constructed an image. The image was perfect in every detail from all angles.

"Imagers are responsive. Initiating beam sequence for satellite transference of data stream." LeRonda's hands hovered over her virtual keyboard. "Started." She pressed the button.

The image in the crystal was beamed to a satellite in high earth orbit and then instantly redirected to the test location several miles away.

This was the next crucial step, testing to see whether they could successfully recreate the quantum Jon miles away from the lab.

Everyone sat frozen as they watched the remote site via camera uplink.

Not far away, in a dingy space with poor furnishings, water and air molecules swirled and merged as they were redefined on a quantum level. Similar to a tornado, it swirled unchecked around the small room. What was insubstantial solidified. The cohesion of atoms slowly took on a pre-programmed form. And from the void, a man emerged. A spark was ignited and life began anew.

The image was now "live" and capable of complete interface with living human beings without their being aware that he wasn't a "real" person. Jon's holographic image could be touched. And the virtual Jon could touch and manipulate any solid matter he came in contact with. The projection was as real as the surroundings they placed him in. Jon *lived*.

The manipulation of matter at a quantum level mimicked the miracle of creation. To complete the reality of the subject's world, a job had been secured for Jon weeks before through an online interview process.

The subject "Jon" had been hired and outfitted without ever having met anyone in person. They gave his job assignments to him in the same manner, thus limiting his exposure to any living persons at any one time.

Now, the next phase of the experiment began—real-time interaction to test the subject's ability to blend in with his programmed reality.

"OK, everyone. Let's wake him up and send him to work," Rick ordered. "And don't forget his special friend."

Jon

I just woke up and I'm not sure where I am. Sitting up in my bed, I have that same odd feeling I've been having lately. Of course, the dream I just awakened from doesn't help. Wisps of the dream are still floating around in my head. All I can recall is something about rednecks and wolves.

Was that a nightmare? I can't shake off a recurring sense that there's something ominous, or wrong, some elusive memory that is refusing to come back. The feeling haunts me and I don't know why. I can't completely grasp the smoky wisps of the dream as they are rapidly fading from my mind.

Sitting on the edge of the bed with my head between my knees, I feel a warm kiss on my cheek.

I turn my head to look her in the eye. She is sitting there staring at me with those big brown eyes, the ones that melted my heart the first time I saw them. I can't resist. I grab her gently by her big floppy ears and tousle her head. She wags her tail in response.

"All right, Nikki. I'm getting up."

Nikki is my only real friend. She has a heart of gold and breath that smells like dead fish.

"Move out of the way, you mangy dog." She isn't budging. "And go brush your teeth. What on earth have you been eating?"

She's wagging her tail with obvious pride, no doubt happy with her own unpleasant odor.

An hour later, I am ready to face my day. I check my log-in and find my duty assignments are already waiting.

I grab my sidearm and head towards the door. "Come on, Nikki. We might as well get on with it."

Nikki runs to the exit with a lot more enthusiasm than I have. Maybe I need a vacation? Maybe not.

I lock up my penthouse suite and head down the hallway. It still smells like mildew, even though the landlord has already slopped on another coat of paint. I can see spots he's missed and others where the paint is so thick that it's sagging down the wall. I give him an "A" for effort and an "F" for execution.

Stepping outside, I squint my eyes in the bright sun. It's shaping up to be another beautiful day.

Nikki obviously feels the same way as she runs around looking for her morning spot to relieve herself.

I wait patiently as she goes about her business. I look around at the neighborhood. Not much going on. It isn't the worst neighborhood in the city, but it's far from being the best.

The people are decent, hard-working, and nice for the most part.

I reach for the scoop and clean up Nikki's daily deposit for disposal. "Everything come out okay?" I ask.

She gives me an obligatory wag of her tail with little enthusiasm. I'm guessing it's her way of saying that she doesn't appreciate my sense of humor.

As a CPD Agent, I can choose whatever vehicle I want. Most of the guys like the newest machines available. The flyers are very popular, for obvious reasons. But I don't care for them unless it's necessary to get the job done. Today isn't one of those days. Call me old-fashioned, but I have a fascination with the past.

I assume some white-collar bureaucrat thought it was an excellent incentive for us blue-collar types to drive whatever we want to keep us on the force. Yeah, right. But it works for me—

my choice is a 1968 Chevy Camaro. Go figure. Most people in my generation wouldn't even know what a '68 Camaro is.

Mine is pewter gray, has a set of American Racing mags, and a piston engine under the hood—a complete relic. It burns gasoline.

Gasoline is an impossibility for most of the 7 billion people on the planet. But not for me—Agents have their perks.

I like to drive fast. The boss frowns on my muscle car's high fuel consumption, but he'll live.

Nikki jumps in and settles down on the passenger side's leather bucket seat.

I climb in behind her and take my spot in the driver's seat. Now don't get me wrong, I think Nikki can drive as well as most people, but I've seen her having trouble reaching the clutch and shifting the gears—she obviously learned to drive in an automatic, not a stick shift.

The computer responds to my voice code and I log in to my status board to get my daily assignments. A list of duties scrolls down my screen. I give them a cursory glance. Everything is already sorted by priority, so I pull up a geo-map and outline my route to the first location.

The engine starts and I let it idle for a few minutes, just listening to its throaty rumble.

I move the stick shift into first gear, then pull away, leaving behind twin rooster tails of dirt and a cloud of exhaust coming out of the twin chrome exhaust pipes. Air cars can't do that.

The sun is rising behind the mountains as I edge the speedometer needle up to 90 mph. That's one perk of being a CPD agent—it also helps that I just didn't give a damn.

The highway is an endless two-lane thrill ride that stretches out in front of my modified antique interceptor.

I drop my custom 8-ball shifter down into 4th gear and hear the engine hum as I wind my baby up to 120 mph. In the 1960s, that was this baby's best speed. Man, I love my old hot rod.

Music seemed like a good idea, "What do you think, girl? Pink Floyd?"

I interpret her wagging tail as a clue that she approves. Smiling at my superior deductive reasoning I slip the crystal into the player. Strains from the past echo in the car as the music swirls in surround sound.

As usual, Nikki sings along with the music. Howling out the window of my car, she continues nonstop. Though I don't much care for her style, I never let on. But 6 hours later, I am relieved to be at my first stop. Silence is golden as I get out of the car and stretch. I'm looking at a decrepit house apparently held together by a single rusty nail. Some people just don't care how they live. I knock on the door to this "mansion" of monumental design and architecture careful not to bang too hard. In my mind, I imagine the door falling off its hinges. Just then, the rusty-hinged front door squeaks open. There stands a tiny man with pale skin that is stretched taut over his narrow skull. His deep-set eyes are perched under a big forehead with bushy eyebrows.

His eyes meet mine. "Wow, I have nothing to complain about," I think to myself. Here I am, serving a summons to a Neanderthal-looking husband who's gotten a couple of years behind on some kind of court-ordered payment—another genius lost in paradise.

One look at my uniform is all the guy needs to blow up. He gives me the usual attitude as if it were my fault that he got caught up by a divorce system that always sides with the woman, no matter how insane she may be.

I can relate. I had a bitch of an ex-wife who sucked up my paycheck better than she ever sucked anything that mattered. But I didn't write the laws, and I didn't vote for the bastards who did. I just enforce the laws, so cut me some slack, Jack.

The twerp is still running his mouth when I think about punching him a new third eye. Fortunately for him, I lose interest.

Nikki growls threateningly. That shuts his trap. "Thanks, girl," I whisper. I'm not getting paid enough to get ticked off by every dipshit that I have to deal with.

"You've been served." I hand him the envelope. "Have a nice day," I say as I walk away, thinking of some profanities that would've punctuated the ending of that sentence nicely.

I hate these assignments.

Nikki runs ahead of me and jumps into the car. Clearly, she's ready to leave jaundice-face behind.

Keeping one eye on the dude, I slip behind the wheel. He's just standing there.

I can tell that he's fit to be tied, but he seems like a thousand other guys I've seen many times over who are in the same boat. He'll get over it.

I pull away, leaving behind my fair share of air pollution.

The sun is setting behind the mountains as I edge the needle up to 90 mph. Man, I love my old hot rod. They just don't make them like this anymore.

I'm high in the foothills, looking down at a straight ribbon of asphalt that runs all the way to the horizon. That horizon is very tempting.

I stare out at that far line in the distance as I race along with nothing on my mind but having a few cold brews and watching tonight's game.

Turning on the music player, I relax behind the wheel. The music starts, slow and mystical, flowing smoothly along the rolling slopes of the road. I am on the verge of losing myself in the music's mood when Nikki sings along, again. Ugh. I wonder if being deaf would be better?

I'm not always this cynical about the world. Geez, once upon a time I had a wife, two kids, even a dream about our perfect family and the world we lived in. I actually gave a damn. My ex pulled the plug on all that. All the dreams I had went down with a flush.

I listen to the hum of the powerful engine. The car is telling me she has a little more juice to offer, so I push the pedal to the metal.

The needle cranks clockwise past its 120-mph maximum on the dial and spins its way back towards the zero.

I'm not sure just when I stopped caring about life. It might have been on the night that she left me. But then again, after she was finally gone, I felt great for a while.

My musical selection is soothing me, filtering out the static from my past. I relax and enjoy the ride as Pink Floyd's "The Dark Side of the Moon" fills the emptiness.

"By the way. Which guy's Pink?"

Nikki howled.

"Are you sure? I thought it was the other guy."

My machine screams over the dark asphalt at speeds that the car designers in Detroit couldn't have imagined.

I can hear the wind whistling past my window. Somewhere out there, past the hood of my car, is a destiny I can feel, but can't quite see.

In the back of my mind, I feel the barest hint of a memory—something important, but elusive—that I can't quite pull all the way out of the gray matter in my skull, like an itch that I can't scratch. That itchy feeling is still bothering me hours later as I lay down and am about to fall asleep with Nikki curled at the foot of my bed.

One day closer to death. Run, rabbit, run.

"End simulation." Rick smiled. The test simulation had gone perfectly.

LeRonda jumped up from her console and gave Susan an enormous hug. "Woo, hoo! She yelled with excitement.

Mick almost smiled as he high-fived Chuck. "That was outstanding!"

"That was excellent work, everyone!" Please follow your shutdown protocols and let's call it a day.

Rick slipped into his office while everyone chattered and marveled about the total success of the day's simulation. He returned a minute later holding a bottle of Champaign and five plastic cups. He started pouring. "Come on, everyone. I've been saving this bottle for this special moment."

The others gathered around, smiling and taking cups of bubbly.

Rick raised his cup for a toast. "Today, we successfully crossed the bridge between life and death. Cheers!"

"Cheers!" They all shared in the drink.

"I'd like to propose another toast," Chuck said as he raised his cup. "To Jon!"

"Here's to Jon!" They all tilted their cups towards the medical suite.

Inside, they could see Mary tucking a blanket around Jon's shoulders, making him comfortable for another long night of fitful rest.

The sight, which on the surface seemed so normal, sobered the celebrants with the enormity of how far they still had to go.

The experiment would not be complete unless they could successfully transfer Jon's consciousness into the quantum body. Only then will they have truly crossed the threshold between worlds.

Rick downed his cup, and with a long, shuddering breath, he spoke. "I don't know about any of you, but I'm exhausted and I'm sure our patient could use a break as well. I'll expect reports from all of you on my desk by 0600 tomorrow.

Rick gazed around the room. "Great job, today. We accomplished the unthinkable. Tomorrow, we'll do the impossible!"

Amidst a round of applause, Rick retired to his office and closed the door. He leaned back against the door and felt his legs trembling with nervous exhaustion. He hadn't realized until that moment just how nerve-wracking the simulation had been. But everything had gone smoothly, perfectly. There was reason to celebrate today's significant accomplishment. "We did it!" he said to himself.

Rick sat contemplatively running the test over again on the console in his office when there was a knock at his door.

"Enter."

Phillip poked his head in. "Sorry to disturb you…"

"That's all right, Phillip. Come in. I wanted to speak with you, anyway. Have a seat."

Rick sat quietly, scanning his console for a few moments until he was certain that they would leave him and Phillip undisturbed. He pressed a button under his desk and a soft click issued from the door. The room was now secure for privacy.

"I'm glad you stepped in, Phillip, I'm extremely interested in your assessment of Jon's psychological performance," Rick said.

"Of course." Phillip cleared his throat. "The patient responded as if he were totally committed to the realty of his experiences. The slight change from White Scar the wolf to Nikki the black Labrador was a key factor in establishing the emotional link with his past. Also, the download of his current job assignments will keep him focused on his new life. All things considered, I have every reason to believe that with more time in the simulation, Jon will consciously move from one reality to the other, eventually."

"Have you given any more thought about what's going to happen to his body?" Rick nodded towards the medical suite.

Phillip laced his fingers. "I can only assume that if we are successful in transferring not only his consciousness, but his soul energy into the quantum model, then the empty body will expire."

"Let me pose a reverse scenario. What would happen to a living, conscious person if their quantum simulation were to die?"

Phillip sat back. "That's a superb question. The answer is 'I don't know.' All of our simulations have been mono-directional, focused only one way, placing Jon's essence into the quantum hologram."

Rick sat silently for several minutes, deep in thought. "Theoretically, the body with the soul will be the one to survive while the other ceases to exist."

"Theoretically, I would agree with you," Phillip said. "Perhaps, we can take a measure of knowledge from the ancient Hermetic principles—the All is mind, the Universe is mental."

"I remember something of that religious teaching from my philosophy course," Rick said. "The Hermetic also taught that nothing rests—everything moves, or to be more specific, everything vibrates. In fact, it was the writings of Hermes Trismegistus that gave me the inspiration for my first attempt at quantum vibration transmutation."

"Which brings us to exactly where we are now," Phillip filled chimed in. "This experiment may demonstrate in practice the wisdom of those ancient masters."

Rick steepled his fingers in thought. "Wouldn't it be amazing to prove that our so-called 'primitive' ancestors held the secrets to the quantum paradigm thousands of years ago?"

"I've often wondered where or how that knowledge was lost. It appears an immense piece of humanity's history is missing," Phillip mused.

"It seems that way." Rick ran his fingers through his hair. "I don't know about you, but I'm beat. Thanks for your input, Phillip. You must be as tired as I am, so why don't you head home and rest up for tomorrow's run."

"Until you brought it up, I didn't realize how tired I am." Phillip stood up. "See you in the morning." He collected his documents and walked out.

Rick stayed in his office working on a program that he had co-written with Chuck. He felt that time was running out for Chuck. Then, as if to emphasize that thought, the phone buzzed for his attention. He knew who it was before answering. "Yes?"

"I'm still waiting, Rick. And I am not a patient man. Should I send in my team?"

"I'd prefer to deal with this myself," Rick said.

There was a long silence on the line. "When are you going to deal with this?"

"Soon. I'll contact you when it's done."

"Understood." The line went dead.

Rick called Chuck's number. Chuck answered on the first ring. "What's up, Rick?"

"It's time. Bring your wife and kids to the cube tonight."

Rick hung up on Chuck and set the phone down. He dabbed the sweat that was forming on his brow. It troubled him the way things had changed in the past few hours. "Come on, Chuck. Time is running out!" He urged.

Chapter 21

Max pulled out a seat and spun it around so that his muscular forearms rested on the back of the chair.

"Rick is not cooperating, and time is running out for us. The experiment has entered the next phase, rather successfully I might add," Aaron snapped.

"So, I'm told," Max said flatly. He watched the blood vessel begin to throb on his boss's forehead.

"I see Nathan committed suicide," Aaron said with a smile, pointing to a news crystal on his desk. "Nice touch. But I heard the CPD is not convinced and is sending a crime scene investigator to the house."

"The CSI won't find anything unless they perform a necropsy on some fish."

Aaron glared at him. "What makes you think they won't? We can't take the chance. Send someone over there immediately and clean it up."

"A fire should take care of any evidence," Max offered.

Aaron's voice left no room for excuses. "What about Vid-Tec themselves? Do they still possess the basic program?"

"Unfortunately, yes. In fact, they've improved upon the base program significantly."

"Tell me something I don't already know," Aaron said with growing irritation.

"We tortured Nathan's second in charge—a Mr. Bill Honely. He was very cooperative towards the end. It seems that

Vid-Tec has some very impressive security that will be impossible to hack into from outside the building." Max reported.

"I assume Bill won't be talking anytime soon?"

"Bill had an air-car accident."

Aaron absorbed the information with a smile of approval. "What's your plan for Vid-Tec?" Aaron asked.

"Infiltrate with our beam and hack the mainframe from inside the building," Max stated.

"Will it work?"

"No way to know at this point. Depends on how well encrypted their system is and how much time we can spend on site," Max said.

Aaron tented his fingers. "We'd better make a backup plan just in case things don't work out."

"Sure boss."

"One more thing. I want that SOB who stole our data silenced, permanently! Rick keeps dragging his feet and I'm having doubts about his ability to deal with this problem."

Max eyed his boss. "I'll take care of it. A call has already been made, and a team is standing by to set up a scenario. We'll go in tonight." Max paused. "Of course, the wife and kids will also have to be killed."

"Just make sure that there are no witnesses and that the leak dies with them."

"Consider it done." Max rose from his seat and left the room. He didn't approve of killing innocents, but sometimes there was no way to avoid it.

Chuck's House: Thursday 0300 Hours

"I'm in position, team leader."

"Roger one. Standby. Two, report."

"Entering the backdoor now, the house is quiet. I'm making my way to the master bedroom."

"Unit one, enter the front."

"Wilco. I'm in the front room. Heading towards the kids' rooms now."

From the back of the trailer home came the sound of a soft whoosh, followed by another a second later. "Both targets have been darted."

A few seconds later, two more darts found their targets, "Kids are down. House secure."

"All right, team. Let's get to work. We haven't got much time. The sun will be up in a couple of hours and we need to be long gone by then."

The men worked in silence. Dragging the parents from their bed and carrying the kids into the kitchen. Over the next hour they set up a murder scene complete with dead bodies. The only merciful act was that the wife and kids had been darted, so they never felt the silenced bullets end their lives.

The men felt neither remorse nor pity. To them, it was just another job, and they were seasoned professionals.

They propped the drugged husband on the sofa with the murder weapon and a bottle of whiskey. When they were far enough from the house, they would call in a shooting.

The Agents arriving on the scene would assume the husband was the culprit, and he would be off to the recycling vat by noon. Case closed.

"Let's pack it up." The team leader said routinely as he made for the door.

The three men slipped like wraiths back into the darkness of the early morning hours.

Chapter 22

The Cube: Thursday 0600 Hours

Everyone was busy at their consoles getting ready for the day's run.

"Hey. Where in the world is Chuck?" Susan asked.

The others must have been thinking the same thing because all eyes turned to Rick.

"He called in sick. I guess you guys de-stressed him a little too much." Rick said with a calm smile. "I'll fill in as a replacement."

Rick watched carefully as all eyes turned towards him. He saw only mild curiosity on their faces.

Rick walked over to Chuck's station and sat down, ignoring the interested looks from the others.

What they didn't or couldn't know was that Rick had been training on Chuck's terminal for the past week. With Chuck's help, he'd become well versed in the program.

Each of them had hours of cross training in their respective fields as well. It was all part of the security procedures put in place before the program started.

Rick had never believed that he'd have to resort to using the other team members as replacements. But things rarely go according to plan.

The team fell into their normal routine.

"Brainwave activity is within the norms. I am bringing the subject up from induced delta to theta range. Blood pressure is normal. Respiration is normal; heart rate is normal; Activating aural implants and olfactory stimuli. Visual cortex input and oral stimulators are operational. The subject is ready and waiting," Susan reported.

"All monitors show *clear*. We are flying solo," Mick replied.

"Quantum projectors are online. Satellites are in geo-synch and waiting on standby. All other backup systems show *green* across the board. Access to all geo locations is at 100%. We are ready for initialization, at your command," LeRonda stated.

"Program is running at 100%," Rick said. He casually inserted a crystal into his computer console. Nobody saw what he was doing—not that it mattered. When the time came, he would implement his override and take control of the subject.

"Subject is aware and functioning. I am preparing the transition from induced delta to theta at your command," Phillip reported.

Rick gave the last command and remotely activated the quantum projector. "The cradle of life" he mused quietly to himself.

In a shabby room, water and air molecules swirled and merged as they were redefined on a quantum level. What were insubstantial motes of dust become solid. The cohesion of atoms took on form, and from the void a man emerged. A spark was ignited and life began anew.

Jon

I'm barely awake. My brain feels like two pounds of mush in a one-pound container. Note to self—no more canned Bud.

I swing my feet off the bed and hang on to the side for dear life. My head is spinning.

Nikki barely raises her head off the floor. She must be holding on to that spinning platform like a carnival ride.

I just made it to the toilet in the nick of time. It's going to be one of those days.

After a long, cold shower, I am finally feeling alert enough to venture out into the world and work the swing shift.

Nikki and I are motoring down the old interstate listening to "Breathe"—which I have to admit Nikki howls with nicely—when I think I hear a distant voice call my name.

I turn down the music. It's dispatch. I'm only half listening, not interested in the slightest.

"Agent Doe. Do you read me? Over."

Shit. My boss Agent Doherty is trying to reach me. I have yet to meet him in person, but he seems OK.

Pink Floyd is going to have to wait. As I turn off the music, I can see the disappointment on Nikki's face. She loves to sing. "Don't worry, Nikki. I'll turn it back on in a minute."

I key my headset. "Go ahead."

The radio call is full of unusual static and I can barely make out the message between all the squeals.

I hear Doherty say something about gunshots being fired. The report was phoned in by a concerned neighbor in district D. It hardly seems worth the call. There are always gunshots being fired in that district.

The address comes through loud and clear. As fate would have it, I am only a mile away. Go figure.

"I'll check it out. Over," I reply.

I wonder if Doherty can sense my lack of enthusiasm.

"There goes our dull day, Nikki."

Nikki's tail thumps once on the seat.

"Where's your eagerness?" I tease.

She buries her snout under a paw and closes her eyes. I want to do the same, but I drive faster. I don't bother with the lights and siren. There's nobody around to appreciate the show.

Minutes later, I pull into a dirt driveway with my music blaring, "Run rabbit, run." My thoughts exactly.

A cloud of dust billows around me towards the decrepit-looking temporary location house in front of me. I wait a minute for the dirt cloud to dissipate.

The last strains of "home" fade away with the coming twilight. I turn off the music.

Just for kicks, I flip on the flashers concealed behind the front grill. The blue and red blinking lights give the front of the trailer house an eerie look, as if a UFO is about to land. Who knows? Maybe it already did.

I get out of the cruiser and just stand there taking in the scene.

Nikki hops out after me and presses against my leg. She is all business. "Stay close, girl."

I hate domestic calls. Mostly because they bring back too many of my own memories that I've been trying really hard to forget.

This type of call is always the most unpredictable. Usually, the worst is already over by the time the authorities show up. But sometimes, they erupt into a savage free-for-all which could end in a bad way for us good guys. By the way, that's me—white hat, gold star, heroic chin—only my hat isn't white and I am certainly no hero. But I do boast a gold star as one of my uniform accoutrements. One out of three ain't bad.

The yard is a dirt field covered with scattered toys in various stages of decay, and piles of garbage that never made it to the trash recycler.

An old sofa sits to the right of the door. The pile of crushed cheap beer cans next to it makes a rather impressive-looking pyramid. I already don't like this guy. Only a suicidal werewolf would drink the Silver Bullet.

The trailer still has all of its wheels. Of course, they're all flat. Not a very "mobile" home.

There's an old rusted-out pickup truck parked half way around the back with the hood up and engine parts stacked on the fender. I get the impression that it died right where it sits over a hundred years ago.

The tires have rotted away, and it has weeds coming out through the body and engine compartments. It looks like a scene right out of the retro sci-fi movie "The Day of the Triffids."

But everything isn't decrepit in this picture. A shiny new satellite dish sits on the roof, looking like some kind of alien homing device. It stands out like a beacon of incongruity.

I absently note the name of the provider emblazoned on the satellite dish: "VTS" Underneath the logo is the name spelled out in smaller print: "Vid-Tec Systems." It figures that this candidate for Darwinism would have a new video system and no car. He probably watches a lot of porn and needs high-speed interweb to keep up with his hand.

The only thing missing around this god-forsaken place are bloodhounds and a rickety porch for them to sleep under.

Hmm. Maybe there were dogs here at some point. I suspect they probably ran off looking for better lodgings elsewhere.

"Looks like your friends have run away," I joke looking at Nikki. She doesn't laugh.

What a dump. Makes me feel sorry for his wife and kids. Maybe they ran off, too. I know I would've.

The front door is open slightly and there's no screen door. Judging by the steady drone of a million tiny wings, every fly within a hundred miles knows it.

It's unnaturally silent, except for the sound of a holovision coming from inside. I can see the blue glow through the front window.

There's an icy feeling in my gut, like I'm already too late.

I grip my Colt 45 revolver.

Some other guys on the force gave me a hard time about its old-fashioned six-round capacity versus their boxy CPD issued ten-millimeter automatics.

I have one of those, too. For me, it's a backup. I like the punch power of my two-hundred-fifty-grain 45-caliber rounds. Shooting through a wall is a capability I've found useful on more than one occasion.

Walking up to the door, "Agent!" I announce. "Come to the front door where I can see you."

"Nikki. Scout," pointing towards the back of the place. With her ears perked up, she slinks off behind the trailer.

I try to temper my voice on the off chance that there are kids in the house. I'm hoping there aren't. The kids don't need to see mommy and daddy ripping into each other. But maybe they don't have any kids. That would be a blessing in more ways than one.

The world already has enough jerks in it.

My instincts scream that this whole deal has already gone south.

I creep up alongside the front door and take a quick look inside, trying to avoid making myself into a target. That's difficult for me to do at 6 feet, 200 lbs., of mostly muscle.

In that split-second glance, I spot the wife and two kids on the floor in the kitchen lying in an expanding pool of blood.

I'd seen death before, and those three didn't look like they'd be walking away from this house ever again.

I can feel my anger building like a volcano about to erupt. It's always the innocent who pay the ultimate price in this insane world, and I'm tiring of it.

"Agent," I yell. "Come out, now!"

No more Mr. nice guy. I'm furious.

I hear nothing. No angry retort. No shouts of defiance. But I can hear the holotube broadcasting in the background. It sounds like that retro game show with its host Bob Barker asking for a bid on a washing machine. Bob is long gone, but his white-haired noggin is still haunting the airwaves. Sometimes, I think that those computer recreations have gone too far. I wondered if this was hell.

It's time for me to make a choice. I can wait for backup or I can do what I always do.

Mom always said I wasn't the brightest bulb in the lamp.

So far it has been a dim bulb day. I can't help but wonder if my ticket is going to get punched. What a terrible place to buy the farm. As if any place would be good.

I whistle for Nikki. She bolts around the corner and runs to my side. "Guard," I command.

Nikki stands at attention and watches the yard. I step up to the door.

It's funny the thoughts that pop into your head when the grim reaper is inviting you in. My world was all grays and blacks with little going on except for work. I knew there was more to life. How do I know this, you might ask? Because I saw it on the holotube, so it must be true.

Somewhere over the rainbow there are sandy white beaches crowded with bikini-clad beauties strutting around in the bright sun without a care in the world. That's where I want to be, but instead, I'm here at this idiot's house hoping that this won't be my last day on planet earth.

Bob Barker's voice echoes from inside. "You've picked door number two! Let's see what you've won!" I don't feel like a winner right now.

The open trailer door is beckoning me inside. I have little choice in the matter. At least that's what I tell myself as I step through the doorway. Sure. No one is forcing me to do it, but I get a sense of urgency that I can't ignore.

Yeah, maybe later I might reflect on this moment and think what a dumb jerk I was. If I survive my own stupid choice.

The front door swings inward and partially blocks my view of the living room. The concealment works both ways. He can't see me and I can't see him. Not an ideal situation but do-able.

I have an itchy trigger finger. I'm not sure what that means, exactly, but I heard it once in an old western. My plan is to shoot first and ask questions later. I heard that one in a movie, too. Maybe I should just start slinging lead through the door.

I glance to the left down the hall and glimpse an unmade bed at the end of the trailer. I had lived in a replaceable home once upon a time, and this one was the same. There's got to be a factory out there somewhere that punches these things out by the millions.

There is a master bedroom with bath at one end, kitchen and living room in the center, and two smaller rooms up front with a small bath. I'm guessing the small rooms were where the kids lived.

Viewing the kitchen, I need no more reason to shoot the man of the house than the bloody bodies on the floor. I avert my eyes from the pool of blood around them.

The house reeks of cigarettes and booze. Underlying that is the coppery smell of ebbing life.

My stomach is knotted up with tension as I slowly push the door back on its hinges with my right foot. The living room reveals itself like a reluctant stripper, one inch at a time.

I can feel the presence of someone else in the room with me. It's that same tingle right at the base of my skull that saved me many times.

I step out from behind the door, gun at the ready, as quietly as a church mouse. Though this mouse isn't saying its benedictions.

The house is lit by the bluish glow coming from the holotube. Shadows are dancing on the walls, giving the place the feel of some bizarre creep show.

There's a guy just sitting on the couch looking as if he's watching the holotube. But I can't see enough of his face to tell if he's awake or asleep.

I can see Bob Barker's simulated face staring back at me from a brand new Ultra Grade Holo unit. The four-D graphics are a little too real for my taste—you'd swear the beamed-in people were standing right in the room with you.

There's a pistol on the end table next to the guy on the couch, along with an overflowing ash tray filled with tobacco cigarette butts and roaches—not the kind that crawled around but the ends of hand-rolled pot cigs. Not a big deal since pot had been legalized decades before, but on the floor was a pile of crushed beer cans—Coors. Now that should be illegal.

There are fast food wrappers and empty chip bags and who knows what else littering the floor. The place is a disgusting sty. No offense to pigs. I wonder if the wife had been a slob or was just overwhelmed.

This guy is a runner up for Good Housekeeping's dump of the decade award for sure. And husband of the year, no doubt in my mind. I almost shot him right then.

I have my gun trained on him as I move up cautiously. He doesn't seem to be aware of me, or maybe he just doesn't care.

I creep closer, with my sights centered on the brown mop of hair on his oversized melon. If he so much as twitches, I am going to splatter the wall with the contents of his head. Given his intellect, I figure it probably wouldn't make much of a splatter.

I walk right up to him and stare at him down the sights of my pistol. The guy is out cold. A bottle of Jim Beam is sitting in his lap, empty.

I stare down at the miserable cuss and feel hate and revulsion well up inside me.

I look over at the kids and the mother. The kids certainly didn't deserve their fate. The wife probably didn't either, whether she was June Cleaver or Satan's sister.

Satan's sister made me think of my ex. But that probably isn't fair to Satan.

It's funny what the mind will do. Mine chose that moment to remember my ex-wife and our kids who she would never let me see. They don't even know who I am.

It's an even bet she's said nothing nice about me. All she ever cared about was the alimony check I sent her once a month. She acted as if I owed her back-pay for every time we did the hip grind. By my count, she's been overpaid.

If I had it to do over again, I would have run long and hard into a quagmire of quicksand.

She was a looker, though. I confess that's what hooked me. But she hadn't aged well. All the ugliness inside had oozed to the surface.

It's funny how the mind works.

I glare down at sleeping beauty with his white pork belly peeking out from under his blood splattered shirt.

I'm picture the whole horrible event in my mind ending with him just plopping down on the couch and watching the holotube while his wife and kids bled out.

I feel my rage building.

My heart is thundering in my chest as I clench my fist around the custom walnut grip of my pistol.

My finger tightens on the trigger.

Glancing at the holo, I wish Bob would shut up. I don't need the distraction. But he's hard to ignore.

I stare at the projected back of a ninety-year-old grandmother's head. She is bidding on a new appliance. I think her price is way too low.

Funny where the mind will go.

I see the desperate futility of the human condition. We are nothing more than crows gathering shiny baubles to place in our nests.

I foresee the coming years wasted on appeals in courts where lawyers argue the virtue of law while pretending that justice is being served. And all the while, this miserable slob will be watching holo in prison.

The rest of us will be feeding him and providing him with toilet paper to wipe his butt. Compared to this crappy abode. he'll be living like a millionaire.

He'll still be alive while his wife and kids will have been melted in the vats and turned into fertilizer. That thought sickens me.

Something snaps inside me like a balloon popping. I know what I have to do. I feel myself putting my piece back in its holster. It's almost as if I am just a spectator looking out at the world through my eyes while watching someone else move me around. I feel like a puppet dancing from a string.

Bending down, I pick up a potato chip bag off the crusty carpet while never taking my eyes off of prince charming.

Bob is blabbing away in the background. I barely hear him.

Slipping the chip bag over my hand like a glove, I can feel how greasy it is inside. It feels as if I've just stuck my hand into a bucket of lard.

Slowly and gently, I pick up the guy's right hand. He snorts a little, but this guy is out cold. A nuclear blast probably wouldn't awaken him.

This guy looks like he could kill that fifth of Jim Beam easier than I could swallow a glass of milk. But you never can tell with drunks.

I move his limb ever so slowly off of his lap and over to the end table where I lay it on the gun and carefully wrap his pudgy digits around the grip.

Placing my chip bag gloved hand over his, I guide his index finger into the trigger guard with the utmost care.

I dared not even breathe. A part of me watches the entire scene as if it is happening to someone else.

Then slowly, with the patience of Job, I raise his arm and place the gun up to his temple. My hand holds the hand that's holding the gun, and I put my finger over his on the trigger.

My world is a surreal, slow-motion place at that moment.

Bob Barker is asking a lady named Ruth, who's from Kansas City, what her favorite color is.

I read the chip bag. To my surprise, I discover they are made with real potatoes and that they have ridges. That they are baked fresh every hundred days seems ludicrous.

They smell like crap. The stink burns its way into my nostrils.

The drone of the flies has an incessant background buzz that drills its way into my ears.

I sense several things happening simultaneously. The holo loses its signal. Bob goes silent, and the screen turns to snow.

The scumbag on the sofa must have felt that something was wrong. Maybe he felt the laser-like intensity of my scowl. Or maybe he just missed the sound of Bob's voice. I don't.

For a brief second, I wonder just what in the world I'm doing.

The holo comes back to life. Bob points to curtain number three.

The perp's bloodshot eyes open and I watch those peepers try to focus. I sense the exact moment that he realizes someone is holding a gun to his head. He looks at me.

Bob yells, "This is what you've won!"

The guy's empty eyes look through me as if I don't exist.

Bob says, "The price is right!"

I help couch potato pull the trigger. The blast makes my ears ring, giving me a few blissful seconds without Bob.

Half of the drunk's head makes a Rorschach ink blot on the wall. The splatter looks like a bird or a butterfly, hard to tell which. But I was right when I thought that there wasn't much in there.

I let his arm fall while shaking the greasy chip bag off of my hand. It drops to the floor. I step away in a daze.

"What the hell" keeps running through my mind over and over as I walk out of the house. I can hear Bob's voice again on the holo. It sounds like he's laughing.

I sit in my cruiser for a long time, trying to figure out what happened.

Not enough clues, so I call in. "44 to base."

"Go ahead, 44."

"Better send the meat wagon. We've got a triple homicide and one suicide."

"On their way, 44. Do you require backup?"

"Negative. The party is over."

"Copy. The computer ETA is 5 minutes for the meat wagon. Have a nice day!"

The dispatcher is a beautiful young lady, but her sense of humor, unlike her bosom, is underdeveloped.

Speaking of humor, it's funny what the mind will do. I want that cold beer now more than ever. There are probably several in *the guy's fridge. Me, drink a Silver Bullet? Nah. There'd be two suicides if I did.*

Nikki looks at me like I've done something wrong.

"I know," I said. I close my eyes and wait for the meat wagon.

"End simulation," Rick said. While the others were busy with their shutdown protocols, Rick casually removed the crystal drive he'd inserted at the onset of the simulation. He whispered under his breath, "You're welcome, Chuck."

"What the heck. Maybe making him an agent wasn't such a good idea," Phillip wondered aloud.

"Did we do that?" Susan asked.

Rick cut in before anyone else could question the simulation. "Jon's psych profile showed a 93% success ratio compared to, let's say, assigning him a job as a garbage collector for a profession. We should've known that this job might entail something other than serving warrants to deadbeat husbands."

"I just never imagined that Jon could be so cold-blooded," LeRonda added. "That thing with the chip bag…"

"Let's not forget that Jon was a soldier. I'm sure he's done worse things in his life," Mick added. "Besides. The guy Jon shot was a murderer, not a saint."

Hours later, Rick sat alone in his office postponing the inevitable. Finally, he picked up his phone and pressed autodial.

The phone on the other end was answered on the first tone. "Talk to me."

"It's done. Chuck, his wife and kids. They're all dead."

"Any problems?"

Rick hesitated before he answered. "Some. But we were able to contain the situation."

"You'd better be sure. We don't need any more complications. You know what will happen to you if there are."

"Yes, sir. I understand."

"Just make sure that you do."

The line went dead.

Rick disconnected. After a few minutes of silence, he walked to the door that led into the back rooms and his studio apartment. He rapped on the door with a single knuckle and then returned to his desk. Seconds later he heard the door open and felt someone enter the room. He looked across his desk. "It's done. But for now, Chuck, you and your family had better stay here for a while. You can live in my apartment behind this office until this complete mess gets sorted out."

"I don't know what to say," Chuck said, fumbling for the right words.

"I do," Elizabeth said. She walked over to Rick. "Thank you for saving my children." She kissed him on the cheek. She turned away and went into the studio apartment where the children were fast asleep.

"What happens to the quantum bodies?" Chuck asked.

"You and I have a long night ahead of us. We've got to re-awaken Jon and finish the scenario. If we're successful, they will take the quantum doubles to a Vat location where they'll be decomposed. No one will ever know they weren't actual people."

<h1 style="text-align:center">Chapter 23</h1>

The Cube: Thursday 2130 Hours

"Chuck. Initiate the program," Rick said from LeRonda's console.

"Program is running."

"Let's wake him up," Rick said.

Jon

I'm hovering somewhere between sleep and awareness while I'm waiting for the meat wagon to arrive.

My mind fills the time by bringing up memories of my ex-wife and our kids. They weren't the happiest memories, that's for damn sure.

If there's a Devil incarnate, then she's his daughter. Of course. I was too young and stupid to realize how screwed up she was in the head. But sex was like there was no tomorrow, and I was just 20 years old, so it's a no-brainier which part of my body I was thinking with.

Well, at least I didn't blow her away while watching the holotube, so I guess I'm a step up from the asshole inside this trailer. Not much of a step, even so, it's something.

I'd be a liar if the thought of ending her reign of terror hadn't crossed my mind a time or two. Fortunately for her, I wasn't that kind of creep. Or was I?

What the hell just happened in there? The arrival of the refer truck interrupted my thoughts of the past.

A boxy red truck pulls up and with a loud hiss from the airbrakes, it squeals to a stop.

The driver and his attendant ooze out of their van like they don't have a care in the world. Of course, why would they? The dangerous part is over.

"They're here," I say to my faithful, ever-vigilant partner.

Nikki barely opens one bloodshot eye and goes right back to sleep.

"Don't worry. I got your back, Nikki."

She's still snoring. Oh, well. I'll take what I can get.

I climb out of my cruiser and lean back against the front fender.

Touching the brim of my hat I give them my best imitation of an old west Marshal I'd seen on the holotube. "Howdy, gents."

With my arms folded across my chest, I wait for the driver and his lackey to say something. They always do. Sometimes I wonder if they actually have a training program for smartass remarks.

"What's the scoop?" The driver steps closer and offers his hand. "Name's Gerry," he says with a southern drawl.

I keep my arms folded and don't shake his hand. "Jon," I answer, nodding my head in greeting as I size up the two.

Gerry pulls his hand back a little self-consciously and points at his partner. "That's Dickerson."

Gerry doesn't seem like a bad guy, but his partner looks like a jerk with a capitol J.

The capitol J must have read my mind.

"Did he draw on you, Marshall Dillon?" Dickerson says with a snicker.

Gerry rebukes his partner. "Come on, Dickerson. Don't make this harder than it has to be."

"Did I say capitol J? Well, howdy, Jag-off. Is that bullshit on your boots or is that stench your aftershave?"

"You can't talk to me like…"

I just glare at him from beneath the flat brim of my hat. He must have noticed the look in my eye, or more likely the Colt in my holster, but in either case, he stops flapping his jaw. Wisely, he finds something else to focus on.

I shift my gaze back at Gerry, "The party's in there. See for yourself." I tilt my head towards the door.

Gerry puts his hand on his juice kit, but I just shake my head. "Don't need it. They're all dead."

He grunts a reply, "Well, at least there won't be any bullshit paperwork about cause of death." He disappears into the house with Gomer on his heels.

Global-Gov had made it against the law to bury a corpse. There just isn't enough open land for that anymore. Hence the juice kit, just in case someone wasn't all the way dead yet.

The two freezer techs come out a minute later and unload a gurney when I ask, "How many stiffs can you stack on one of those?"

Dickerson looks like a cow watching a passing train while his mind catches up to my question.

"One," he answers as if he's thinking I'm the stupid person in the group.

"There are four in the house. What are you going to do? Stack 'em like cordwood?" That got his attention.

"Jackass," he grumbles as he pulls his steel contraption towards the house.

I don't offer to help.

I wait outside, thinking about nothing in particular other than my life.

My mind immediately jumps back to where it left off.

Yeah. My ex was a bitch.

I finally called it quits when I was awakened one night by a patrol officer who told me my wife and kids had been involved in a car accident.

Hell. I didn't even know they had left the house. I could see it in his eyes. Pity.

That made me sick to my gut.

What was she thinking? Sure enough, the whack job had packed the car with everything in the house including the damn ice trays from the freezer and was making a dash for Texas when she got broadsided not more than a block from home by a drunk driver. There's karma, again.

I had a rude awakening that night in more ways than one.

The following morning, I threw her pathetic butt on a bus. And since she would never leave without "her" children, they got a ticket, too. They deserved better, but what was I supposed to do?

I close my eyes for a moment and wait for the freezer techs to do their job.

Gerry steps back outside, swatting flies as he exits the house. "That's one insane mess in there."

"Yeah," I say. Man of a thousand words. That's me.

He leans on the car next to me and takes off his hat. His face is prematurely lined from too many years on the job. As he stares off into the distance, I notice that he also has the eyes of a man who's seen too much.

I answer his unspoken question. "I figure the guy popped the wife and kids, then just sat down in front of the holotube and vegged. He must have done himself when the game show came on. I would have."

Gerry just stares into the distance. "Yeah. That's probably how it went down."

"Who the frag was he?" I ask.

I realize it's a stupid question as soon as the words leave my mouth. Nobody cares. Nobody ever does.

Gerry looks sideways at me. "Did you notice that there is an out-of-date Vid-Tec ID badge on the couch next to the vic.?"

"No. But he had to work somewhere."

"Seems kind of odd to me," he says.

"What's odd about it?

"I hear that Vid-Tec pays pretty well. So, why this?" He points with his chin at the squalor.

I can see his point. "Who knows? Maybe getting sacked caused him to snap. It seems pretty cut and dried. He snuffed the family and then himself. Maybe living in this hell hole finally got to him," I suggest.

"Maybe."

I look at him. "So, what are you thinking?"

"Just wondering about that ID, is all," he says. "Name on the ID is Charles Adams. According to the badge, he was some kind of programming tech."

"Maybe he sucked at his job, too."

"I suppose. Hell, it doesn't really matter, now. Sometimes I forget I don't care anymore," Gerry says.

"Maybe I should talk to his friends at the company." I offer.

"Somebody paid for that fancy holo set. Last time I checked, they were extremely pricey," Gerry says.

"He sure didn't buy that with Global-Gov benefits," I banter back. "If this guy worked, then how did he get back and forth? It wasn't in that piece of garbage," I chin towards the rotting auto in the yard.

"He's got to ride share with somebody," Gerry suggests.

"I'll run his retinas as soon as I get back—see who Charles' boss was over at Vid-Tec," I say. "Not that the Vat factory is going to give a damn."

He just shakes his head. "Know anything else about what went down here?" he asks.

"I know he's dead," I say. "That's a start."

He slips his hat back on and gives me the look. "Smartass," he says, shaking his head.

"You got this?" I ask.

"Sure."

"Great. Just submit a copy of your report for the record," I say.

"I'll send it up tomorrow."

"Thanks," I say. "I'll see you around."

I climb into my cruiser just as Gomer comes bumbling out of the trailer with the gurney stacked two bodies high.

The gurney must weigh a ton.

I watch as he loses his footing, and the bodies tumble off onto the ground.

Gerry curses a blue streak as I slowly pull away.

I don't think they can hear me laughing, but I don't really care.

It's been a mother of a day.

I go back to my empty domicile and fall asleep in front of the holo with a beer in my hand and Nikki curled by my side. Paradise.

Rick cut the quantum feed, ending the simulation. "That should do it. Tomorrow, we can get back on track."

Chuck stepped over to Rick. "Thanks, Rick." He said awkwardly.

Rick looked away. "Just don't do anything stupid like this again. Now, go join your wife and kids. I'm going home so I can try to get a couple hours of sleep. See you in the morning." Rick hesitates for a moment. "And Chuck, don't mention this to anyone."

Chapter 24

CPD: Friday 0430 Hours

Agent Doherty couldn't sleep, so he went to work early. The station was quiet at this time of the morning. Besides himself, there were just two deputies and the dispatcher.

"Morning, Clara," he said to the night shift dispatcher. "Anything interesting happen last night?"

"The all-night donut shop was closed down for its annual maintenance," she replied.

"That explains the long faces around here." Doherty poured himself some coffee and took a sip. "This stuff tastes toxic. Did I miss a warning label somewhere?"

"Thanks. It's my special brew," Clara offered. "It's only been roasting for eight hours. Give it another four and it'll smooth out," She said with a wink.

"This stuff is peeling back the lining of my stomach," he said as he took another big mouthful.

"You're lucky. Higgins used a pot to unclog the sink in the restroom," she bantered. "He said it worked better than commercial drain cleaner."

"I believe it," Doherty said as he sat down at his desk. He logged into his computer and sorted through the long list of reported crimes for the last twenty-four hours.

He saw one that interested him and opened it. Murder/Suicide: They found a woman and her two children murdered in their home at approximately 7:30 p.m. last night. The shooter was identified as Charles Adams and was suspected of taking his own life as reported by CPD agents at the scene. The agent on site, Jon Doe, reported the crime and ordered Vat services for cleanup.

Doherty continued to read the incidentals with little interest, noting that Jon had filed the report in a timely fashion and that it was written professionally. Then something caught his interest. Charles had worked for Vid-Tec.

He leaned back in his chair. Vid-Tec was sure popping up a lot lately. Doherty didn't believe that it was a coincidence. He sat forward and requested a full background file on Charles Adams, aka Chuck.

The report came back almost instantly. Doherty scanned through the file. Chuck had a very ordinary upbringing, did well in school, and apparently was a genius of sorts in computer programming.

At the age of 25, he married Elizabeth Hartford. They had two kids, a boy and girl. No pets. Lived in a modest two-bedroom pre-manufactured home like most of middle America. He bounced from job to job until about a two years ago when it looked like he'd hit pay dirt when he landed a job at Vid-Tec. Not much happened for about a year—no traffic violations, nothing that was worth noting in the file—that is, until about eight months ago, when Chuck quit Vid-Tec and seemed to have fallen off the grid. No job or reportable income of any sort. He wasn't on unemployment or using G-script to buy groceries. Not easily done these days. Not without some serious inheritance of which there was none on either side of the family. That left one of two things, hard-core criminal activities or Government involvement. Chuck did not come across as a criminal, so that left only one thing. But what was he doing for the government?

Doherty tilted his chair back and laced his fingers behind his neck. Vid-Tec. Why is a holo provider having so many deaths, lately? Hard to believe the big shots over there would start offing themselves over programming issues. If it could be believed, Chuck's death made the total three alleged suicides in only a few days, and all victims with ties to Vid-Tec. So maybe he didn't buy it.

Doherty reached for his phone and punched up the number for the ME. A woman with a short fuse answered the call. "What!"

"Morning Nancy."

"Is it? I've been up all night trying to scrape together enough of that Bill Honely character to do a toxicology screening."

"What have you found out?" Doherty asked.

"The guy didn't have a drop of liquor in his bloodstream."

"Drugs?"

"Nothing turned up. Bill was as sober as a newborn baby," Nancy mumbled, exhausted. "If you ask me, and you most likely are, I figure his air car must have suffered a catastrophic computer failure of some sort. How else can you explain the accident?"

"I'm not sure. Have you discovered anything further on Nathan?"

"Don't you have anything better to do?" Nancy mocked. "Nathan Watkins died from a blunt trauma to the head. The gunshot wound was delivered postmortem by persons unknown. I haven't been able to identify any DNA other than the victim's, but..."

"I know that tone of voice. You found something, didn't you?" Doherty sat up a little straighter.

"It's weird, but there's a quantum element mixed in with Nathan's blood that I can't account for. And frankly, I do not know how it could even be there."

"What about Bill? Is the same thing showing up there?" Doherty asked.

"I didn't screen for it." Nancy sighed. She knew what he was going to say next. "But I will, since you asked me so nicely."

"Thanks. Let me know when you get something." Doherty said.

"You *owe* me," Nancy snorted as she hung up.

Doherty was grasping at straws and he knew it, but sometimes straws paid off. Quantum particles were pretty high-tech stuff. Not something easily found at the market. First Nathan, then Bill, and now Chuck—all of them had worked for Vid-Tec and all of them are dead.

Doherty got Clara's attention. "Contact Vat disposal and see if you can put a hold on the pickup from last night. I want the bodies from the Adams' residence sent over to the ME for analysis."

"I'll get right on it," Clara said. She punched in the number. A female voice answered, "Thank you for calling Vat recycling. Your call is important to us, so please stay on the line. If you know the number of..." Clara waited. Her call was answered and recorded for quality assurance. After speaking with the scheduling manager, she hung up.

"Doherty, I spoke with the Vat people and they said that it was too late on your request for the entire family. Some type of screwup at the factory has them listed as misplaced."

"Thanks, Clara. Get in touch with the meat truck driver that picked up the bodies. I want to talk to him."

"I'll schedule a meeting. Here or at the Vats?" Clara asked, although she already knew the answer, Doherty hated the vats.

"Here, of course," Doherty answered absently.

"Chicken," Clara teased.

"Shrewd," Doherty answered with a smile. "Is Spinoza in yet?"

"No. He's not scheduled to be in for another hour."

"What about that new guy? What's his name, Doe?"

"Doe is one of our field agents. We never see them in person. Do you want me to contact him?" Clara asked.

"No, don't bother. I'm heading out for breakfast. I'll be back in about an hour. Have Spinoza contact me when he gets in."

"Got it, boss. See you later," Clara said.

Chapter 25

Top Secret Lab: Friday 0445 Hours

Max lay down on the table while technicians wired him to the quantum projector. This was the second time he'd been to the facility, but the newness of what he was doing unnerved him. He'd been an operative with the Agency for more than a decade. And in that time, he'd killed people without regret, traveled around the globe to topple foreign powers, and to assassinate world leaders. But nothing in his career compared to what he was doing, now. He kept his nervousness to himself.

What bothered him wasn't the work—he excelled at that. No, it was something else, but he wasn't sure what that was, exactly.

"Open your mouth, please," The technician said neutrally.

It came to him as the techs were making the last connections, and the IV was inserted into his vein. It was the idea that his body was lying here without his consciousness. He would never admit that to anyone, but the concept of separating his essence from his physical body was the most terrifying thing he'd ever done. He supposed it was the vulnerability that he felt. While he was in the quantum projection, his body lay on this table completely at the mercy of the techs. And *that*, he realized, was the part that scared him— the feeling of vulnerability.

Max could hear the techs beginning the process and was aware of a mild sleepiness overtaking his body. He knew drugs were being injected into his bloodstream and felt a moment of panic, and then that, too, faded away. His eyes closed.

Max opened his eyes and looked around. It took him a few seconds to get his bearings. He was in the sub-basement of Vid-Tec, surrounded by banks of computers.

He stood immobile for a few minutes, absorbing the feeling of his quantum body. It was a strange, almost unearthly, sensation that gripped him.

The thought of his body lying in the lab was disorienting in a way that words can't quite describe, although when he'd been to Nathan's house, he remembered how he'd felt in the projected body—indestructible, like a god.

Max studied the layout of the room. The sub-basement facility was huge. The banks of computers stretched nearly out of sight.

He walked down a row, studying the computers. Lights blinked in random patterns like Christmas ornaments. He had no way of knowing which computers were for research materials or were broadcasting holo shows. His task seemed impossible.

After an hour of fruitless searching, he finally gave up. Time for Plan B, he decided.

Just then, he heard a door open and shut at the far end of the room. He sensed a presence. Max was no longer alone. He could hear voices.

"Come on, Bill. We don't have all day," Tom said impatiently.

Bill scanned his security badge at the checkpoint. "Last time I checked, we had until 2 a.m. Besides. What else are we going to do?"

"Grab some coffee in the break room for starters," Tom replied. "Then maybe catch part of the game from last night on the holo re-broadcast."

"I can tell you who won," Bill taunted.

"Don't even think about ruining my game time," Tom said with a sneer.

The two security men walked towards the next checkpoint. The routine of the job made them unaware that they were not alone in the facility.

Max tracked their passage by the sound of their voices. They were getting closer, and it limited his options. He could request removal, but his mission was incomplete. Max never left his job unfinished. He prepared himself for his next step.

Max moved down a parallel aisle until he was behind the two guards. Silently, he made his way down the cross corridor. Slowly, he peered around a computer bank. The two unsuspecting men were only a few feet away with their backs to him.

Max moved as silently as a wisp of wind. He stunned Tom with a sharp blow to the side of his neck and then, before Bill could react, Max grabbed him in a headlock and snapped his neck. He let the body fall to the floor. Turning back to the first man, he dealt a lethal jab at Tom's windpipe. Tom died in seconds, unable to draw his last breath.

Max listened. The room remained deathly still. No alarm had been sounded. Feeling certain that his presence was still a secret, he set about making preparations for Plan B.

Fifteen minutes later, Max double-checked his improvised explosive. Everything looked in order. He set the device inside one of the computer towers and started the bomb's timer. In five minutes, the basement would become an inferno. Finished with his work, he walked to a desk and picked up the phone. He dialed a number from memory. "It's time." He tossed the phone down.

Seconds later, his quantum body dematerialized.

Vid-Tec, 12th Floor Office: Friday 0805 Hours

Peggy walked into Jan's office. She was the last one to arrive for this important meeting.

She took her seat as Jan spoke. "I've called this meeting because of some serious events that have come to light. Someone is more than a little interested in our new project."

"Shouldn't Nathan be here? Or Bill?" Bruce, the lead scientist in charge of development asked.

Jan let the question hang in the air for a moment. "Nathan is no longer with the company."

"You can't just fire him! He…" Bruce blurted out, but Jan cut him off.

"If you'll let me finish." She stared at Bruce and the other executive board members seated at the table. "As I was saying, Nathan is no longer with the company—he's dead. They have informed me that he took his own life." Jan glanced down at the news report on her desk.

A stunned silence filled the air.

"Even more disturbing is the fact that Bill also died recently. Apparently, he died in an air-car accident," Jan said somberly. "I know that we all respected Nathan and Bill. The brilliance that they brought to our company cannot be easily replaced. But thanks to their efforts, we are on the threshold of this new technological breakthrough. I know that some of you might have even considered them as friends, but this loss, no matter how disturbing, must not impede our moving forward with the new project. We have billions invested in this. And no matter what happens, we will not lose this investment to a competitor."

Nobody said anything for a few minutes while each person silently thought over the implications of Nathan's death. A few mourned his loss, but most saw an opportunity where none had existed before—an opportunity for advancement.

"Bruce. You're now the head of the R&D section until a suitable replacement can be found," Peggy announced. "Report to HR after this meeting to discuss your new position and benefits package."

Bruce acknowledged the promotion with a slight nod. He tried hard not to smile.

Jan resumed the meeting. "Bruce. How close are we to broadcasts featuring our new Tec?" she asked.

"We're very close. Maybe just days away from our first broadcast. But we still haven't picked our first product for the test screening."

Jan nodded towards the marketing director. "Larry. Do you have someone in mind?"

Larry cleared his throat. "I thought we'd invite our top 10 accounts to the test screening and do a demo of the broadcast with full-sensory simulation. Then, we let them fight it out to see who will be the top bidder for the first airing."

Jan smiled. "An excellent idea, Larry! They'll be crawling over each other to be the first to use the new technology! All we have to do is stand back and make a huge profit from their voracity."

Larry smiled. "I'll set up a meeting for the day after tomorrow."

Jan switched her gaze back to Bruce. "Can you be ready?"

Bruce was about to answer but was distracted by his water glass on the table. The clear liquid inside was trembling. "What the… "

A muffled boom echoed around the room, shaking the windows and furnishings. A fine layer of dust floated down from the ceiling tiles.

Everyone started talking at once. "Is it a terrorist attack?" someone asked amidst the confusion. Others had reached the same conclusion as unmistakable fear blossomed in their questioning glances and worried looks.

Jan hushed the group. "Quiet, people!" She looked at Peggy. "Find out what's going on, now!"

Peggy was already on the intercom talking with the security desk in the lobby. "Has anyone been down there to confirm what's going on?" She listened for a moment. "Well, do it, dammit! And get back to me, immediately!"

Peggy shifted her attention to Jan. "There's been some kind of explosion in the computer basement. The fire system seems to be malfunctioning, and no one can get near enough to the room to determine how bad it is."

"Has the fire department been notified?" Jan asked, feeling as though idiots surrounded her.

"The automatic alarms are tied in with the fire suppression system. If they're not working, then I doubt we have notified the fire department," Peggy surmised.

"Well, call them!" Jan's patience was wearing thin.

"I'm trying! I can't get a signal." Peggy stabbed at her phone in frustration.

"Anybody have a signal?" Jan demanded.

A chorus of "no's" circled the room as everyone frantically tried to make a call.

Another explosion shook the windows. This one louder than the first. More dust rained down from the ceiling grid. Screams could be heard coming from the outer offices.

The situation was deteriorating rapidly. The men and women in the office squirmed with nervousness, but remained seated, waiting for Jan to dismiss them from the meeting.

"Bruce. Get out there and find out what's going on!" Jan said in a shrill voice.

Bruce knocked his chair back in his haste to comply with Jan's command. He hurried to the door and pushed the pad, but the door refused to open. Fighting down panic, he jabbed at the electronic pad again and again, "It's not responding!" he shouted, failing to keep the tremor out of his voice.

More explosions erupted in rapid succession, each worse than the last. Acrid smoke started billowing into the room from the air conditioning ducts.

"Everyone, stay seated!" Jan demanded in a typically uncompassionate way. But, as the nauseating smoke filled the room, all semblance of order quickly vanished as each person scrambled for relief from the choking fumes.

More shouting and screaming could be heard from outside the room. Bruce began pounding on the door, while screaming for help. The room suddenly felt hot. A tiny wisp of steam floated up from the water urn.

Peggy panicked. "I can't breathe!" she gasped. She stumbled towards the windows and pounded her fists against the reinforced glass.

Someone else threw a chair against the pane. It rebounded without causing so much as a single crack.

The smoke was so thick that it was difficult to see across the room, let alone breathe. The toxic fumes were already taking a toll as one by one, the people in the room succumbed.

Jan shrieked in shocked surprise as the handset for the interoffice phone turned into a puddle of hot molten plastic that stuck to her hand.

Peggy screamed.

The incredible temperature continued to rise. Panic registered on the faces of those who had yet to be overcome by the smoke. A group was jammed at the door, climbing over each other to bang and beat on the unyielding surface as they scrambled to get out of the room to escape the intense heat.

"Let me out!" Larry screamed as he shoved Bruce out of the way. He fell to the floor where his clothes immediately caught on fire. Bruce writhed, screaming in agony as the flames engulfed him.

The carpeting smoldered then blackened before bursting into flames. The flames crawled up the walls in fiery tendrils that snaked out across the ceiling in search of more consumables.

Peggy's hair burst into flames. She ran screaming and threw herself against the window. She fell back, twitching uncontrollably as the hungry fire consumed her.

Jan watched as Peggy burned. Not wanting to end up like Peggy, she ran to the smoldering table and snatched up the water pitcher, dousing her hair. Too late, she realized, the water had been boiling in the ewer. Jan screamed as the steaming fluid scalded her eyelids and blistered the flesh on her hands and face. She ran blindly across the room, seeking relief from the torturous heat. Jan smacked into the wall with a sickening splat.

In seconds, the room was a blistering inferno that ravenously consumed everything and everyone inside. The windows exploded outward from the tremendous heat and pressure. The raging fire swept through the entire structure from the concrete sub-basements to the roof.

There was no place of refuge. The lobby was packed with the dead and dying as security tried in vain to open the doors. Gunshots rang out as one guard tried shooting through the armored windows. His last shot he fired into his own head to escape from the terrible fate that awaited them all.

The building was a roaring firestorm. Most suffocated as the fire sucked up all the oxygen. But a few, such as Jan, died horribly as it cooked them alive.

The building trembled as its structure weakened. Moments later, the building collapsed in on itself.

A smoking crater now occupied the site. The once beautiful structure had been turned into a crematorium.

The mournful wailing of sirens could be heard in the distance.

Chapter 26

Global-Gov Capitol: Friday 0845 Hours

The camera lights went out as a round of applause circled the Global-Gov office. The reporters pushed their way towards the Presider. Eager to get answers, with hands outstretched holding microphones, they shouted their questions. But she was hustled out of the room by a screen of bodyguards.

As soon as the door was secured behind her, she shoved her bodyguards aside. "Get away from me, you friggin' idiots!" she shouted angrily as she slipped into her private study.

She sat down at her desk. And as soon as the door was closed, picked up the phone and punched in a secure number. It was answered on the first ring.

"Madam Presider. What a pleasant surprise."

"Cut the crap, Glen. When do I get what I paid for?" she snapped.

"The project is coming together, but there's still work to be completed. It's a long way from being perfected," Glen responded. As the head of Global-Gov security, he wasn't used to being talked down to and had to swallow the retort that almost escaped his lips.

"I'm not a patient woman, director. This project of yours is the greatest gift humanity has ever seen. Virtual immortality will be my legacy. I'll be able to rule the globe for generations. I want it! And I want it, now!" she screeched, slamming down the phone.

Glen let the ringing in his ear fade and then pressed a pre-programmed number.

The Agency: Friday 0853 Hours

Aaron went into his office and closed the door. He sat down with a sigh.

Max twisted his chair around and sat with his arms folded on the seat back.

Aaron's phone buzzed. "What next," he cursed under his breath as he recognized the caller. "Yes?"

"Well?" was the only word exchanged, but Aaron was completely aware of its meaning.

"Everything is going according to the plan." Aaron said.

"What about Vid-Tec?"

"Unfortunately, they were collateral damage," Aaron said.

"Perhaps in the future, you will keep a better eye on your people," Glen remarked.

Aaron glared at the phone. "This project is not without its risks."

"Maybe *you* are one of them?" Glen said sarcastically.

"That's your opinion."

"Careful, Aaron. You can be replaced, too," Glen said harshly.

Aaron digested the threat before answering. "Are we finished?"

"Your program is being followed closely by some powerful players. In short, they want what you have."

Aaron chose his words carefully. "We have nothing yet. The process is incomplete."

"I've heard differently."

"Well, you heard wrong," Aaron snapped.

"I hope for your sake that you produce some results, soon." The call was disconnected.

Aaron hung up his phone. "Max! Was there a problem?"

"No," he replied. "Just a minor glitch that's been handled. Vid-Tec has been eliminated and all of their data has been destroyed."

Aaron glared at him for several long seconds. "You'd better be right. I'll castrate you and nail your nut sack to my office wall. Do I make myself clear?"

"Not a pretty picture. By the way, what do you call that kind of art? Wall-nuts in situ?"

Aaron glared across his desk. After what seemed like an eternity later, he said, "Fill me in."

"I infiltrated Vid-Tec early this morning using the quantum tech. However, my attempts to gain access to their computer network were unsuccessful." Max paused. "Security interrupted my attempts with a routine patrol. After eliminating the guards, I opted for Plan B.

Aaron waited.

"I improvised a bomb. The detonation was successful, and the ensuing fire destroyed the building and killed everyone inside. There were no survivors at the site," Max reported.

Aaron tilted back in his chair and digested the report. "That's the first good news I've heard since this shit storm started. Is it safe to say that we have destroyed all of the data?"

"They'll be roasting marshmallows over that smoldering pit for weeks, if not months. Nothing could have survived. It was their only source for data storage. Vid-Tec was so paranoid about data theft that they had no offsite backup systems.”

“Excellent work. What about Nathan’s house?”

“I’m sending in a team tonight,” Max said.

“Don’t use any of our people. Send in some expendable assets, just in case the CPD gets there first.”

“You’ve got it, boss.”

“I have another assignment for you.”

“You’re a real nut buster, boss.”

“Someone is putting pressure on the director of Global-Gov security. This person wants something from us. Something that I will not share. Apparently, they think we have a working quantum projector.”

Max thought about the chain of responsibility. “The only person with that much power would be the Presider herself.”

“That’s my assessment as well.” Aaron said. “I want you to verify this information and neutralize the source.”

“And if it is the Presider?” Max asked.

“You know what you have to do,” Aaron said. “Make it look natural.”

“Sure, boss. I’ll just ask her out on a date,” Max said sarcastically.

“Get out, jackass.”

Some days, Max really hated his boss, and today was shaping up to be one of those days.

He placed a call; it was answered after the third ring. “It’s your money,” a bored voice said.

“I’ve got a job for you,” Max explained what he needed done and hung up ten minutes later.

Chapter 27

CPD Headquarters: Friday 0857 Hours

Agent Doherty walked into the precinct to find it in a state of bedlam. "What the hell is going on?!" He called out to no one in particular.

An agent ran past, donning a ballistic vest. "Terrorists have bombed a building over at Tech Plaza Park!"

Doherty hurried to his desk.

"It's about time you showed up!" Spinoza said.

"When did this happen?" Doherty demanded.

"Reports just started coming in a few minutes ago."

"Get a team out there," Doherty commanded.

"Already on their way," Spinoza replied. "The bomb squad has been dispatched and more units are converging on the site as we speak."

"Which building was attacked?" Doherty asked as he scanned the reports.

"Vid-Tec," Spinoza answered.

Doherty stopped what he was doing. "Vid-Tec? What the…?"

"Yeah, that's what I thought."

Doherty grabbed his vest. "Let's go."

The two officers climbed into Spinoza's cruiser and took flight. Ten minutes later, they were circling over the smoking ruins of Vid-Tec's headquarters.

Spinoza sputtered. "My god, there's nothing left!"

Doherty stared out his side window. "Circle around once more. I want to get a good look."

Spinoza hovered in a slow loop as heat waves buffeted the cruiser. "What could have caused so much damage?"

"Let's see what we can find out," Doherty said. "Land near the Chief's car."

Spinoza circled lower and landed their cruiser next to the burnt stump of a tree. The smoldering ruins of the Vid-Tec building were spread out in front of them.

"What'd they use? A micro-nuke?" Spinoza asked, stunned by the extent of the destruction.

"Had to be something like that to cause this much damage." Doherty answered. He climbed out of the cruiser. The air was smoky. The faint smell of tainted meat hung on the lazy breeze.

Doherty walked towards a group of fire fighters. "Hey, chief. Got a minute?"

The fire chief turned towards the sound of Doherty's voice. "Hi, Doherty. What brings you guys down here?" He stuck out his hand and grasped Doherty's in a firm handshake. The two men shared a professional relationship honed from years of duty in their respective fields.

"Hi, Jim," Doherty replied. "We got the call. It was reported as a terrorist attack." Doherty gazed around at the bustling activity. "I know you haven't had time for a full investigation, but can you tell me what happened here?"

Jim issued some commands to his men and then turned back to Doherty, "I can tell you this. That's the hottest fire I've seen in a long time. Must have been an accelerant of some type used."

"Not much left," Doherty said, pointing out the obvious.

"There's something else that's odd," Jim added. "We never got so much as a single call for help. Usually someone gets a call through, but not this time."

"That's odd. Is the cell network down?" Doherty asked.

"No. That's just it. Everything seems to be working fine. So why no distress calls?" Jim worried.

Doherty ran some scenarios through his mind and came to a speculative conclusion. "It's possible that the signals were being jammed."

"If that's true..." Jim was interrupted by a young firefighter who ran up to him.

"Chief! You've got to see this!"

The unfamiliar man looked a little ashen as he led them towards a spot in the rubble.

"We were digging for hot spots when we discovered these." The man pointed to a charred mass.

Doherty stared uncomprehendingly at the mass of smoldering rubble, but then something caught his eye. "Oh my god. They're bodies!"

Jim had seen burn victims before, but never on such a large scale. "By the looks of things, hundreds of the poor souls had perished."

"They must have crowded in the lobby trying to escape the fire." Doherty said. "But why couldn't they get out of the building?"

"I don't know," Jim groaned. "And I doubt we'll ever be able to figure out why."

They spent the next few hours combing the wreckage, looking for survivors, but it was hopeless. The intense heat had consumed everything organic. Most of the steel girders had melted, and the concrete had literally turned to dust.

Astonishingly, the damage seemed to be limited mostly to the building site itself. The surrounding area was fairly free of debris, although cars in the lot had a saggy half melted look to them and were layered in a fine coating of ash.

At the end of a long day, Spinoza and Doherty returned to the station with more questions than answers.
It was turning out to be a hell of a day.

Doherty smacked his hat on his leg to knock some dust off that had collected during the day. In uncharacteristic silence, he filled his coffee mug and sat down behind his desk. A heavy sigh escaped his lips as the horrible scope of what he'd seen weighed on his mind.

Spinoza sat quietly at his desk. His face wore a mask of barely contained emotions. He'd never seen such horror before and knew that he could never get those gruesome images out of his head.

The two agents sat in silence, each lost in his thoughts.

Doherty broke the spell several minutes later. "Sure, seems like Vid-Tec has gotten involved in something big."

"Yeah, but what? It's just a damned holo company," Spinoza said, equally puzzled.

Doherty sipped his coffee as he recapped the events of the past few days: "First, we get a call about Nathan's suicide, which wasn't a suicide at all. Then Bill, his partner, dies in a freak air car accident."

"Then following that is the triple homicide and suicide of Chuck and his family—strange that the bodies have conveniently disappeared," Spinoza added.

"And everything ties back to Vid-Tec somehow," Doherty finished.

"It sure seems like someone is covering up their tracks," Spinoza said, pointing out what they were both thinking.

Doherty sat forward. "You're right. Somebody is. Let's get our asses over to Nathan's house and see what the CSI team has uncovered."

Thirty-eight minutes later, Agent Spinoza hovered through the security gate and entered the private community where Nathan used to live. Two minutes later, he floated down Waverly Drive and was just about to turn into the cobblestone driveway when he spied a pair of red taillights disappearing around the next corner. At first glance, it seemed to be an ordinary sighting, but something about the car nagged at him. "Did you see that car?" he asked Doherty.

"Just a glance. Why?" Doherty's attention was on the mansion. There was a reddish glow coming from the upstairs window that struck him as being odd.

"I don't know. I guess it was nothing." Spinoza turned into the driveway. The CSI van was parked in front of the garage. Its rear door was open, but there was nobody around. "Where are…"

His words were drowned out by a massive explosion that tore the roof off of the house and sent the CSI van toppling sideways like a child's toy.

Flaming debris rained down on the cruiser.

"Back up! Back up!" Doherty yelled.

Spinoza jerked the car backwards, nearly clipping the gate post as he reversed out of the gap.

Doherty was already on the radio calling for backup and alerting the fire department.

Spinoza slammed the air car into forward and accelerated, heading in the direction of the other car.

"Where are you headed?" Doherty shouted.

"That car we saw! It must have been them!"

They crested the hill and spotted the car racing away from them.

"That SOB is racing away from the scene!" Doherty said as he gripped the dash.

"Call it in!" Spinoza said through gritted teeth as he rounded a curve, barely keeping the cruiser above the road.

"Station 9. Spinoza requesting backup. We are in pursuit of suspects of bombing on Waverly Drive. Suspects are heading north on old highway 32 just past route 198 in ground vehicle."

"Copy that. Air patrol is responding. ETA three minutes."

Both agents stared through the windshield as the fleeing car raced ahead of them. Its red taillights bounced in the darkness as the ground car swerved around corners at speeds the driver could barely control. He was obviously desperate to escape.

Doherty pointed out the side window. "Here comes our backup."

The air patrol swooped down over the road, passing the other car and then turning around, blocking the road.

The driver tried to swerve under the jet copter.

Doherty and Spinoza watched as the car clipped the guardrail, sending a shower of sparks trailing behind. The driver fought with the wheel, but the car bounced off the guardrail, careening diagonally across the road, crashing through brush and into the trees. It disappeared for a moment, then there was a blinding flash as the car exploded in flames. The surrounding trees caught fire and instantly the area was an inferno.

Spinoza slowed to a stop. They could feel the heat through the windshield even though they were some distance away.

"That person's toast," Spinoza stated matter-of-factly.

Doherty looked askew at his partner. "I'll notify the fire department and tell the air patrol to stick around. We're heading back to the house." Spinoza turned the cruiser around as Doherty made the call.

They arrived back at Nathan's house and entered the drive ten minutes later.

The fire department had arrived and was dousing the burning structure with Aerosolized Fire Fighting Foam. There wasn't much left of the once beautiful home.

Doherty stood next to the cruiser, taking in the scene of destruction.

The fire chief walked over. "Doherty. Why is it you always end up at one of my fires?

Doherty turned to him. "Hi, Jim."

"Busy day," Jim answered in a world-weary tone. "Is it just a coincidence that you're here, or is there something else going on that I should be apprised of?"

Doherty let out a heavy sigh. "I wish I knew." He looked Jim in the eye. "I've got a CSI team in there, somewhere."

Jim looked at the house and then back at Doherty. "We'll find them," He said with sorrow. Both men were aware of what they'd find.

Chapter 28

The Cube: Monday 0600 Hours

The following Monday morning was bright and clear. Inside the lab, the team had just assembled for the day's run.

Rick exited his office looking sleepy-eyed.

"Where's Chuck? Is he sick?" Susan inquired.

Rick turned to Susan as he jerked his thumb towards the closed office door. "He's in there."

LeRonda stared at Rick curiously. "What's going on, Rick?"

Phillip watched the interaction between the team members and felt the unasked questions hanging between them. He could tell that Rick was hiding something, but he did not know what it could be. He knew he would have to talk with Rick at some point to avoid potential problems in the future, but for now, he said nothing.

Rick could feel the unasked questions as he panned his eyes around the room before he spoke. "Chuck won't be with us, today."

Rick went to Chuck's control station and sat down with a sigh.

Phillip made a mental note for later.

"Come on, Rick. What's going on here?" LeRonda said, expressing the number one question that was on everyone's mind.

Rick faced the group. He looked at each team member and knew he owed them an explanation. They'd been through too much together to be lied to. But what could he say? If the truth about Chuck ever leaked out, his family would be hunted down and killed without mercy.

At that moment, the door to Rick's office opened and Chuck stepped out, followed closely by his wife.

"I asked you to stay in my office," Rick scolded.

Chuck raised his eyes to Rick's. "I know. But we didn't want you to have to lie for us." Chuck pulled his wife closer.

"You realize what's at stake here?" Rick stressed.

Elizabeth answered, "Yes we do." She looked at the others. "Chuck has told me so many stories that I feel as if I know every one of you, even though we've just met. So, we owe you the truth—we can't lie to our friends."

Phillip raised a finger. "Perhaps if you tell us what's going on, we can help," he encouraged.

"Well, this is difficult to explain," Chuck began. "I'll start from the beginning." He told the complete story from the sweet beginning to the bitter end, concluding with the faked death of his family.

Susan covered her mouth in stunned surprise.

Mick raised his eyebrows in a silent query.

"No way," LeRonda said. "I don't believe it. That was you who Jon shot in the head?"

"A quantum image without a personality," Rick corrected. "Basically, an empty shell suited for our purpose."

"You went along with this, Rick?" Susan asked.

Rick nodded. "Yes, I did. Chuck may be an idiot but he's our idiot, and that makes him family. I could not sit by and let him be murdered. Although if he screws up like that again, I'll do it myself." He glared at Chuck to make his point. "But there are more important issues that need to be discussed at the moment. What you don't know and must now be told is that the Global Intelligence Agency is after our project."

"The GIA? They have no jurisdiction," Mick added.

"That's never stopped them before. And I don't think it will stop them now," Rick countered.

"What about the Agency? Can't they keep the GIA at bay?" Susan asked.

"The Agency has its own agenda for this project and is just as much of a threat to us as the GIA—maybe more so." Rick continued. "I know they were the ones who wanted Chuck eliminated. Should they discover what I've done, I'll be killed along with Chuck and his family. I don't think any of us will be safe."

"I hate Monday's," Mick muttered under his breath.

Rick held his hands up in supplication. "I know how you all feel. That's why, now more than ever, we must push forward and complete what we've started for Jon and Mary before we get shut down, or worse. If any of you feel that the risk is too great, speak up now."

The room went silent as everyone weighed the consequences of their actions and the possibilities that might come from them—good or bad.

"I'm in for the duration," Susan said firmly.

LeRonda looked at her friend. "If she's in, then I'm staying."

"I've got nothing else to do," Chuck blurted.

Phillip sat up a little straighter. "Quitting is not an option. Count me in."

Rick looked towards the last person in the room, "Mick?"

"Looks like we're all in this together," Mick said.

Rick swept his gaze around the room. "Let's get to work, then. Start your program sequences and prepare the quantum simulation."

The team went to work.

Rick pressed the intercom button on the arm of his chair. "Mary? How's our friend?"

Her tiny voice came from the built-in speaker. "He's doing fine. We're ready when you are."

"Good. We'll be starting the simulation momentarily," Rick answered.

"All systems are up and running. We are *green* across the board; waiting for your command." LeRonda informed Rick.

"Initiate program," Rick commanded as he inserted the crystal into the cradle.

In a darkened room nearby, water and air molecules swirled and merged as dust became redefined at the quantum level, forming into solid matter. The cohesion of atoms took on form and from the void, once again, Jon emerged.

Jon

This morning, a tiny bird apparently felt it was his duty to roust me from my slumber by pecking on the windowpane. I'm wide awake, now. Fortunately for that little pecker, my gun is out of reach. But, thanks to my unwelcome avian alarm clock, I'm off to an early start.

Truth is, I didn't sleep very well. My recurring dream is really frustrating me since I can't seem to remember any details about it the minute I wake up. And that pisses me off to no end.

My head is filled with questions that I can't answer— questions about my troubled sleep, my life, and most recently about my killing a man in cold blood.

On the other hand, Nikki looks ready to meet the day.

"Come on, girl."

She trots through the door ahead of me and jumps into the car.

I drive around a while, trying to get a handle on what the hell had gone down in that house.

My head aches. It feels like a tightly filled water balloon, ready to burst. The way I've been acting lately, you'd think my peanut-sized brain had created a lot of extra room in the old cranium.

Ten hours have gone by and I'm no closer to figuring out the fuzzy details of what happened in that house, so I do what most people wouldn't do; I decide to go back to the crime scene.

Nikki is looking at me as if I'm crazy.

"Don't give me that look. I feel bad enough already."

She thumps her tail on the seat.

"Easy for you to say," I chide.

As I'm pulling in, I see that the place is dark and empty. No doubt they have hauled the bodies out and the meat wagon has definitely been long gone.

The only thing that seems out of place is the crime scene tape stretched across the door. It's a sad banner to those who died in there.

I shut down the cruiser and sit there listening to the ticks of hot metal as the engine cools off in the early evening.

I can't shake my gut feeling that something isn't right.

An agent's instinct is what they call it.

Everything looks quiet, but I'm having that familiar tingle at the back of my neck.

I've learned to trust that feeling and I will not ignore it, now. So, I start the car and back out of the driveway and head back down the road.

Stopping about a hundred yards from the house, I reach over to the dash and turn off the dome light. I ease my door open and quietly slip out of the car.

Nikki follows. Her black fur blends in with the darkness of the night.

I leave the door slightly ajar and move back to the trunk.

Carefully I open the lid and grab my ballistic vest and slip it on. Nikki's has one too. "Come on, girl. Time to armor up."

What I grab next is an 8-gauge sawed off that I nicknamed the "defoliator."

Lock and load—I drop in two shells and cock back both hammers.

Nikki is all business. She stays by my side, alert and protective.

We walk towards the house, slow and easy. My eyes watch everything.

After the heat of the day, the air feels cool and smells sweet.

There are no sounds at all—no crickets, no owls, no barking dogs. It's as if the world has stopped and everything is waiting to see what I'm going to do next.

I feel a strange sense of déjà vu.

The two men are waiting. They saw the car pull in. Now they are deciding what to do. Their instructions are to erase any evidence that might connect the recent death of Chuck to the Agency. But killing a CPD agent isn't part of the deal.

"We've got to get out of here!" Jimmy whispers.

"It's too late for that," Billy whispers back.

Both men hunker down behind the counter that separates the kitchen from the den. They have their guns cocked and ready.

"Look. He's leaving," Billy says to his younger brother Jimmy. "Let's get this job done now and get out of here!"

"I'll search the back rooms," Jimmy mutters.

Billy searches the living room. He isn't worried about keeping it neat. He pulls knickknacks off the shelves and dumps them on the floor. Pictures, candle holders and other bric-à-brac go flying as he circles the room like a tornado.

Jimmy does the same to the bedroom. He opens a dresser drawer and starts rummaging through a pile of women's underwear. He's a little embarrassed but slightly excited at the same time. Near the bottom of the drawer, he feels something tubular and rigid. For a moment he thinks it's a flashlight. He pulls it out and almost drops it when he realizes just what he's holding. "Hey. Billy. Look what I found!" he whispers loudly.

Billy glances down the hallway and sees his brother smiling stupidly at him. He's holding up what looks like a flashlight without a bulb. "Put that down, dufus!" he snaps.

Jimmy is only slightly annoyed as he holds the cylindrical object up high like a trophy before tossing it back in the drawer. "What do you think she used that for, Billy?"

"Dude! Get your mind off your dick and find that ID badge!"

"OK. OK. No need to bite my head off."

Jimmy sulks as he continues to ransack the bedroom. But no matter what his brother had said, he can't quite get the mental *image of the woman using her toy out of his head. He is so engrossed in his fantasy that he doesn't notice a fleeting shadow pass by the bedroom window.*

I walk back up the road, quickly. There's still no sign that anything is amiss. When I get near the place, I cut through the yard and use the old truck as a shield.

Nikki is creeping along, almost invisible in the night. Her low growl warns me that danger is near.

I slip quietly around the back corner of the trailer home.

I can see the back door is ajar. And from inside, I catch the briefest flash of a hooded light.

I keep my back to the outside wall as I inch towards the door, holding my weapon up—ready.

I hear harsh whispers from inside, and for a moment, I wonder if it's just kids exploring the murder scene on a dare. If so, they are about to get the scare of a lifetime.

I silently step up to the doorframe, and slowly crane my neck to see inside.

I see nothing at first, but I know someone is in there.

Then, I see him. He must have sensed my presence, or it was just my bad luck, but he turns around and gawks at me. We stare stupidly at each other for a split second that feels like five minutes.

Then he raises his right hand. I see the black outline of his gun rising towards me. I spin into the door frame, raising the defoliator.

He is fast—too fast.

I feel like I'm moving in a tub of molasses. I'm struggling to bring my weapon to bear, all the while watching as his gun muzzle lines up on me.

I see the muzzle flash as he fires.

His shot grazes the right side of my skull. The impact of the bullet spins me to the left, just as I let loose with both barrels of the defoliator.

I see him disappear, blown back into the darkness as I stumble away from the door.

I hear indistinct shouts from inside and know that I am in some serious shit.

Nikki growls a warning for anyone nearby to stay away.

There is at least one more shooter, and I am in a bad way. My world is spinning around in lazy circles. It all fades away, then everything goes black.

I come back from the abyss with one hell of a headache. Nikki is licking my face as I try to clear my head. I don't know how badly I'm hurt, but it's bad enough. The 8-gauge slips from my hand. I think I hear screaming. But my ears are ringing like a church bell on bingo night.

I try to stand up. My legs feel like boneless rubber tubes. The next thing I know, I'm sitting on the ground propped up by an airless trailer tire. My revolver is in my right hand, but I can't figure out how it got there.

I stare stupidly at it for several long seconds. I am slipping in and out of it. This scares me more than anything else. I need to keep my wits about me.

Nikki whimpers in frustration. The second gunman could come out at any moment. And I don't want to be an easy target.

I feel myself fading fast. If this guy doesn't come out soon… I let that thought go.

Sobbing is coming from inside. "I'm going to kill you, you worthless pig! You killed my brother!"

This guy sounds upset. I can hear him tearing through the house like a freight train.

Nikki is staring towards the door, growling and baring her fangs. She sounds ready to kill.

Then I hear a new sound—sirens in the distance. A neighbor must have called in because of the gun shots.

"Shit!" a shout comes from inside. Evidently, the other gunman has heard them, too.

Seconds later, I hear feet pounding through the house followed by the front door being slammed open.

The night grows still. My eyes close. I let my head rest on that old flat tire. I was just thinking that it made a decent pillow when the wailing siren stops in front of the house and I hear car doors opening and slamming.

My world fades to black.

Warning sirens suddenly blared and the room lights flicked from white to red.

Rick jerked up in surprise. "Shut those damned sirens off! Give me status!" he yelled.

"Blood pressure is off the charts!" Susan screamed. "Adrenal output, oxygen levels, everything is maxed out! He's going to crash! Nooo! Nooo! Rick, we're losing him!"

"Shut it down! Shut it down!" Rick screamed.

The others worked frantically, shutting down systems in a cascading rhythm.

Rick saw the blue aura fade from the crystal chamber.

He watched Mary through the glass enclosure. She was busy administering a sedative.

"Brainwave activity has spiked and is oscillating wildly," Phillip reported with concern. "I think he's lost consciousness in the simulation!"

"Keep a close eye on him. We're not losing another one like we did before!" Rick said sternly.

This was how they'd lost the last test subject. The reality of the program could be too much for the subject in times of crisis.

For Jon, getting shot in the simulation was just as traumatic to him as it would be in actual life. And it could prove just as fatal. Jon's mangled body simply couldn't cope with the strain.

Rick knew that somewhere deep inside Jon's broken cavity, his heart was beating wildly.

"Hang on," Rick pleaded.

The room was deathly quiet as everyone waited.

Thanks to Mary's quick thinking, the strong sedatives she administered were taking effect.

"Blood pressure is returning to normal. O2 and other vitals are all lowering to acceptable levels," Susan announced. "I think he's going to make it," she said, letting out an enormous sigh of relief.

Rick digested that tidbit of information. "Shut it all down. I want status reports ready in two minutes. I want to know exactly what happened in there." Rick walked quietly to his office and closed the door.

Mary continued to work her magic on Jon. She placed her hand on his forehead and whispered soothing words into his ear. "Sleep, Jon. Rest now." With moist eyes, Mary looked at her patient. "I can't lose you, again."

Chapter 29

The Cube: Monday 2130 Hours

Minutes later, Rick's team members were seated around the briefing room table.

Rick was already on his second cup of coffee.

"I want answers, people. What have we learned from our near catastrophic failure?" Rick demanded. He absently stared through the one-way glass and watched Mary tending to Jon's needs.

He savored his coffee while he waited for a response to his question.

"It was the programmed reality that triggered Jon's near fatal response to the gunshot trauma. It's the same reason the other test subjects had failed," Phillip reported.

"You mean died," Rick corrected.

Phillip cleared his throat. "Yes. The nature of the program parameters prohibits Jon from differentiating between the waking reality and the programmed reality that we place him in. Therefore, everything that Jon interacts with is as real to him as this room is to us."

Rick turned his attention to the others seated around the table. "There must be a way to buffer the input so Jon can be maintained indefinitely in the simulation."

Phillip couldn't resist speaking his mind on the matter. "The problem isn't in the program, but the nature of the experiment. In order for us to allow our hologram to move and interact with real-world objects and people, we have to provide our projection with solid, real-world abilities; thus, the problem of Jon succumbing to a real-world stimulation that could end his life. Let's take, for example, a car crash…" Phillip was interrupted.

"… or a gunshot wound," Mick stated pointedly.

"Precisely," Phillip said. "This real-world immersion is why we make certain that Jon's day begins and ends at home. This is how we ground the patient in the reality of a normal life cycle between waking and sleeping."

Rick paced the room. "I want some buffers in place, today. We can't afford to have another crisis that leads to failure," Rick said.

LeRonda had an idea. "We can try reducing the photo-refractive crystal's output, but I'm not sure if that's going to change the interface. The triple phase read-beam must still meet the time-density requirements for the beam frequencies. If the three beams of different frequency don't interfere with each other in a precise configuration, then the light and dark particles inside the crystal will fail to excite the free charge carriers, and the photons in the conduction band will become trapped."

"Without the space-charge field, the electro-optic field will collapse. Field collapse will cause our real-world manipulation of quantum particles to cease. Without them, we might as well shut down the project because we won't be able to manipulate matter from our end," LeRonda explained.

Rick remained quiet. His eyes shifted from the team at the table to the glass chamber and back again. "If you make those adjustments, will Jon respond to the new stimulus?" Rick asked with concern.

"Not with any certainty," LeRonda answered.

It was up to Rick to make the call. "Very well, then. We will stick with the program 'as is' for now. The one thing we *can* do differently, however, is to minimize Jon's exposure to lethal situations that could lead to traumatic failure. OK, everyone. Let's move forward. Back to your stations, please."

Rick walked over and stood behind Susan at console number 3. "What's Jon's status?"

Susan's fingers flew over the virtual display as she pulled up the data to prepare for another test cycle. "All bio signs read normal. Jon is ready."

Rick was slightly nervous. This was the first time that Jon had been put through two back-to-back simulations. He tried not to worry and turned towards LeRonda. "Are the satellite projectors in place?"

"Yes. All satellites are in geo-synch and are operating at 100% of the norm. All quantum repeaters are online and actively repeating our signal," LeRonda replied as she scanned multiple screens.

Rick entered his security code and re-inserted the crystal into the cradle.

"Psi-emitters activated," Chuck said.

Rick noticed a pale blue aura envelop Jon's glass chamber. According to the med-techs, the aura should not be visible. Yet, there it was.

A slight shiver ran down Rick's spine, even though the room temperature was comfortable.

Rick thought about the two CPD agents who had arrived just as Jon had blacked out. Were they still on site? Probably.

Had they discovered Jon and Nikki? He hoped not. Rick wondered what had happened to them. He was concerned for their safety, but more importantly, the program's stability. The program was all that mattered if Jon were to have a new life.

"Restart the sequence," Rick whispered. "Let's see if we can get Jon back home."

CPD Cruiser on Site

The car's high beams lit up the front of the house in stark contrast to the expanding darkness of the night.

"Hold on a sec." Doherty reached over and stopped Spinoza from exiting the cruiser. "I don't know what's going on here, but let's do this by the book. I'll take the back. You enter from the front. And for god's sake, don't shoot until you've confirmed your target. I don't feel like getting plugged by my partner."

"I'll be careful," Spinoza replied.

"Let's go." Doherty folded himself out of the car and drew his sidearm. He nodded towards the open front door and the torn crime scene tape. Someone had obviously been in the trailer, and it looked like they'd made a hasty exit.

Doherty circled around the end of the house trailer.

Spinoza moved quickly up to the side of the open door with his gun held at the ready. "CPD agent!" he warned. "Come out with your hands where I can see them!"

There was no answer from inside. The place seemed deserted, but he wasn't taking any chances. He pulled the LED light from his belt and flicked it on.

Taking a deep breath to steady his nerves, he peeked around the doorframe and let the beam of his light wash over the room.

He scanned the scene through the sights of his gun. The place looked deserted.

He stepped into the doorjamb and called out, "I'm armed!"

Spinoza tried to push the door all the way open with the toe of his boot, but something was blocking it.

Agent Doherty could hear his partner hollering at the front. He turned the far corner of the trailer and stopped in his tracks.

He heard a rustle from the trees to his left. Shining his light into the bushes, he thought he saw a pair of feet sliding backwards through the dense brush as if being dragged.

There was something wrong about the dark shape, as if the light and dark were playing tricks on his eyes. It was difficult to make out the shadowy form in the darkness.

He glanced behind to make sure he wasn't being followed, but when he turned back, the scene was normal and what he'd thought he'd seen was gone.

Shrugging off the illusion, he slid down the side of the trailer until he reached the open back door. Cautiously, he aimed his light into the opening. The beam fell on a pair of legs that ended below a torso that looked more like fresh hamburger than a human being. He swallowed down some bile, "This one's vat sauce for sure."

"Spinoza! Get in here!"

Spinoza kicked the front door all the way open and rushed inside to find his partner standing over the lower half of a human corpse. He quickly scanned the room only to discover what had been holding the door partially shut. He choked back some vomit. A string of entrails, intestines and general gore ended with the upper torso slightly tilted against the wall. The head stared back at them accusingly. "I wish I hadn't eaten chili for dinner." Spinoza groaned.

"Check the front—I'll get the back rooms." Doherty ordered.

Spinoza forced himself to follow procedure and forget about the gruesome sight as he moved forward. "Clear!" He hollered from the front.

Doherty came from the back. "Place is empty. Call it in. Tell them we need the refer truck."

"And a bucket," Spinoza remarked as he wiped his chin with his sleeve and headed out to the cruiser.

Agent Doherty and Spinoza were still investigating the murder in the trailer home an hour later. The freezer techs had removed the body, but a pool of blood remained.

The place looked like they had ransacked it. Drawers were open and their contents strewn about on the floor. They had swept shelves clean of knickknacks.

It looked like a tornado rolled the dilapidated home down a mountain side.

"What is so important about this shit hole?" Spinoza mumbled to himself. "And how is Vid-Tec tied to this guy?"

Doherty looked at his partner. "Somebody sure wanted something, badly." He looked at the chalk outline where the victim had died. The white marks crisscrossed over several other outlines. "But what were they looking for? And who pulled the trigger on the corpse? One of his own people?"

His foot crunched down on a large bright yellow potato chips bag that had been tossed on the floor. "What the...?"

He reached down and picked it up. The bag reeked of potato grease and something else that shouldn't be there—gun powder. He put it in an evidence bag for later analysis and stuck it under his arm.

Doherty was about to turn away when he noticed the corner of a card sticking out from under the sofa. He bent down and picked it up. It was an ID card. It was high tech with no identifying marks of any kind. But Doherty had seen something similar when he was in the military—he recognized the telltale signs of a government-issued badge. The picture didn't match the victim who had just been hauled out—neither half.

Other than the picture, there were no other markings or information of any kind on the ID. They'd have to run it through the scanner back at HQ to see if they could read it.

As Doherty took one last look around, he sealed the card in another evidence bag and slipped it into his shirt pocket.

He then headed out, taking care to lock the door and seal it with a new strip of evidence tape.

Spinoza spotted the chip's bag under Doherty's arm. "What's that, Doherty? Taking a snack home?" Spinoza teased with a stupid grin on his face.

"Shut up, dirtbag. And get in the cruiser."

Jon

Nikki is sitting quietly beside Jon, guarding his unconscious body. She had dragged him into the woods when the others had shown up. Her programmed instinct is to protect Jon.

She is waiting in the trees, quietly watching from the darkness for the other Agents to leave.

Jon stirs.

She licks his face and whimpers softly in his ear, a prearranged signal that danger is lurking nearby.

I slowly come back to my senses. The first thing I notice is a familiar fishy smell on hot breath. The next thing is a soft whimper in my ear. Nikki is warning me to remain quiet. I reach up and rub her head, letting her know I'm all right.

"Stop it girl." I can barely endure the face cleaning that she's giving me. Pushing her aside I raise my head enough to peer over the hedge, just in time to see a CPD car lift off and fly away.

I'm not sure why I feel like I should hide from them.

Blood is still oozing from my head wound, but the dizziness is fading away a little.

Nikki keeps me steady as we make it back to the car.

The drive home is a blur of flashing moments.

I stumble into the bath and wash the blood off my face.

I have a nice crease along my temple, but otherwise, I seem no worse for the wear.

Now, lying in bed, I'm staring up at the ceiling trying to understand exactly what I'm caught up in. There's more to this case than I'm grasping, but what that could be is beyond me at the moment.

I'm not too surprised by my lack of insight. Mom always said that I wasn't the smartest kid on the playground.

Nikki is lying on the floor next to the bed. She's ever vigilant, protecting me. She's my hero.

Nikki has finally dropped off to sleep.

My eyes are closing...

"End simulation," Rick ordered. "Thank heavens we averted a potential disaster. If those agents had discovered Jon on the site, it would have created some seriously unwanted attention. Follow your shutdown protocols and let's call it a night. I'll be in my office if anyone needs me."

As Rick sat behind his desk, he could see through the one-way glass into the work area. It looked as though things were not going well for the team. The shutdown had gone smoothly, but there was still tension in the air because of the disturbing news from Chuck. LeRonda felt the stress from the last several hours overwhelming her. She took it out on Chuck.

"What in the hell were you thinking?" LeRonda snapped.

"I wasn't! Okay?" Chuck said defensively.

Phillip tried to defuse the situation. "Let's not overreact, everyone. It's been a tense day. Let's all just step back a moment and…"

LeRonda cut him off. "Keep out of this, Phillip! What the hell do you know, anyway?"

Susan intervened. "LeRonda. Calm down, please. This isn't helping."

"You heard what Rick said—they could kill us because of what Chuck did," LeRonda said, breathing heavily.

Susan put her hands on her hips and glared at her friend. "Yes. We all heard what happened. But do you remember what else Rick said?" She looked around the room at each of them. "It was the Agency that wanted Chuck eliminated."

Everyone remained silent.

"Don't you get it?" Susan said, exasperated. "They've been watching us the entire time!"

Susan's revelation hit them all like a physical blow.

"Oh, shit," Mick mumbled.

LeRonda sat down heavily in her chair. "They're going to kill all of us," she moaned.

Chuck's eyes filled with tears. "I'm so sorry, guys. This is all my fault." He hid his face and wept silently behind his hands.

Susan took pity on him and stepped closer. She placed a comforting hand on his shoulder. "Take it easy, Chuck. You're not to blame for *everything*. Obviously, the Agency has been monitoring all of us for some time. You did us all a favor by bringing the truth out about our situation. I don't know about the rest of you, but I'm grateful to you, at least now we know that we're marked for death. And maybe now, we can do something about it. There's more going on here than we know about. I, for one, don't like being kept in the dark," Susan said firmly.

"I agree with Susan," Mick said. "Knowledge is the key we lacked before. The Agency is merciless. We would have been killed without warning and without ever knowing why."

"But what can we do?" Susan asked.

Phillip grabbed a sheet of paper and scribbled down a quick note and held it up for everyone to read. "What if they're listening to us right now?" the note said. He looked imploringly at each of them.

The others nodded in silent agreement.

Phillip spoke in a light-hearted sounding tone of voice for the benefit of any hidden microphones that the Agency had placed in the lab. "Come on, guys. Are we going to buy into all this conspiracy theory stuff? Isn't it more likely that we're just overreacting? This past week has been stressful for all of us, including Rick."

"That's true mate," Mick said, playing along with the ruse. "Why would the Agency give two cents about what we're doing? It's all going to go public anyway at some point, assuming we are successful. And if we fail, then what is there to cover up?"

"I suppose you're right, Phillip," LeRonda said, winking. "It has been a trying week. I'm up for pizza and drinks. Anyone else?" she said, feigning happiness.

"Count me in," Mick answered, as did all the others.

LeRonda took the cue. "I'm out of here."

LeRonda grabbed her coat and strutted into the elevator. Susan and Mick weren't far behind her. They held the door, waving at Phillip to hurry.

Phillip gave Mick his best clinical appraisal. "I'll want to de-brief you in my office first thing tomorrow."

"Mmm, hmm," Mick said while nodding his head in agreement.

Chuck quietly returned to Rick's office and the studio apartment where his family was waiting.

Phillip grabbed his jacket and got into the elevator with the others. He looked at LeRonda. "Really!" he said, pretending to be indignant. The tension immediately faded as they all laughed at Phillip's performance.

"Well, did we learn anything from our little show?" Phillip asked.

"Time will tell. Now what?" Mick asked.

"I just realized, if the cube is bugged then they already know Chuck isn't dead." Susan answered.

Chapter 30

LeRonda's Apartment, One Hour Later

Susan set her drink down. "What if a new crystal was inserted into the laser reader? If we could get our hands on the current crystal, we'd have the entire program to use as leverage if the Agency decided to eliminate us."

"This is completely against protocol," Phillip pointed out. "What reason could we give to Rick for doing such a thing?"

"I thought every crystal had to be stored in a vault, or something, so the data could be saved or transferred in case of crystal degeneration?" LeRonda asked.

"That's true," Mick added.

"Could we scan the old crystal? It contains a record of previous test events. Maybe we can access the data and make a copy."

"I don't have access," Mick answered. "Only Rick has the code."

LeRonda looked at her peers. "There must be another way."

Susan stared back at her friend before answering. "They store the data in a second location—a backup crystal."

"Are you sure?" Phillip asked. "I've never heard of that."

"Neither have I," Mick said. "And I thought I knew everything—at least as far as security is concerned."

"It's classified. I'm sorry, but I couldn't say anything," Susan said apologetically.

"Where's it kept?" Mick asked.

"Chuck's console automatically records everything that goes on in the simulation. It's all still there. We just have to access it," Susan answered.

"Can you access Chuck's station?" Mick asked.

"No. It will require a bypass code to circumvent the security password. I don't have that type of programming skills, but she does." She tilted her head towards LeRonda.

All eyes turned to LeRonda. "Piece of cake. But I'll need access to his terminal in order to hack into the security program and make a copy."

Mick offered to help. "I'll find a reason to keep Rick busy and out of your way. How much time will you need?" Mick asked.

"An hour or less to get the program. Once I get what I need, I can work offsite to change the database. Then, I'll need about ten minutes at his terminal to upload the changes and then test them," LeRonda answered.

"Let's plan for the day after tomorrow. The scheduled security sweep on Tuesday will buy us some extra time," Mick said.

"Shouldn't we just tell Rick what we're planning to do?" Susan asked. "After all. He *warned* us about the Agency."

"We can't take the chance," Mick added. "Besides. We don't know just how deep Rick's involvement is or where his true loyalties lie."

"I'd venture to say he's in as deep as we are or deeper. Let's not forget that he protected Chuck and his family—if the Agency found out, they'd never stop looking for them," Phillip said, reminding them of what he considered being the important facts. "Let's pray they haven't."

At the Agency: Earlier that Day

Max entered Aaron's office, wearing his typical black suit. Aaron was on the phone and motioned for him to sit down. He sat down at the desk and started fiddling with a glass egg that was carefully balanced on a delicate stand.

Aaron gave Max the evil eye. "Make it happen, today." Aaron said before hanging up. "What have you got for me, Max?"

"The team has accessed Jon's DOD file."

"Hmm. What's your source?" Aaron asked while watching the glass egg teetering precariously.

"One of our operatives caught the request for the file while reviewing daily activities on a proxy server that the team is unaware of. They flagged the file. We just got notified."

Max sat quietly while his boss vented. "It makes no difference. Jon's background won't help them, now."

"Maybe it's time we shut down the civilian side of this project," Max offered.

His boss glared back at him. "That's the only smart thing I've ever heard you say."

Max let the snide remark go unanswered.

"What about the team?" his boss pointed out. "We can't let them just walk around. They know too much. God help us if a foreign agent got ahold of them. Our tech advantage would be compromised, or worse—used against us."

Max smirked at his boss. "We couldn't have that."

"You're a real pain in the ass, you know that Max?"

"Just trying to keep it light, boss," Max said in his typical sarcastic tone. "All this talk of murdering people can be stressful."

Aaron glared across the desk. "Take out the whole damn bunker. I want every trace of them and their project wiped out. Including Rick, his team, the test subject, and his doctors. Everything and everyone! Is that clear?!"

"Yes, sir. It'll take a day to set it up."

"Why so long?" Aaron snarled.

"Well, I can't just beam in there with a micro-nuke, now can I?" Max replied. "You *do* remember that they harden the cube against electronic intrusion, right?"

"Hmm. I'll shut down the project for twelve hours. They're due for a scheduled security sweep. That should give you enough time to penetrate their security and plant some explosives."

"Pushing it right to the edge, aren't you, boss?"

Aaron stared at his most-trusted agent. "You've got a six-hour window starting Tuesday at 0800 hours, not a minute longer, or I'll add your name to that list."

"There's still the matter of the missing money," Max added.

"I thought your team recovered the briefcase?" Aaron asked.

"They did, but it was empty."

Aaron sat back and pursed his lips. "It's insignificant." He glanced at his watch. "Right now, I need to inform Rick of the security shutdown for tomorrow. Make whatever preparations you need right away."

"Yes, sir."

"And, Max. Set the charges for Friday at noon."

Aaron picked up his phone and punched in a number.

The Cube: Monday night 2300 Hours

Mary checked Jon's bandages. When she was done with that, she checked his vitals. Everything looked good. But Jon still existed on a plane between two worlds—unconsciousness and reality.

She whispered a prayer that he would come back to her. But then worried about what would happen if that prayer were answered. The consequences of his awakening might be more than he could take.

Would he want to live knowing that he could never be free from his connection to a machine? Could she do that to him? There had to be a way for them to be together again.

As she worried about the question, the viable solution formed in her mind. Was it possible?

He shifted slightly. Perhaps it was a reaction to her ministrations. Time would tell. She adjusted his sheets and thought about what needed to be done.

A sheen of perspiration glistened on his forehead. She wiped his brow with a cool cloth. "Shhh, Jon. Rest, now. I'm here."

Mary could see Jon's eyes moving behind his lids. She wondered what he was seeing in his dream state. It appeared he was having a nightmare, and it pulled at her heartstrings that there was very little she could do about it.

She thought about the last time they'd been together— before the war. Before the night she had told him to leave. Before he'd become what he was now.

A tear rolled down her cheek.

Her replacement was due in a few minutes, and she didn't want the night nurse to see her like this. She exited the chamber and slipped off her protective suit and hung it on a hook. She wiped away the tear and straightened up the front of her scrubs as best she could.

Moments later, the elevator doors opened. The swooshing sound alerted Mary that she wasn't alone anymore.

The night shift nurse entered the room, "Hi, Mary."

"Oh. Hi, Janet."

"How's our patient doing today?" Janet asked as she set down her purse and started to don her sterile suit.

"It was another hard day for him. I wish..." Mary left her thought unfinished.

Janet gave Mary a sympathetic look. "You go on home, honey, and get some rest. Don't you worry. I'll take good care of him."

Mary cast one last look at Jon before she turned away. "See you in the morning," she said tiredly as she exited the room.

Janet entered the chamber through the airlock and made another check of Jon's vitals. Seeing that everything appeared normal, she dialed down the sound level on the monitors.

The late-night shift had become routine for her, and so far, there had never been any problems. Jon usually slept soundly through the night, and Janet had no reason to believe that tonight would be any different.

Upon exiting the chamber, she sat in a comfortable chair. Janet need only shift her eyes to the right to see all the readouts and monitors at a glance through the window. She kept her bio-suit on just in case she had to make an emergency entrance and set her helmet on the nearby table.

Turning on the reading lamp she pulled out her latest book. It was a book entitled, "Dreams of Betrayal." Although it was not her genre of choice for reading material, the storyline had intrigued her. She'd started to read it after a friend insisted she would like it. Janet quickly found herself so drawn into the story that she couldn't put it down.

She flipped through to her bookmark and read. "*Laktos held Inga close and gazed into her beautiful eyes…*"

An hour later Janet was quietly snoring. Her book lay open on her lap. It was at that moment Jon's vital signs flatlined.

Chapter 31

Jon

I'm coming to awareness, as if from a long sleep. Lying motionless I try to remember my last waking thought. Nothing is coming to mind. No surprise there.

I sit up and swing my legs off the bed, then stand up.

I'm confused. Nothing seems familiar. I don't recognize any of my surroundings. Where am I?

I look around the room, taking in all the medical apparatus and monitors, and I wonder how I ended up in a hospital.

Red lights are flashing on most of the surrounding monitors. The strobing effect reflecting off the glass enclosure makes the room feel like I'm inside a kaleidoscope.

Being the observant genius that I am, I sense that something is wrong.

I turn and see a dark-skinned, heavy-set woman sleeping in a chair on the other side of the glass partition.

"Hello, miss? I think something needs your attention," I said, a little worried as I walk towards the glass intent on waking her.

My reflected image seems ethereal mirrored on the glass wall. Behind me, I see someone else. I turn around. A man is lying on a bed covered to his neck in white hospital sheets.

Wires are snaking out from beneath pristine linens and are connected to various machines that surround him.

The red lights must have something to do with him, I reason. Sometimes, I'm smart. This isn't one of those times.

Curious as a cat, I move a step closer. I know I shouldn't have. Curiosity killed the cat, after all.

My eyes are transfixed on the bed.

There is something familiar about the patient.

I take another step closer, and then another, as if in a trance.

The stranger's face is turned slightly away from me and partially covered by the linen.

I can feel myself getting anxious, afraid of what I might find.

Now I circle the bed, taking notice of the glass chamber that cocoons the patient.

I also notice that the sheet is unusually flat from the chest towards the feet, as if... Then the significance of what I'm seeing dawns on me. The patient is grotesquely mutilated.

I walk slowly around the foot of the bed, inexorably drawn to the patient—like a moth to a flame.

I'm fearing what my mind is trying to tell me. There is something oddly familiar about the small scar on the back of the patient's neck.

My hand is shaking as I reach for the sheet. I pick up the corner between my thumb and index finger. Slowly, so as not to disturb the sleeping man, I pull the cover back.

The sheet feels warm in my fingers. My chest feels constricted, as if my blood has stopped in my veins.

I can't draw a breath as millimeter by millimeter his face slowly reveals itself to me.

Nooo! My face looms in front of my eyes! Nooo! I reel back in horror.

Suddenly my mind is flooded with memories of the war, the micro-nuke and the explosion.

Mary. I have to see her.

A sense of panic fills my soul. abruptly, I feel a desperate need to see her, to find her. But how?

I run blindly towards the exit and then through it.

Up ahead, I spot the elevator. At the top of the shaft, I run through an airport terminal. No one notices me as I fly past. Airports are accustomed to seeing people running.

I dash outside and run through the darkness. Then suddenly I find myself in our apartment.

Mary is sleeping with my pillow clutched in her arms. I can see that she's been crying.

"Mary. Mary, can you hear me?" I kneel by the bed and reach for her. "Oh, God! Mary, I'm here! Please! Can you hear me?" My heart feels as though it would burst.

Mary stirs in her sleep as if maybe she can hear me.

I'm afraid to touch her. If my hand should pass through her, it would prove that I am dead—a ghost.

I'm not ready to face that possibility, yet.

"Oh, Mary. I miss you so much!"

I can't stop myself.

My hand moves ever so slowly as I reach for her. I touch her lightly on the cheek and feel the warmth of her skin. "Mary, I love you."

Mary's eyes flew open. The room was empty. What had disturbed her slumber she wondered? She thought she'd heard Jon's voice, but that was impossible. It must have been a dream.

She squeezed her eyes closed and willed herself to go back to sleep, but sleep wouldn't come.

She rolled over and looked at the empty side of her bed—Jon's side.

Mary faces me and I swear she sees me kneeling beside her. She looks like an angel to me.

I feel a constriction in my chest as if a thousand volts of electricity are passing through my body. Suddenly I feel myself being drawn away from Mary's side. I try to hold on, but the force that pulls at me will not be denied.

My vision is darkening around the edges.

"Mary, help me!"

Janet's eyes flew open. Something had awakened her from a peaceful dream about dragons and handsome swashbucklers.

It took her a few moments before she realized that the monitors were softly beeping a warning alarm.

She looked through the window and to her shock, she saw the medical monitors all flashing red warning lights.

She jumped up from her chair and raced into the chamber. One look at the monitors confirmed her worst fears.

"Oh, no!" She went right to work. In seconds she had the defibrillator charged and ready. "Clear!" She said more from training than necessity as she applied the paddles.

Jon's lifeless body jerked from the charge of electricity.

She checked his vitals. The heart monitor still showed a flat line.

She upped the voltage and hit him again.

The heart monitor spiked and then showed a weak, but steady beat.

"Oh, my dear lord!" She breathed a sigh of relief as she re-hung the paddles with shaking hands.

Janet let out the breath she'd been holding.

"Come on, Jon. You just have to be all right."

She checked all of his vitals and watched him closely until she was sure that he was out of danger.

"Thank the Lord almighty," she whispered.

She looked around the room, feeling guilty about her lapse, and to reassure herself that her actions had gone unobserved.

Her phone started vibrating, startling her. She gasped with her mouth wide open in fear. "What else, Lord? Oh, Lordy, you're going to be my undoing tonight. She checked the caller ID and saw that it was Mary.

Janet took several deep breaths and tried to calm herself. "Hello, Mary," Janet said barely able to speak.

"Hi, Janet."

Mary's voice sounded shaky to Janet's ears. "Are you all right, hon?"

"I don't... I mean... Yes, I think so," Mary said with uncertainty.

Janet knew something was bothering her friend. "Why don't you tell me what's going on?"

"It's silly. Really. Now that I think about it. I must have been dreaming," Mary said with a steadier tone.

"What were you dreaming about?" Janet asked.

Mary hesitated. "Jon—I swear I could feel him in the room with me, talking to me. For a fleeting second, I even thought that he touched me. That's what woke me up. Pretty screwy, huh?"

Janet spoke softly. "Not really. I know how much you love him and how difficult it must be to see him the way he is now."

Mary started to cry. Her soft sobs sounded so lonely to Janet's sympathetic ears. "The good Lord must have a plan. We just can't see it, yet."

"Yes, I suppose so." Mary didn't sound convinced.

"I have faith that everything will be all right. Have faith, dear."

"I'll try. I'm so sorry to have bothered you. Sometimes I feel like I'm being silly," Mary said softly, embarrassed by her outburst of tears.

"Now, don't you fret one little bit; I'm here for you whenever you need me. That's what friends are for." Janet's voice was reassuring.

"Thanks, Janet. I don't know what I'd do without your strength to lean on." Mary paused. "Is Jon all right?"

Janet glanced over at Jon. His vitals were strong and he appeared to be resting comfortably. She decided not to say anything about what had happened. Poor Mary was under enough stress already. "Yes. Jon is fine, just fine. Now you get some sleep and I'll see you in the morning."

"Good night," Mary said before disconnecting.

Janet put her phone down while deep in thought. She stared at Jon and wondered if it was possible that he had in fact gone to see Mary at the moment he flatlined. She had heard stories of patients who'd had near-death experiences—every nurse has had at least one NDE story to tell in their career, especially those like herself who worked in trauma units.

She crossed herself. "God almighty."

She spent the rest of her shift wide awake.

Chapter 32

The Cube: Tuesday 0815 Hours

Mary was alone with Jon. Chuck and his family were quietly asleep in Rick's studio suite, and the lab was empty. Everyone had been given the day off for the annual security sweep.

Mary went about her usual routine. Her thoughts were about last night's dream. It had seemed so real. Maybe she would talk with Phillip about it at some later date.

The elevator chimed, and the doors swooshed open.

She barely took notice as the security team started their routine sweep for possible hidden microphones and miniature spyware.

Max made his way around the room while surreptitiously keeping an eye on Mary. She was a looker, all right. It was a shame someone as good looking as her had to die, but it was just another job.

The two others on his team went about their assigned tasks, hiding explosives under the consoles where they wouldn't be noticed, while pretending to be searching.

The entire process took only fifteen minutes.

"Max," one man quietly called to get his attention. "What about in there?" he nodded towards Rick's office.

"Don't bother. We've planted enough to seal this place tighter than King Tut's tomb. Finish up and let's get out of here."

Max waved to Mary, signaling that the routine sweep was completed.

Mary casually waved back as the men gathered their gear and entered the elevator.

The Cube: Wednesday 0500 Hours

LeRonda was the last to arrive. She stepped out of the elevator to see Susan, Mick and Phillip already at their consoles.

"You're late," Mick scolded.

"I know. I had to make a few improvements to this." She held up a small crystal drive.

"Let's hurry before the others arrive," Mick urged. "I can only buy us a little time." Mick locked the elevator doors.

Susan saw what he was doing. "Won't that make them suspicious?"

Mick entered a last keystroke on his virtual keypad. "For just the occasion, I added *this*."

A female voice purred from the overhead speakers. "The elevator is temporarily out of service. I have notified maintenance. Assistance is on its way. Would you care to listen to Mozart while you wait?"

Phillip smiled. "Perfect. Elevator music while you wait for the elevator—the supreme torture. Now I've seen it all." Phillip glanced at Mick. "I'm glad you're on *our* side," he said.

LeRonda moved quickly to Chuck's console. She slid into his seat and inserted the crystal drive into its slot. The console booted up quickly as she typed in her activation code. "How far back should we go?"

"Let's go back to the phase one test," Susan suggested.

LeRonda searched for the time in question. "I've got it—duplicating, now." She clicked on the recording.

The monitors lit up, showing the recorded data stream. LeRonda pressed fast forward. The images flew past their eyes rapidly.

"What was that?" LeRonda blurted out. "I thought I saw something weird.

"What did you see? Susan asked.

LeRonda played with the crystal again. This time she focused her attention on the data stream. LeRonda reviewed the data once again. Her finger flew to the controls, and she hit pause. "There! Look at the data stream. It's been changed," she said excitedly.

"Maybe there's something we've overlooked," Mick suggested.

LeRonda was only half listening to the others' stunned comments as they watched the feed. She backed up the loop and played it forward again.

LeRonda didn't answer as she concentrated on the data. She suddenly sat up straighter. "What the heck!"

By now everyone was looking over her shoulder to see what she saw.

"What does it mean?" Phillip puzzled.

LeRonda looked up from the console. "It means that someone hacked our program and captured the feed. In other words, someone else has been using all of our data."

"But who could have done that?" Susan asked with concern.

"Only the Agency could have done it," Mick said, "That's how they've been watching us." LeRonda said gravely.

Mick said what they were all understanding, "Chuck! Chuck did it when he copied his data."

"No!" LeRonda's hands were a blur as she discontinued the program data replication and yanked the crystal from the console. "If they were watching Chuck, then we're dead meat for sure now."

Mick chimed in. "Speaking of dead meat, Rick is approaching the elevator. What should we do?" Mick said as he watched the security cameras.

"We can't let on that we know what happened," Phillip urged. "Unlock the elevator before he gets there."

Mick took Phillip's advice and quickly reactivated the controls to the elevator.

"But I need more time!" LeRonda protested.

"How much?" Mick asked as he watched Rick enter the elevator.

"Just one minute. I want to insert my control virus into his system so we can hack the Agency and download their feed anytime we want." LeRonda worked feverishly at the controls.

Mick monitored the time. "The elevator is almost here.

"Almost there," LeRonda reported. "Got it! I'm done."

She shut down Chuck's terminal and rushed to her station as Mick heard the elevator chime its arrival. The doors opened seconds later and Rick stepped out.

Rick was slightly taken aback by the presence of everyone. "You're all here early today. Did I miss a meeting or something?"

Susan put on her best smile. "Just eager to get started on the new day, boss."

Rick looked at her questioningly but made no further comments. "Very well, then. Let's get this show going." He took his seat on the center dais and paged Chuck. "Come on, Chuck. You're late for work."

Chuck exited the office and took his seat a minute later.

The team went through their startup protocols. "Waiting. On your mark," LeRonda stated.

"Begin the simulation."

A spark was ignited and life began anew.

Jon

I just woke up and I'm covered in a cold sweat. Everything in my world feels wrong, somehow; but I can't pin it down.

If I have to define it, I would say I feel as though a part of me is missing.

I swing my feet to the floor and head for the shower.

My head feels like a lead balloon, and my mouth tastes like old leather. And not the good kind.

After a 20-minute shower, I almost feel human again. Although my reflection still looks like hell.

Nikki is whining at me. She obviously agrees.

I guess what I am really trying to do is to not think about what I'd done recently. Was it murder? You betcha.

Was I the bad guy in this movie? Some people might think so, but when it comes right down to it, I would do the same thing again if the need arose.

But what if I was wrong?

I keep seeing the vacant expression in his eyes. He hadn't acted afraid. I'm not supposed to take justice into my own hands. My job is to enforce the laws.

I am not supposed to be the judge or the executioner, let alone all three.

Maybe it's time for me to walk away from this job.

It's beginning to dawn on me that everything might not be what it seems to be.

I get dressed and do what millions of other people do every day; I go to work. I needed a job when I took this one. One day, I saw an ad for a law enforcement position as a CPD agent.

I remembered Marshall Dillon from the old television shows that were popular during the retro wave and thought he was cool. So, I figured it would be cool to be like him.

I applied for the job and got hired. Then I aced the training program. I was issued a badge and a gun and was assigned to the greater 36.

I remember when there were 48 states, but that was some years back before the revolution.

It wasn't an awful job. The pay was weak, but most of the time the job was boring as all get out. At times, interspersed with a few tense moments just to remind me how underpaid I was.

I guess deep down inside; I knew I was just marking time.

It's odd how we go along in our lives thinking that everything will be the same day after day. But change is inevitable. So why do we act surprised when it slaps us in the face and mocks our attempts to fight it?

My cruiser is right where I left it.

Nikki jumps in and curls up on the passenger seat. She tucks her muzzle under a paw and immediately goes to sleep. She's got to conserve her energy for the exciting day ahead, after all.

I'm driving around in a daze, looking out at the world as life passes me by. It's hard to do away with years of habit, so I watch everything and everyone around me from behind my dark sunglasses.

I stop at the Diner to grab a bite. I'm not making this up—that's what it's called. How original?

The Diner is a converted railroad car that has seen better days, but the coffee is always hot and the food wont kill you—so I've heard.

"Morning, Jon." The waitress greets me the same as a thousand times before. "The usual, sweetie?"

"Yeah, Dolly."

I go to a table near the end and sit with my back to the wall. It's easier to watch people when you can actually see them.

Dolly saunters over with a mug of coffee. "How you doin' today, handsome?"

Dolly has a southern drawl that is sweet as molasses. And a flirty attitude that holds an unspoken promise of pleasure unimaginable. She is a looker, and someday, I might just give in to her advances. But not today. "Just another perfect day in paradise." I say as I smile up at her over the brim of my cup.

She winks back at me. "Pure honey."

I sweep my eyes over her backside as Dolly walks away. She has a delightful walk.

I survey the Diner. There's a bald guy in a bland business suit sitting in a booth with his head bent over his touch screen, flicking his fingers up and down. He probably sells pet rocks.

Two tables down is a couple. They look married, but you never know. The guy keeps watching Dolly bend over to clean the tables whenever he thinks his lady isn't looking. His behavior isn't that odd. The way his lady keeps watching Dolly, I think flames are going to shoot out of her eyes. Normal.

At the counter are two men with an empty seat between them. Both are on their touch phone thingy's oblivious to all the drama playing out around them. Neither man seems to have the slightest awareness of the other. Or maybe they're deep into texting about the world economy. No way to tell.

I slide my gaze around to the other tables. Two ladies who are dressed up in pastel summer dresses with finely quaffed, fresh-from-the-salon hairdos, are sharing a table just beyond the two suits.

These two are more my type, but my chance to give them my winning smile never opens up because they're busy texting or something.

I wonder if they're texting the two businessmen? Or maybe just each other?

"Oh, Maybelle. Your hair looks divine."

"I know! Jenny did an absolutely fabulous job... blah, blah, blah..."

Maybe they're texting about me—that handsome single man in the corner booth? Somehow, I don't think so. More likely, "Who's the dweeb without a touch screen? He's so twentieth century. Insert giggle snicker emoticon."

Even the kid waitress is leaning on the counter, texting away as fast as her tiny thumbs can go. She must have felt me staring at her, because she just looked at me with a pouty scowl.

The door to the diner opens, and another customer comes in.

I feel that tingle on the back of my head.

This guy looks way out of place, and it isn't just the weird black suit that gives him away.

He grabs a stool down at the far end of the counter.

Pouty face drops her phone into her server bib and sidles up to the guy.

"What'll you have?" she says with impatience. Clearly, she has more important things to do.

"I'd like a cup of coffee and a glazed donut," he says.

She wrinkles her nose at him as if she's just smelled some flatulence and walks away. Apparently, his charms are wasted on her.

I can almost feel this guy trying not to look my way.

Dolly slips into my view. "Here you go, hon."

She sets my plate of bacon and eggs down with flourish, and a lot of cleavage. "Would you like anything else?" She smiles invitingly.

"No thanks. I'm good."

"I'll bet you are," she says and sashays away.

My chivalrous demeanor is faltering.

I'm eating slowly while keeping an eye on the man in black. He doesn't fit. But then, neither do I.

That lifelong feeling of being different is creeping in around my carefully constructed bulwark of personal defenses.

Everywhere I look, there is not a single person who isn't preoccupied with some type of handheld phone gizmo. Not just in the Diner, but those walking on the sidewalks. I don't get the fascination. Who the hell are all those people communicating with? And why don't they just talk to each other?

I am the only one not on a cell phone. No, that's not true— the man in the suit isn't on one, either.

He's staring straight ahead as if the meaning of life is engraved on the coffee urn.

I'm feeling uneasy. I have this overwhelming desire to get away before he notices me.

Fighting the urge to panic I leave my food uneaten and, walk out of the diner making fast tracks down the sidewalk.

I whistle for Nikki. She jumps out of the car through the open window, and pads along with me. She loves going for walks.

I leave my '68 in the lot. I'm not too worried about getting a parking ticket.

We keep walking. It's only a few blocks to the heart of our little town. When we arrive, I see there are several people out walking, too.

I pass them by without giving them much notice. Nikki wags her tail at them, but nobody notices her either.

But unlike me, they are not troubled by an inner preoccupation. They are occupied by an odd fixation for their hand-held telephones.

No matter where I look, everybody has their heads down and their eyes focused on their tiny screens.

The only signs of life are the twitching of their thumbs as they text some unseen recipient.

Alexander Graham Bell would roll over in his grave if he knew they had turned his invention into a portable typewriter. Wouldn't talking be easier? I think so., But, apparently, I seem to be the only one.

I keep walking.

They all seem content. Maybe it's just me, the only person in the world without a cell phone.

I see a guy with a phone thingy stuck in his ear like Uhura used to use on retro TV's Star Trek. I guess he's old school.

The current fashion still seems to be handheld devices with touch screens, just like when my dad was still around.

I vaguely recall overhearing someone talking about the next upgrade for the iPad. I'm sure I am not the first guy to think the MaxiPad, but that name was taken a long time ago.

My heart is pounding from an irrational sense of fear. But there's nothing to be afraid of, or so I keep telling myself.

I have to fight the urge to look back, half expecting to see an angry mob of cell phone zombies trudging along behind me with outstretched arms grasping tightly to their electronic souls while their thumbs type away in a blur of motion: "Fresh meat ahead. Eat him."

Using gargantuan self-control, I don't turn around. I'm seeing the scoreboard: Zombies: 1—Self Control: 0.

I turn around. There is no one ready to zap me with a cell phone. Maybe, I should switch to decaf.

That's when I catch his reflection in a store window—like a shadow on the glass.

He's a block back on the opposite side of the street. It's the man from the Diner—the man in black.

My senses haven't failed me. I am being paranoid for a reason. At least that's something.

Mom always said I wasn't the brightest bulb in the lamp.

I unsnap the clip on my holster, so I can pull my colt in a hurry if I need to. Then I start back up the street towards the guy.

He just stands there, watching me get closer. For a second, it appears he can't believe I'd be that stupid. Believe it, buddy.

I cross the street. He's about 30 yards away, just standing there as if he is waiting for some sign.

Then he makes his move. It isn't what I'm expecting.

He slips around the corner and disappears.

"Come on, Nikki!"

We run to the corner. Nikki gets there a second before me. "Hold, girl." She stops and sits, waiting for me to catch up.

A moment later, I peer cautiously around the corner, but the man in the black suit is nowhere to be seen.

"Geez, what's going on?"

Nikki remains silent.

"Nikki search."

She darts out, eager to be working at what she does best. But as she sniffs the ground, I sense confusion in her movements. She returns to my side and pushes on my hand with her muzzle, showing that her search has produced no results.

Nikki is an excellent tracker, and I find it strange that she hasn't picked up a scent. That thought bounces around in my skull as we walk back towards the Diner to get my cruiser.

Nothing seems to be going my way, today.

The people on the sidewalk are still techno drones who pay no attention to me or to Nikki.

As we pass by an antique shop, I casually glance inside. In the back corner, I see something that gets my attention. "Is that for real?" I'm thinking.

I go inside. As we enter, an old-fashioned bell attached to the door rings.

An elderly guy is standing behind the counter. He looks as though he's been standing there since the turn of the last century.

"Hello there, young fella. Nice dog. Is she friendly?" he says to me with an authentic Mid-western twang.

"Only to people she likes," I reply with a grin.

Nikki goes up to him and licks his hand.

"I guess she likes you. Or she's tasting you. Too soon to tell which."

The old guy pats her head and smiles. "Help you find something?"

I have a weakness for antiques, especially for what I'm eyeing in the back. "Does that thing still work?"

The old guy turns around to see what I'm staring at. "Yep. She sure does. Takes a while to get her going, though. You gotta give her time to let her tubes warm up."

Vacuum tubes? Wow. The object of my desire is older than I imagined. "Do you mind?"

"Not at all. Let me plug her in." The old guy does something behind the set.

I move closer.

He moves around to the front of the antique TV and pulls on a knob until it clicks. No remote control for his generation.

He chuckles as if he's read my mind. "We had to get up off our behinds to change the channel when she was new," he says with a twinkle in his eye.

I stare at that old TV set and think about what the world was like then.

"What circa is that old set? 1980s?"

"No, no," he laughs. "A lot older than that, young man. 1950s."

"I wonder what she would say if it could talk," I say, not really expecting an answer.

"She has sound, that's for sure. But I don't suppose that's what you meant." He's looking at me with an odd expression that makes me feel out of place.

Suddenly, I feel like such an idiot.

Nikki wags her tail as if to say, "You got that right."

The old man smiles as if he has a secret worth telling. "Yes sir. I remember the old days. Before the world changed and everything went to hell in a handbasket."

His eyes have that faraway look in them, as if he's replaying scenes from the past in his head. "The world was a lot simpler, then. Mind you, not perfect by any means. We had our problems. Like those Commies who wanted to take over the world with their red scourge."

"Those heathens!" I say, caught up in the moment, though I didn't have a clue what he was talking about.

The old guy's mind is faraway, now. Lost in another world only he can see.

"I was just a kid when we got our first television set. In fact, this here set is that very one!

"I loved watching TV at first. We used to sit around that thing every evening and watch whatever was on, good or bad. You see, there were only three channels back in those days."

He looks at me, and for a second, I can see the pain in his eyes as he is recalling his memories. He's longing to be back there again—back in the world where he belongs.

"But TV changed us. We just didn't know it at the time. We stopped seeking the factual truth about any world issue because it was so conveniently broadcast right into our homes. No wonder we called them 'boob' tubes. We just suckled away on all the mindless gibberish while drooling over our TV dinners."

A tear forms at the corner of his eye. He absently wipes it away with the back of his hand while he keeps reminiscing. "Behind all the glitz and glamour of TV sat the men who decided what we should and shouldn't see and hear. Nobody knew or cared who those guys were. We blindly trusted them to show us right from wrong. We allowed them to forge and mold us with their version of what our morals and attitudes should be. They force fed us their opinions as if they somehow knew what was best for us. All the while, we just sat back and let them change the way we viewed our world, never even suspecting just how much we were being programmed. Of course, it wasn't long before the powers that be saw the potential. The first lie they convinced us to believe is that everything on the TV news is true. How do we know this? Because 'they' said it was against the law to broadcast untruths. If we only knew better, we'd have asked for the number to call when we felt we'd been lied to by the newscasters."

I could visualize his world through my eyes, and although it had been a long time ago, things have changed little; at least where media manipulation is concerned.

The old man continues in that far away voice. "I saw all this happening around me because I differed from everybody else. But I ignored what I was seeing because somehow, I felt as though I was missing out on something that everyone else was enjoying. Meanwhile, out in the actual world, some professors were inventing the computer, then the smaller version they dubbed the personal computer, and finally something they named the World Wide Web."

He comes back to reality and looks at me as if he is seeing me for the first time. "It's the web that snared all of us. I should have known better. You can never trust a spider."

The old TV set is warming up, and somewhere in that mass of vacuum tubes, a dormant antenna comes to life and searches for a signal.

I hear a buzzing noise and my head goes fuzzy, like I'm going to pass out.

Nikki whimpers as though she's in pain.

I can see the old guy's eyes grow wide in the screen's reflection. He looks like he's seen a ghost. "My word!"

I reach for the counter to steady myself, but I miss the mark. The next thing I know, the old guy is staring down at me.

My world goes gray. The last thing I hear is the old guy yelling at the top of his lung's "Jeezus! What's happening?!"

My world goes black.

Rick jumped up from his chair. "How did that happen?!"

They were all moving frantically at their stations, trying to find an answer.

"We have signal degradation at the projection point!" LeRonda shouted. "We're losing image control!"

"Get Jon out of there!" Rick commanded.

"Boosting signal!" LeRonda yelled. "He's fading in and out of the quantum field! I can't hold him!" Panic crept into her voice.

"Chuck! Reboot the program!" Rick roared.

"Almost there. Got it!" he reported.

"Signal is stabilizing," LeRonda said with a sigh of relief. "Jon is firming up, solidifying. Quantum field is re-established."

Jon

I can't remember how I got outside the shop. Not a good thing.

Peering through the window, I can see the old guy puttering around inside, so I shuffle through the door.

The bell on the door tinkles. The old guy looks up. "Well, I'll be damned. I thought I was going crazy when you disappeared."

I don't know what he's talking about. "Thank you for helping me out."

"Wasn't much I could do," *he said with an odd look.*

"Still, you must have done something. How else did I end up outside? By the way, my gun is missing. You know anything about that?"

"That wasn't the only thing you left behind," *the old guy remarked. He reached under the counter and pulled out the revolver and my gun belt.* "Here you go, sonny. I wasn't sure you'd be back, all things considered."

I started reaching for the gun when the old guy grabs my wrist. He holds on for an awkward second and then let's go. "I just needed to know if you were real."

I close the belt buckle and tie the leather string around my thigh. Armed and ready.

"Of course, I'm real. What else would I be?"

"What else? That's a good question, sonny. Don't you remember?" *he asks with that same odd look in his eyes.*

Now, I'm feeling really uncomfortable. "Well, yeah. I guess so. I passed out. Right?"

The old guy chortled. "You did more than pass out. You disappeared completely!"

My head was spinning. "What? What do you mean, I disappeared?"

"Just like I said, friend. You fizzled out like a TV set with a bad tube in it. I was staring right down at you when you and your dog just faded away—like ghosts," *he says, shaking his head.* "I've seen some strange things in my time, but never anything like what just happened."

The words "like a ghost" slam me hard. I feel my head whirling. A memory is forcing its way to the surface.

I have to get out of there. "Thanks," I say over my shoulder as I make a hasty retreat from the shop.

But I don't get very far. I lean against the wall and try to keep from falling over. My brain is spinning like a top.

A name filters up from the dark recesses of my mind, "Mary." Suddenly I remember Mary. I can see her face in my mind's eye.

But what happened? Why aren't we still together? I can't remember if we'd broken up or what. But I don't think so.

My heart skips a beat as I realize that I have to find her.

Another memory is forcing its way up through the fog in my brain. It's more of a feeling than any clear thought, but it feels like I'd just seen Mary recently.

I stagger back to my cruiser in front of the Diner.

Nikki hops in and I notice she seems a little out of it. "Rough day, huh, girl?"

She lays down without so much as a half wag of her tail. I can tell she doesn't feel right. I know I don't.

Turning the key fires up the gas-guzzling piston engine. I punch down on the foot-shaped throttle, and leave twin black tire marks on the pavement, along with a swirling cloud of burnt rubber that's fading in my wake.

I don't have a clue where I'm going, but I sure seem to be going there in a hurry.

As more memories flood over that invisible dam inside my head, my heart is thumping so fast, you'd think it was in a race with my car, and probably winning.

With each passing mile, I'm feeling more clarity come to light. It's stripping away all the dimness of my past, finally.

I whip into the lot outside my apartment and run up the stairs with Nikki close behind.

The door slams behind me. And for a brief second, I wonder why I've come back to this place. I know I'm headed somewhere else, but I can't remember where.

Suddenly, I feel exhausted. A quick nap sounds like a plan, so I lay down.

Lights out.

Rick studied the readout. "Is he shut down for the night?"

"All systems are offline. Shutdown protocols are nearly complete," LeRonda answers.

"Susan. How's our subject doing?" Rick asked.

"All bio readings are slowly returning to normal. He's responding to induced sleep mode."

Phillip gave his report. "Brainwave activity is at 0.5-4 Hz and holding at delta frequency."

"Chuck. What's your status?" Rick inquired.

Chuck hit the last key. "I'm shut down. All systems are offline. I have secured all data."

Rick sat quietly, contemplating his next question. "Phillip. Did you notice anything peculiar about this last run?"

Phillip didn't answer for a few seconds. "My first impression was that Jon seemed to have conflicting memories with his programmed reality."

Rick considered Phillip's opinion. "Did any of you notice anything uncharacteristic right at the end of the simulation? Anything at all?"

Chuck interjected. "For a second, it appeared Jon was becoming self-aware."

"Self-aware? Isn't he supposed to be aware of his surroundings as if living a normal life?" Rick inquires. "That's the whole point of this experiment, isn't it?" Rick offered.

"Yes! But he's not supposed to know that he's inside a simulation. And that's what I mean. For a moment he seemed to realize that it wasn't real," Chuck said in an irritated voice.

"But that's impossible. The programming is supposed to *prevent* that from happening. That's why we created his false identity and implanted memories of a life that fits with his new reality," Phillip stated. "Is it possible that his consciousness is transferring to the quantum model?" he proposed.

"It seemed as though he was confused for a moment at the end," Susan said. "If his conscious mind is interfacing with the quantum Jon, then we could be on the verge of a breakthrough," Susan speculated.

"It's entirely possible," LeRonda agreed.

"The more time he spends in the simulation, the more receptive his mind will be to accepting the simulated world as reality, and his sleep world as insignificant," Phillip conjectured.

"Do you think he's ready to cross over?" Chuck offered.

Phillip glanced at him. "Maybe."

"Any ideas on what caused the quantum signal to deteriorate while Jon was in the antique shop?" Rick asked.

The room remained quiet while everyone replayed the scenario in their minds.

Chuck was the first one to add his thoughts. "About a minute before the interference, Jon was talking to the old man about the antique TV."

"That's right," LeRonda confirmed. She turned to her console and typed furiously. "Those old TV sets had a dual receiver for picking up broadcasts."

"So, you're thinking that it's what caused the interference with Jon? From what I know about holo sets, it couldn't have." Chuck responded. "They still operate on the same frequencies as the old sets," he added.

"Found it," LeRonda said. "Look at this frequency spike right at the moment we lost the signal." She pointed to her graph. "Those old sets also operated on ultra-high frequency bands—or 'UHF', the term they used in the day."

Rick sat forward in his chair. "Can we shield our signal to prevent this from happening again?"

"It may be possible," Chuck answered. "I'll look into it."

Rick thought about the implications of what he'd just heard. "I want detailed reports from all of you on my desk by 0630 hours tomorrow. That's all for today." He glanced towards the glass enclosure. Mary was fussing over Jon as usual, but today she had a worried expression on her face. Rick wondered if she knew that something was different. He made a mental note to ask her later. "Go home, everyone. I'll be expecting those reports first thing in the morning."

Rick went into his office and closed the door.

In the glass's reflection, Mary watched the team gathering their coats. She turned and watched Jon sleeping peacefully.

Mary leaned close and whispered in his ear. "I love you. I'll figure out a way we can be together again. I don't know how, but I will, I swear." She touched his lips with her gloved finger, holding back the tears that threatened to spill down her cheeks.

Chapter 33

Agency Office: Wednesday 1645 Hours

Max entered the room, closing the door quickly with a shove of his foot. He approached Aaron's desk. As usual, he pulled out the chair, turning it so that it was facing backwards. He sat down and leaned forward on crossed arms against the back of the chair. "We've got more problems," he said succinctly.

Aaron put his elbows on his desk. "Talk to me."

"Rick's program is farther along than we believed," Max reported.

"How so?"

"I followed their programmed subject, today. And if I hadn't known that he was a quantum projection—no one else did either—his interactions were totally natural. Rick's crew has perfected the process. The quantum guy even has a mascot."

"Mascot? What do you mean, a mascot?" Aaron questioned.

"He has a programmed dog as a companion."

"A dog? What are those guys up to?"

"I don't know. But whatever they're doing, it can't be good for us," Max retorted.

"So, what does *that* mean?"

"This Jon person who they've programmed is a real bona fide hero," Max said.

"I've read his file. He was killed on his first mission along with the rest of his team. Hardly worth mentioning as a genuine threat." Aaron snapped.

"Did you read the part about how his team wiped out almost an entire battalion of heavily armed enemy troops? That's not a simple task, if you ask me," Max countered.

"Hmm. I see your point. But he's not who he *was*. He's just a ghost of himself. And he doesn't even know it."

"Sure, boss," Max agreed. "But he believes he's a good guy—like a hero in an action-adventure movie."

"Doesn't matter who he believes he is. We can kill him just as easy as the next guy."

"Sure, boss," Max paused. "There's one more thing."

"Go on," Aaron urged.

"I followed Jon to an antique shop in town that's run by an old guy. After Jon left, I paid a visit to the old man's store. There were some pretty interesting things in there..."

"Save me the rundown about the inventory—anything to report about the old man?"

"He told me an interesting story."

Aaron glared. "Does he know anything important?"

"Not really. But he witnessed Jon and his dog fading out."

Aaron leaned closer. "Now that's important. Maybe Rick's project isn't as perfected as you thought it was. What did the old guy say about seeing them fade out?"

"He said it scared the shit out of him. He was a pretty smart character, too, and seemed close to figuring out how it happened."

"Where is he, now?" Aaron asked.

"On his way to the vats," Max replied unemotionally.

"Are the bombs set?" Aaron demanded.

"Friday, at noon. Per your orders."

Aaron leaned back in his chair, "It doesn't matter how far they've come. In a few days, everything they know will be dust. In the meantime, monitor them. I want a report on everything they do."

"On it. I'll count all the rolls of toilet paper, boss."

"Get out of here, ass wipe."

"That's what the toilet paper's for," Max retorted. "There's one more item on your wish list."

Aaron glared at him.

"The presider has been eliminated. That should put an end to any inquiries from Global-Gov concerning the project."

"What happened?" Aaron asked.

"Apparently, her train derailed while in route to a campaign rally. There were no survivors." Max smirked as he walked out.

Aaron leaned back in his chair and stared out of his office window, smiling. "Finally, something is going my way."

Chapter 34

The Cube: Thursday 0640 Hours

Chuck submitted his report for the previous day's work and was just about to leave Rick's office when he noticed how quiet the room had become. He casually looked at the others, who were all studying their own reports. Usually, it was full of banter and mindless conversation revolving around what to do for dinner and drinks. But this morning was different.

LeRonda was the first to speak. "What do we do, now?" She was hoping that one of them had the answer.

Mick glanced towards Rick. "You never told us what happened with your meeting with Mary."

Phillip seemed distracted as he watched Mary fussing over Jon.

"It's as we thought. Mary is Jon's fiancée," Rick answered.

"It occurs to me that the one person who might be able to help is standing on the other side of that glass partition," Phillip stated.

Everyone looked towards Mary.

"But what does that mean to us? How can that help us?" Mick asked.

"I'm not sure, yet. But if there's one thing I'm certain of, it's that a woman's love is nothing to be trifled with," Phillip mused. "Perhaps, it's time we all had a serious talk with our resident doctor."

"I think its best we call her in for a chat," Rick said as he pressed the intercom. "Mary. Please come to my office."

"We can't talk to her here," Susan blurted.

Rick looked at her with questioning eyes.

LeRonda wrote a note and held it up for everyone to see. "We think the Agency bugged the Cube."

Rick was taken aback by that—he should've suspected as much, but hadn't thought of the possibility himself. He grabbed a tablet and wrote a message for the others to read—*Search the cube.*

CPD Headquarters: Thursday 0854 Hours

Doherty sat behind his desk nursing a cup of lukewarm coffee reading the latest news reports. A train derailment caught his eye when his phone rang. "Doherty," he answered.

"The results are in from that ID badge you asked us to analyze."

"Speak to me," Doherty said briskly.

"You're not going to like this. It seems the owner worked for the government on some kind of top-secret project. The details of which we don't know because the card is highly encrypted. We weren't able to break the code. But we were able to get a site location from the key code."

Doherty set his coffee aside, suddenly interested. "Where?"

"We believe it's the Agency."

"Are you sure?" Doherty asked.

"As sure as we can be. Like I said, the card is highly-encrypted. We were lucky to get that much."

"Thanks. What about that chip bag I turned in? Anything important come back on it," Doherty queried the lab tech.

"Your suspicions were right. The bag was coated with powder residue from a gunshot."

"How would powder end up on the bag?"

"We asked ourselves the same question. After we discussed several scenarios, we came to one conclusion. So, I ran some further tests, and they confirmed it. The bag appears to have been used as a glove by the shooter."

"A glove? Pretty damned inventive. Were you able to get any prints or DNA from the bag?" Doherty was curious.

"From that greasy mess? Ugh. No. And, I don't think I'm going to be eating chips again. At least not any time soon."

"Thanks for the update. If you learn any more, you know where to find me." Doherty disconnected.

Spinoza looked quizzically at his boss. "What's the scoop?"

"It seems our victim was a government employee. His ID card was Agency issue," Doherty answered with a sigh.

"No, way," Spinoza muttered. "You won't believe this, look." Spinoza handed over a crime alert.

Doherty looked at his partner after he scanned the report. "An explosion in D.C. destroys Agency H.Q. No way is right. We're not going to get any intel from the Agency."

"The only other leads we had went up in flames when Vid-Tec was destroyed," Spinoza added.

"I wonder if we'll ever know what they were working on," Doherty wondered, then sat back in his seat.

"Whatever it was, it must have been important. Somebody killed a lot of people to keep it quiet," Spinoza added.

"I have a feeling the killing isn't over," Doherty said quietly. He picked up the file and placed it in a case drawer labeled *Pending*.

Mary's Apartment: Thursday 1643 Hours

Mary entered her apartment and closed the door behind her. She stood in the entryway for several minutes, numb from another day of too much stress and worry. Mary did not know how she could help Jon. She missed him so much that it hurt, and she was feeling guilty about what the experiment was putting him through.

Mary set her purse and keys on a small foyer table and started for the kitchen. She wasn't hungry, but knew she had to eat something. If she was going to help Jon, she had to keep up her strength.

She had barely taken a step when there was a knock on the door. She was expecting the others to meet with her, so the intrusion into her routine was a welcome diversion.

Mary turned back and peered at the security feed from the door camera. She was pleased to see that it was Susan and the others from work, fidgeting in the hallway.

She opened the door. Mary was hesitant. Rick had asked her to speak with everyone, but she was still unsure about what they wanted to know.

LeRonda greeted her. "May we come in?"

"Yes. Of course. Please, come in. I didn't mean to be rude. It's just that I'm exhausted and I..." Mary stammered.

Susan stepped close to Mary. "No need to explain. We understand."

The group filed into the apartment.

"Please make yourselves at home." Mary led the somber group into the living room.

The apartment was immaculate and nicely decorated, but it had an air of emptiness that made it feel as though something were missing.

Mary sat on the sofa next to Susan and LeRonda, while Mick and Phillip took seats across from them. Rick sat in a chair by the window.

"You're probably wondering why we're here," Phillip said.

"I guess it's safe to assume it has something to do with Jon," Mary said, trying to ease the tension.

Susan replied. "Yes, it is. We were wondering what you could tell us about his personal life. Obviously, we just want to help him, but we need your input."

Mary looked at each of them before answering. With a heavy sigh, she began. "Jon is my fiancée. We were going to be married, but the war interrupted our plans. They drafted him."

She stood up and went over to the small table where she picked up a picture. It was of Jon and herself. She looked at it lovingly, wishing she could go back to that moment and live there, forever. "This picture was taken just a week before he left." Mary paused, barely able to keep her emotions under control. "I tried to stop him. But..." A couple of tears rolled out from the corners of her eyes. "He said it was his duty. That he had to go."

"We're so sorry," Susan comforted.

Mary's eyes brimmed with tears. "Those first few months after he left were the hardest of my life. I couldn't talk to him because of his training program, and then because of his deployment. All of it was so secret." She grabbed a tissue and dabbed at her eyes. "I hated the government for taking him from me. All I wanted was that he come home. I kept imagining that day—our lives together again—how happy we'd be." She cried.

"Then, I got a letter. An honest to god paper letter with gold filigree trim and official seals stamped all over it. I knew it wasn't good news—government letters never are. I could barely make myself open it," she sniffed. "It said he was dead—killed in action. A few cold words to sum up the end of a young man's life. But what else could they say?"

"We had no idea," Phillip said.

"How horrible," LeRonda whispered.

Mary looked at LeRonda with a strange expression, "The genuine horror started a few weeks later. I heard about this program from a friend of a friend who worked with me at the VA hospital. For the life of me, I can't remember her name, but she leaked information to me, stating that Jon wasn't dead but actually involved with this top-secret study for wounded soldiers. It stunned me when I first found out about it, but then I became furious. After being told he was dead only to find out, he was still alive... well, I called in every favor owed me and got myself transferred to the project so I could be with Jon. I did not know what I was going to find."

"Dear lord," Susan muttered.

"Now I see what's left of him... it's...," Mary wept and couldn't go on.

Susan put her arm around Mary's shoulder and tried to comfort her.

"Now that I know he's alive, I can't bear the thought of losing him, again." Mary could barely continue. "It's difficult for me to share what happened. It's so personal."

"Don't worry about a thing. We won't breathe a word," Mick assured her.

"I know you must think I'm a terrible person. I should just let him go. It's not fair to keep him alive as he is. That's not living." Her shoulders quaked as she cried.

"As it so happens, that's why we're here," Phillip said reassuringly.

Mary looked at him with red-rimmed eyes. "Really? How so?"

"We all agree that Jon shouldn't be put through any more tests," Phillip said.

Mary said nothing, because she knew in her heart what had to be done. "I'll do it. I'll set him free."

"That's not what we mean. That may not be necessary," LeRonda said.

They confused Mary. "I don't understand?"

"The project has taken a different direction than what they led us to believe," Mick said. "But we think that there may be a better alternative for Jon."

"Mary, we want to attempt something that will save Jon, but the risk is very high. He might not survive," Susan stated honestly.

"Why did you come to me with this? I mean, how did you know?" Mary asked.

"We didn't until we read through Jon's military records." Rick said. "Even then, we weren't sure. At least not until after you and I talked."

"Go on," Mary said.

"We also need your help to do what we have in mind," Phillip said.

"What do you need me to do?" Mary asked. She found herself conflicted with feelings of hope, a hope that she dared not let blossom for fear of losing her one chance to be with Jon.

"Here's what we have in mind," LeRonda began.

Chapter 35

Agency Headquarters: Friday 1115 Hours

Rick exited the elevator and strode down the familiar corridor. Even though it had been years since he'd last set foot in the building, nothing had changed.

He set his briefcase on the security scanner and slipped between the detectors.

Stepping to the guard station, he held up his ID.

"Good morning, sir." The guard was all business. "One moment while I check your entry authorization." He tapped on a computer terminal that was facing away from Rick.

"Sure," Rick replied in a bored tone. He may have sounded bored, but he was actually boiling over with nervous tension. This was the most dangerous part of their plan—if LeRonda's program hadn't worked, he would spend a long time explaining himself to some very unsympathetic people.

During their search of the cube, they had not only found listening devices planted on every console but also enough explosives to vaporize the cube and everyone in it.

The others had been furious, but rather than vent uselessly, Rick was already planning retribution. He'd outlined his idea when LeRonda confessed to him about her infiltration program that she'd inserted into Chuck's console.

Rick was astonished at her audacity, but what else could he have expected from such brilliant people. It made him smile.

It turned out that LeRonda had a better plan. Now all he had to do was get past the most highly secured facility in the world carrying a briefcase full of explosives.

The guard kept clicking on his computer screen while Rick's briefcase slid out of the scanner. He reached for the handle, trying to hide the slight tremor in his hand.

"I confirm your 1130 appointment with the Director, Dr. Denzer. Do you require an escort?"

"No, thanks. I know the way." Rick pulled his case off the tray and started walking away from the guards.

"Just a minute, sir." The guard said brusquely.

Rick's heart jumped into his throat. He turned slowly, expecting to be arrested.

"You forgot your visitor's badge." The guard handed him the laminated card. "Please wear this at all times while in the facility."

"Of course," Rick said as he clipped the card to his shirt pocket. He turned and walked away before the guard could notice that his knees were shaking.

He walked down the endless corridors with doors on both sides, etched-glass windows, and gold inlaid name plaques.

Finally, he reached the one he was looking for—*Director of Field Operations.*

Rick turned the old-fashioned knob and pushed the door inward. He stepped into a tastefully decorated outer office.

Ten paces in front of him was a beautiful secretary who was busy working at her computer. Rick knew she was studying the biometric readout taken from his palm as he'd turned the old-fashioned doorknob, which concealed some very high-tech equipment.

"Good morning, Dr. Denzer."

"Please call me Rick," He said while smiling.

"Yes, sir. The director will see you, now." She ushered him to a set of double doors which were made from polished hickory. The automatic doors opened easily with a touch of her finger. "This way," she beckoned. "Rick."

He stepped through the doors, which closed silently behind him.

The director got up from behind his desk and extended his hand. "Rick. It's good to see you."

Rick grasped the offered hand. "Aaron. How have you been?"

"Always busy, as you know—what with the new Global-Gov trying to take over the world." Aaron said with a grin. "Sit down, please." He gestured towards a comfortable antique chair. "Anything to drink?"

"No, thanks. I'll be flying back to Denver within the hour." Rick replied, making himself comfortable. He set his briefcase on the floor.

Aaron eyed the black valise. "Is that what I think it is?"

Rick sat back in his chair, pretending that he hadn't heard the question. "Nice view," he complimented, staring out at the Washington monument.

Aaron walked back behind his desk while looking at the view. "I never tire of it." He sat down, his attitude changing. The cordial smile and the politically correct good humor vanished. "Let's cut the bullshit. Why did you come all the way here? It surely wasn't for the view from my office."

"I've brought you something that you've been asking for," Rick said with an expressionless face.

"Is that the data crystal? The experiment was a success, I take it?" Aaron couldn't hide the self-satisfied smirk from his voice.

"Yes," Rick answered as he picked up the case and set it on his knees.

"Congratulations, Rick. I can't wait to have our tech boys get a look at what you've done!" Aaron held out his hand again.

Rick was fiddling with something on the front of the case while looking at his watch. It read 1157 hours local time zone.

He set the briefcase back down. "This is embarrassing. I can't get the combination to work. Do you mind?" Rick pointed towards the phone on the director's desk. "I've got to check in with the lab and see if I've got the right code."

Aaron could barely hide his disparagement. "Sure." He nodded towards the phone, while watching the clock tick away the precious minutes of his day.

Rick walked slowly towards the phone, checking his watch once more. He picked up the handset and dialed his office number. His phone was answered on the first ring. "Yes?"

"Hi, Phillip. It's me. I'm here with the director and he wanted me to tell you he is proud of our efforts and says congressional recognition and top scientific awards will be presented to each of us." Rick paused and glanced at his watch, then at Aaron and smiled. "Now would be a good time."

Aaron watched in stunned shock as Rick dematerialized right before his eyes. The phone made a loud clatter as it hit the desk. "What the...!" The clock on his wall rang the first of twelve muted bells, signaling the time. Aaron looked at the clock with a sudden sick feeling in his gut. He reached for the phone just as his office door opened and Max entered. "I was just about to call you. The bomb you placed in the lab... what time did you set it for?" Aaron urged.

"Twelve noon. Just like you ordered. Why?" Max answered as he sat down next to the briefcase.

"Which time zone!"

"Our time zone. Of course. It should go off any second." Max smiled wickedly.

"Nooo....!" Aaron screamed, as he bolted towards the closing office door. He didn't make it.

The explosion shook the entire building destroying the entire wing, including the secondary project lab two levels below Aaron's office.

At that same moment in the cube, "End simulation." LeRonda said.

"All systems are shutting down and Rick is offline." Chuck and Susan reported in unison.

They looked towards the medical suite to see Mary removing the feeds from Rick's head and body.

Chapter 36

The Cube: Saturday 0730 Hours

Janet looked at the clock. It was past the end of her shift and neither Mary nor the scientists had shown up yet. She had dozed off, but only for a moment. She glanced through the window into Jon's medical suite, having a sudden moment of apprehension. Everything appeared normal and Jon was sleeping peacefully. "Thank you, Lord."

Janet got up from her chair and went to the water cooler. She was wide awake now, as adrenaline pumped through her veins with the memory of what had happened the last time she had fallen asleep on the job.

Janet heard the elevator door open and turned to see who was coming in at such an unusual time of the morning.

The seven conspirators stepped off the elevator and went quickly to their assigned stations. Chuck went to station one and immediately started inputting LeRonda's override program.

Mary went to the medical suite. "Hi, Janet," she said a little nervously. "You can go home, now; I'm sorry for being late."

"That's, OK, hon. I'm sure you needed the extra rest. Are you sure you're OK? You look a little peeked?" Janet asked wearily as she picked up her jacket and purse.

"Of course." Mary said as she gave Janet a friendly hug.

"OK, hon. Call me if you need anything," Janet offered as she headed to the elevator before disappearing behind the closing doors.

Susan powered up her console. "Are we sure this is going to work?" she asked to anyone who was paying attention.

Phillip filled in the silence that followed. "There is no way to know until we try."

"And if it fails? We'll be murderers," Susan stated.

Mick chimed in. "It's for sure we'll be murderers if we *do* succeed." He scanned his security feeds. "All systems are online and security protocols are in place. Locking out the elevator… now." Mick pressed a flashing red icon.

Susan fell into the routine and began the sequence. "Brainwave activity is at 0.5-4 Hz and holding at delta frequency.

Temperature is 98° F. Heart rate is normal, holding steady. Respiration normal. Blood pressure is 119 over 77.

Phillip looked at Rick. "Now's the time to work your magic."

Rick went to the safe where the crystal was secured and began to work. This was the first hurdle that had to be made. If they were to have any chance at all of succeeding, they needed the crystal. The safe opened at Rick's prompting. He reached in and removed the crystal and then inserted it in the cradle.

LeRonda reported her status. "Quantum projectors are online. Satellites are in geo-synch and waiting on standby. All other backup systems show *green* across the board. Access to all geo locations is 100%. All communication towers, quantum relay and photon-wave relay stations are online. We are tapped into every bandwidth of broadcast capability and are ready for initialization." She looked over her shoulder to see how Rick was doing.

Meanwhile, in the medical suite, Mary was preparing to do something she would have never believed possible just a few weeks earlier.

She prepared a series of injections that, when combined, would stop Jon's heart. His brain would remain active for a few precious minutes. They hoped that his consciousness could be inserted into the crystal's matrix where he would live on, theoretically.

Rick watched closely as the cradle clamp closed gently around the precious gemstone. Its robotic arm swung the crystal into position beneath an array of lasers where it was locked in place with a pneumatic hiss.

Rick was so nervous he could barely speak. "Ready."

Susan and Phillip looked in at Mary.

Mary stood next to Jon, stroking his face gently. "The time has come, my love." She had prepared emotionally to accept this moment. The thought of him existing as he did, to be used as a puppet for lab experiments, was not living. She knew that, nevertheless, it had not been a simple choice to make. She dared not hope that he would find a new life inside the crystal. It would crush her if he didn't.

Phillip spoke. "Patient is entering an induced state of subjective consciousness. I am monitoring brainwave activity. All indicators show patient is responsive to external stimuli.

LeRonda started the computer sequence. "Everything is ready, Rick."

Rick looked around the room. Every eye was on him. What happened next would rewrite all of human history, or it would end the life of one human being.

He walked to the intercom on the medical suite wall and pressed the button. "Are you ready, Mary?"

Mary stroked Jon's face with her bare hand. There was no more need for gloves and all the other precautions she had taken to protect him from infection.

Her fear was gone. If this didn't work, she had secretly prepared a second dose of the lethal injections for herself. She would be with her beloved Jon one way or another. "I'm ready," she answered.

Rick returned to his command seat. "Initiating program. On my mark; five, four, three, two, one."

Water and air molecules swirled around a tiny vortex of quantum matter in the center of the medical suite.

"I can feel the energy like a thousand ants crawling on my skin." Chuck had to raise his voice to be heard above the din.

"It's amazing!" Susan said, smiling.

"I never realized that there would be so much static charge!" LeRonda said with awe.

Atoms merged as they were redefined on a quantum level. What was insubstantial became solid.

"There he is!" Phillip pointed as a ghostly outline of Jon's quantum body took shape.

The cohesion of atoms took on form and from the void, a man emerged. A spark was ignited and life began anew.

Mary inserted the second syringe into Jon's drip tube and pressed the plunger in slowly. The heart monitor behind her beeped a warning as it registered heart flutter and erratic rhythm.

"I'm registering abnormal heartbeat." Susan confirmed.

"Brainwave pattern is still within norm," Phillip added.

LeRonda worked steadily at her console. "I'm almost ready to start beam transferal."

Phillip watched his readout. "Brainwave activity is spiking above norm!"

Mary kept a careful watch on Jon's vitals. But something strange was happening. She noticed a deep blue aura coalescing above Jon's prone body, as if they had turned a pale beam of light on.

"My readings are going wild!" Susan shouted. "I've never seen anything like this before!"

Mary screamed from the medical suite. "LeRonda, now! Do it, now!"

Multiple alarms sounded from the sterile room as Jon's life signs flatlined.

"I'm initiating, now!" LeRonda shouted over the bedlam. "Imagers are responsive. Starting beam sequence for satellite transference of data stream." LeRonda's hands hovered over her virtual keyboard, "Mark." She pressed the button.

The quantum image in the crystal was beamed to a satellite in high earth orbit and then instantly redirected to the medical suite.

Jon

I have this funny feeling, as if I missed something important. I'm still only half awake. It's taking my eyes a few seconds to focus on my surroundings. Where am I? I'm not in my room.

I remember this place. I'm almost afraid to look around. It scares me to think about what I might see.

Mary stood quietly watching from behind a rack of monitors as Jon walked around the room. Her hand covered her mouth. She was too afraid to hope that this was really her Jon.

Jon

I see the patient lying under a sheet. I remember that it's me, or had been me, or is still me. Man, this is confusing.

I glance at the monitors and see that the silent alarms are going off. I see the flatline racing across the heart monitor screen—I'm, he, or whoever is dead.

Am I a ghost? I don't feel dead.

Ow! I stubbed my toe on the bedpost. I am definitely not a ghost because it hurts like hell.

Someone has pulled the sheet over the body's head. Slowly, I reach toward the sheet. But this time, I'm not afraid to look underneath.

As I lift the sheet, I look at the body. It looks different. Oh, it's not because of the horrible shape it's in. It's more than that. It's as though I'm looking at a stranger. Not me, not this time.

I don't feel any connection to that body like I did before.

Rest in peace, buddy. It sounds stupid to me, but isn't that what I'm supposed to say to a dead person?

I hear the soft whisper of cloth and stupidly realize that I'm not alone.

Her reflection shimmers ghostlike in the glass dividing wall.

"Jon?" Mary asked with a puzzled look on her face. Her heart started beating wildly.

"Mary!" Jon turned his head towards her sweet voice with a smile already spreading on his face.

He reached for her as she fell into his arms. She felt so warm and alive. He raised her chin and kissed her soft lips. He felt her body relax against his. Enfolded together, they were a perfect fit.

Mary looked up into Jon's eyes. "I've missed you so much." She wept tears of joy as she pulled him closer and put her head against his chest. She could feel his heart beating in rhythm with her own.

His breath felt warm on her cheek. His arms wrapped around her in an envelope of love. She was with her beloved Jon and she would never allow herself to be parted from him again.

"I love you, Mary," he said softly.

Then his tear-filled eyes followed the sounds of cheering. Outside the room, a small group of people were smiling and slapping each other on the back. He heard corks popping and saw champagne flowing. He figured that there must be a party going on, although he wasn't completely sure what it was all about. "Mom always said I wasn't the brightest bulb in the lamp," he thought to himself.

Other Books by Steve R. Romano

Science Fiction

Dreams of Betrayal: The Vortex (Book 1)

Dreams of Betrayal: Realm of Nightmares (Book 2)

Dreams of Betrayal: Satellite of Doom (Book 3)

Dreams of Betrayal: Battle for Capernaum (Book 4)

Juvenile Fiction

Mike and Scrag

Mike and Scrag: The Avalanche

Mike and Scrag: Thunder Mountain

Tony and the Haunted Goldmine

Children's Picture Books

The Adventures of Amerina: The Garden

The Adventures of Amerina: The Doll

The Adventures of Amerina: The Horse

The Adventures of Amerina: The Sled

Author website: SteveRRomano.com